Final Round

By William Bernhardt
Published by the Ballantine Publishing Group:

Primary Justice
Blind Justice
Deadly Justice
Perfect Justice
Cruel Justice
Naked Justice
Extreme Justice
Dark Justice
Silent Justice
Murder One

Double Jeopardy
The Midnight Before Christmas
The Code of Buddyhood
Legal Briefs *(editor)*
Natural Suspect *(editor)*

William Bernhardt

◆ ◆ ◆

FINAL
ROUND

BALLANTINE BOOKS ◆ NEW YORK

A Ballantine Book
Published by The Ballantine Publishing Group
Copyright © 2001 by William Bernhardt

All rights reserved under International and Pan-American Copyright Conventions. Published in the United States by The Ballantine Publishing Group, a division of Random House, Inc., New York, and simultaneously in Canada by Random House of Canada Limited, Toronto.

Ballantine is a registered trademark and the Ballantine colophon is a trademark of Random House, Inc.

www.ballantinebooks.com

Library of Congress Cataloging-in-Publication Data
Bernhardt, William, 1960–
Final round / William Bernhardt.— 1st ed.
p. cm.
ISBN 0-345-44962-2
1. Masters Golf Tournament—Fiction.   2. Golf—Tournaments—Fiction.
3. Augusta (Ga.)—Fiction.   4. Golfers—Fiction.   I. Title.
PS3552.E73147 F5 2002
813'.54—dc21   2001043389

Manufactured in the United States of America

First Edition: April 2002

10 9 8 7 6 5 4 3 2 1

ACKNOWLEDGMENTS

FIRST, I WANT to thank my friend and literary agent Robert Gottlieb for suggesting a crime novel set at the Masters tournament. The research alone has made this book a personal favorite. And I want to give equal thanks to my friends at Ballantine, Gina Centrello and Joe Blades, for being receptive to this departure from the courtroom and all my usual stomping grounds. I want to thank my wife, Kirsten, for her always invaluable contributions, including her assistance with the considerable research necessary to steep this book in the history and ambience of the Masters tournament.

Finally, I must thank my golf experts, Richard T. McNeil and Frank Hurka, for reviewing an early draft of the manuscript and making many priceless suggestions. Any errors, however, are mine, not theirs, and they are similarly not responsible for the occasional dramatic license I have taken. I know, for instance, that the par-three tournament is usually played on a different course, but the allure of the legendary Masters course was so great I decided to let Conner and his friends play it out there. Similarly, I am aware that Conner makes some spectacularly long drives, and that the Masters players typically do not stay on the Augusta National Golf Club grounds, but I preferred to keep the suspects on the premises of that magnificent golf course whenever I could.

Readers are invited to e-mail me at: wb@williambernhardt.com. You can also visit my Web site (www.williambernhardt.com) and learn more about this and my other novels.

Best of luck on the links.

The Club wants no publicity except with respect to the Masters tournament. Our members wish to enjoy the seclusion of a private club and prefer their visits at the Club not to be publicized . . . It is expected that [members] shall actively discourage any form of publicity pertaining to the Club, about which they have advance knowledge, if it is unrelated to the tournament—and especially if it is to be commercial in form.

    —from The Annual Report to Members

Tuesday Night

DEATH CAME SO suddenly he didn't even have a chance to scream. All at once, the lights were out—as if someone had thrown a switch inside his brain. Blood and bits of flesh burst from the side of his head. He was dead before he hit the ground.

The man standing over him swung his golf club in the darkness, smiling with satisfaction. Dead in one stroke—not bad at all. Almost like a hole in one, in a perverse sort of way.

Why hadn't the man listened to him? he wondered. He swung the club angrily back and forth, chopping at the air. A boiling rage consumed him. Why, why, *why*? He hadn't wanted it to happen this way. But what choice had the man left him? None, that's what. None at all. He had tried to be reasonable. He had offered to be accommodating. But in the end, it had made no difference. In the end, he simply had no alternative.

Now there was the question of what to do with the corpse. It would have to be disposed of in some way or another. He peered down at the motionless body. Blood still poured out of the huge gash on the side of his head, seeping into the white sand, creating a sticky sanguine pool. Dark and . . . disturbing.

A thought occurred. Why do anything at all? He'd had no time to plan for body disposal, and anything he did now would create a risk that he would be seen. Why not just . . . leave it where it was? Sure, the body would be found in time, but that was inevitable in any case. The key was not whether it would be found—but when. And who would be around when it happened.

Yes, that was the solution. All he had to do was scrape the sand around in this unusually deep bunker until nothing was visible . . .

That worked perfectly. And how could anyone complain? They were called *hazards*, after all. His victim probably didn't realize that meant it could be hazardous . . . to his health.

The man smiled, laughing to himself at his little joke. And there was a certain pride in having once again taken care of himself, once again protected himself from those who would bring him down. Those who fought him. Those who tried to deprive him of what was rightly his. Who wouldn't take pride in that? He was a self-made man, after all. In every possible sense of the word . . .

Somewhere behind him, back on the fairway, he heard something. He froze. What was it? Was anyone out there? Was someone listening? Could someone see what he had done?

He whirled around, trying to look in every direction at once. He didn't spot a soul. Perhaps it was a bird, perhaps just the rustling of the branches on that huge maple tree. Or nothing at all. But he couldn't be sure. There could have been a witness.

He hoped not, though. Because if someone had seen, if someone had the slightest hint of what he had done . . .

Then he'd have to do what was necessary. Again. And again and again, if it came to that. Whatever it took.

The Bastion of Excellence

◆ ◆ ◆

In the 1947 Masters, as Freddie Haas lined up a putt on the eighth green, Johnny Bulla (who was in the group behind him) hit a ball onto the green. This was not only a breach of golf etiquette but a safety hazard. "Hey man," Haas said to Bulla, "you hit into me. Someone could have gotten hurt."

Club chairman Cliff Roberts immediately summoned not Bulla, but Haas, to his office. Haas had violated the Augusta National rules by raising his voice above a conversational level. "Fred, we don't tolerate that kind of attitude around here." Roberts promptly yanked his credentials and tossed him out of the tournament. "If you will write a letter of apology," Roberts added, "we might have you back again." Haas thought he was more sinned against than sinning, but he learned an important lesson. At the Augusta National, it seemed, it was more important to be well behaved than to be right.

Haas wrote the letter. To the surprise of many, he was invited back the next year.

CHAPTER

1

Monday

"It's Silly Putty," Conner Cross said with an air of finality that defied anyone to disagree with him. "I'm certain of it."

"It is not," John McCree replied. He'd been defying Conner since they were kids and had no trouble doing it again. "It's a specially treated ball of monofilaments, packed and compressed for maximum durability and flexibility."

"Monofilaments! Give me a break. It's Silly Putty."

"You're wrong."

"I'm not. This is a subject on which I have a certain expertise."

"You can't even spell *expertise*."

"I'm telling you, it's Silly Putty. I was reading a magazine article about this just last week."

"I find that highly unlikely, unless maybe it was mentioned as some playmate's pet peeve."

Conner raised his hands to his mouth and shouted. "Fitz!"

An older man sporting a shoeshine-boy cap and toting a large bag of clubs strolled toward the two men at the first tee. "You called, Master?"

Conner Cross smiled. "Look, Fitz, we need you to settle an argument."

"Caddies don't settle arguments." Fitz, ever the dapper dresser, was attired in a Lacoste golf shirt, a Lyle & Scott cashmere sweater, and Italian gabardine light wool slacks—quite a contrast to Conner himself, who sported a bright floral Hawaiian shirt, yellow bicycle shorts, and a tattered Panama straw hat. "We counsel. We strategize. We tote. But we don't settle arguments."

"Be a sport."

Fitz folded his arms across his chest. "No," Fitz said emphatically. His full name was Daniel Fitzpatrick, but he'd been caddying forever, and everyone had long ago reduced his name to the single syllable.

"C'mon. For me?"

"Definitely not."

"What, are you afraid you'll be fined by the caddies' union? Look—if you'll just settle this dispute, I promise I won't make fun of that silly yellow sweater."

"What a charmer."

"Puh-*leeze*?" Conner wheedled.

Fitz twisted his craggy, weathered face. "I caddied for Gary Player for six years and he never once asked me to settle an argument."

"Then you're overdue. Here's the thing: what do you think they put inside golf balls—Silly Putty, or super-compressed monofilaments?"

Fitz rolled his eyes. "I assume you stand in the Silly Putty camp."

"I shouldn't say. It might prejudice your decision."

"For your information, you dimwits, they put rubber inside golf balls. That's all it is. Rubber."

Conner Cross and John McCree looked at each other. "Rubber?"

"That's right," Fitz said emphatically. "Plain ordinary rubber."

Conner and John continued staring.

"He says it's rubber," Conner said.

"I heard that," John replied.

Conner's eyes crinkled. "Nah. Can't be."

"Definitely not," John agreed. "No way."

"Can't be," Conner said, making a clicking noise with his tongue. "Doesn't make sense."

"Agreed," John said. "If golf balls had rubber inside, they'd bounce all the way down the fairway. Or in Conner's case, the rough." The two golfers exchanged a look.

Fitz threw up his hands in despair. "I don't know why I even bother talking to you two reprobates!" He marched past them toward the first tee. "C'mon. If you don't get your practice round started, you'll lose your tee time. And if you don't log enough practice hours, they'll toss you out of the tournament."

It was possible, Conner groused, as he followed his caddie to the tee. Anything was possible at the Masters. This annual event, hosted by the Augusta National Golf Club, was one of the most prestigious, if not *the* most prestigious, of the tournaments on the tour. But it was also a pain in the butt. The Masters was full of rules, regulations, and hoity-toity guidelines of decorum, all of which drove Conner crazy.

During his three years on the tour, Conner had developed a reputation as the PGA's bad boy. According to the press, he was the "gonzo golfer" who delighted in flouting convention. This had made him the hero of some—but not the PGA authorities and officials, and definitely not the top dogs at the Augusta National Country Club. Safely ensconced in the deep South, the Club—which still only accepted male members—was determined to maintain the high standards of a more genteel era. It made Conner want to barf.

John nudged him in the side. "Smell that?"

Conner inhaled deeply. "Cheeseburgers?"

John looked at him pitiably. "Honeysuckle."

Conner sniffed again. John was right, of course. The sweet scent of honeysuckle permeated the course. Much as the Masters tournament got under his skin, Conner grudgingly had to admit that the Augusta National course was magnificent, particularly when the tournament was held each year in April—often culminating on Easter Sunday. He gazed out at the flowering crabapples, the graceful dogwoods, and the blazing streaks of azalea, all set against a magnificent green expanse of turf and trees. It was a spectacular view.

"Not much like back home, huh?" John said, grinning.

Conner silently agreed. He and John had grown up together in the wheatfields and tall-grass prairies of western Oklahoma. They were inseparable throughout junior high and high school. They did everything together—bombed the same classes, got bombed on the same six-packs, and, of course, played golf. Back then, golf had held a special allure for Conner, who'd grown up with his father on a not-very-prosperous farm near the small town of Watonga. Its scruffy nine-hole course was an enchanted oasis in the midst of the red dirt and yellow plains that surrounded it. He and John both fell in love with the sport there.

After high school, John went off to college in California, while Conner stayed near home and went to OU. After college, John made the PGA tour. Conner didn't—but John did everything imaginable to get him in, including loaning him money and arranging private golf instruction from Harvey Penick and other golf giants. Ultimately, Conner won his PGA card. John lived in Georgia now and was a member of the

Augusta National Golf Club—whereas Conner probably couldn't gain membership with a recommendation from Robert E. Lee. John was in nearly all respects the antithesis of Conner, but Conner liked him anyway. Fact was, even though Conner hated to admit it, he pretty much owed John for everything good in his life.

Today was Monday; Conner had flown into Georgia last night. The actual tournament would not begin until Thursday, with a par three mini-tournament on Wednesday. Between now and then, he needed to get in as much practice as possible.

Conner winked at his caddie. "Shall we get started?"

Fitz stared at him, appalled. "You mean, you want to play golf now?"

"Isn't that what I normally do on golf courses?"

"Matter of opinion, I suppose." His eyebrows knitted. "You can't play golf dressed like that."

"And why not?" Conner asked. "All my private parts are properly covered, aren't they?"

Fitz's lips tightened. "Conner, when are you going to get it through your thick skull that being on the PGA tour is a big deal? You should dress in a dignified manner. Not like some . . . Polynesian hobo."

"I like this outfit," Conner said, touching the brim of his battered Panama hat. "I think it has panache. I think it says, 'Here's a man who's at peace with himself.'"

"I think it says, 'Here's a man who's about to be thrown off the tour.'"

"Don't be absurd."

"I'm not! You know the PGA has strict rules on decorum and appearance. They don't even allow pros on the tour to have facial hair, for Pete's sake. And this club has even more rules than the PGA. You can't dress like a bum."

"I'll dress any damn way I want to."

"And you can't swear, either. That's an automatic $250 fine."

"Enough chatter," Conner said, turning away. "I'm ready to hit the ball."

Fitz pressed the heel of his hand against his forehead, as if suffering from a severe migraine. "Great. Just great. Try to remember what I told you, okay? Stance. Swing. You're putting too much weight on your left foot. And you're not bringing your backswing high enough."

"Stop being such a mother hen."

"Jack Nicklaus paid me big bucks to be a mother hen!"

"Then go cluck in his coop for a while. You're making me crazy."

"You were born crazy."

Laughing, Conner poked the tee into the ground and removed a club from his bag.

Fitz grabbed his hand. "What do you think you're doing now?"

"I'm getting a golf club. I know that must seem strange, but the ball goes farther than if I just blow on it."

"You took out a wood. You can't use a wood on this hole."

"I can and I will."

"The tee markers haven't been moved back. It's not that far to the hole. That's way too much power."

"I'm warming up, okay?"

"Conner, you can't—"

"Stop telling me what I can't do!"

"But you—"

"Fitz!" Conner raised a finger.

Fitz fell silent.

"All right then." Conner squared himself before the ball and drew in his breath, preparing to swing.

"Stance," Fitz murmured audibly. "Swing."

"Fitz!"

"All right, all right." He buttoned his lip.

Conner brought back his wood and swung. The dimpled white ball soared beautifully into the air, up, up, up . . . and well over the green. The ball dropped onto the cart path, bounced over a retaining wall, and fell into the greenskeeper's storage shed.

"Aaarghh!" Conner shouted at the top of his lungs, thrashing about with his club.

John fell to his knees, convulsed with laughter.

Conner glared at him. "And what may I ask is so damn humorous?"

John rolled on the ground, propping himself up with one arm. "What . . . do . . . you . . . think?" he said, squeezing the words out between guffaws and gasps for air. "You."

"Damn, damn, *damn.*" In a sudden fit of temper, Conner whirled the wood around again and inadvertently pulverized the tee marker—which was a lovely miniature of the Augusta National clubhouse.

"I tried to tell you," Fitz said quietly. "God knows I tried. But would you listen? Nooooo . . ."

Conner pivoted. "Fitz, I'm warning you—"

He was interrupted by the rapid advance of a short man with a whistle around his neck. "Excuse me," the man said, puffing intermittently on his whistle. He was a bit overweight and appeared to have worked up a sweat just crossing the tee. "What do you think you're doing?"

"Excuse me," Conner shot back. "Who the hell are you?"

"Derwood Scott. I'm the associate tournament director."

Conner mouthed a silent *oh*. Fitz looked as if he'd like to disappear into the rough.

"Mr. Cross, you are in violation of four different tournament regulations."

"Only four? Jeez, I wasn't even trying."

John cleared his throat and tried to look serious. "And which four offenses would those be, sir?"

"One, his embarrassing attire. Two, his indecorous language. Three, his shockingly unprofessional conduct. Four, his destruction of club property."

John nodded. "That does add up to four, doesn't it? All right, officer—take him away."

"This is not a joke!" The more insistent Derwood became, the higher his pitch became. Soon only dogs would hear him. "This is the Augusta National! We will not brook with insubordination!"

"Look," Conner said, "why don't we just forget this happened?"

"I don't think so!" Derwood snapped. "First of all, you will be charged for replacement of the tee marker you destroyed."

"Fine, that's fair . . ."

"Second, you will receive a formal reprimand for your indecorous behavior."

"Okay. Consider my wrist slapped."

"Third, because you moved an immovable obstruction—the tee marker—you must take a two-stroke penalty."

Conner's face became fixed and stony. "What's that?"

"You heard me. Two strokes." He snapped his fingers at Fitz. "Write it down."

Conner stared at the associate tournament director with dead eyes. "Let me remind you, Derwood, that I know where you live."

"What's that, some kind of threat?"

Conner took a step closer to him. "Yeah, some kind. The deadly kind."

"I'm not afraid of you, you tin cup ruffian."

Conner kept walking until he was practically hovering over Derwood. "I could change that."

"Two strokes," Derwood repeated firmly. "Plus a third for that shot you lobbed into the storage shed."

"Three shots?" Conner growled, his eyes wide and crazed. "I haven't left the tee yet!" His curled fingers reached for Derwood's throat.

"All right, all right," Fitz said, cutting in between them. "Let's break this up. We'll take the penalty strokes."

Conner looked as if he might have a stroke. "But—"

"What do we care? It's just a practice round."

"But it'll be reported—"

Fitz put his arms around Derwood's shoulder and steered him away from Conner. "This has all been a terrible misunderstanding. You know how it is sometimes. The pressure of playing the world's greatest golf course. No offense was intended, I assure you."

Derwood frowned. "Nonetheless, he—"

"By the way," Fitz continued, "may I say that you look particularly distinguished in that snappy green sweater? What is that, cashmere?"

"Uh . . . no. Camel hair."

"Well, it looks magnificent on you. Truly magnificent."

Derwood looked down at his sweater. "Really? You like it?"

"It's brilliant. Brings out the green in your eyes."

"I thought my eyes were blue."

Fitz squinted. "Huh. Must be the light." He guided Derwood off the course. "Anyway, thanks so much for dropping by . . ."

Derwood stopped. "He'll still have to pay for the tee marker."

"Of course he will."

"And I'll have to report this to the tournament director."

Fitz drew in his breath. "If you must."

Derwood headed back toward the clubhouse. "And tell him to watch the language."

Fitz sighed. "I do every day."

After Derwood had disappeared, Fitz rejoined Conner at the first tee. "I told you—"

"Don't say it," Conner said, as he lined up his next shot. "Just don't say it."

Fitz folded his arms and sniffed. "This never happened to Arnold Palmer."

2

"**S**ILLY PUTTY?" FREDDY E. Granger said, blinking. "I thought it was a blue glutinous liquid. You know, like the stuff they put in the bottom of Magic 8-Balls."

"You're all dead wrong," Harley Tuttle responded. "It's BBs, tightly packed and held together with a thin polymer plastic."

"I thought they were filled with spider eggs,' Barry Bennett said, looking puzzled.

"No, no," John corrected him. "That's Bubblicious Bubble Gum."

"Can't you clowns keep your urban legends straight?" Freddy shot back. "That's McDonald's Quarter Pounders. But only if you get the cheese. I read all about it on the Internet."

"Speaking of spider eggs," Barry said, "have you seen that weird stars-and-moon logo on the back of Procter and Gamble products? I think it's satanic."

Conner's eyes rolled skyward. "And you guys wonder why you don't get product endorsements."

After the practice round, Conner and John and Fitz had strolled down world-famous Magnolia Lane to the white-columned Augusta National clubhouse. The grounds were in their most beautiful season. Conner felt bombarded by flowering flashes of pink and white set against the unbroken green backdrop. The warm April wind whispered through the pines, just enough to cool, never so much as to disrupt the game. Conner recalled that the Augusta National had been constructed on an ornamental-tree nursery. When everything bloomed, it was impossible to forget.

Almost all the pros in the tournament were inside at the bar—big names and up-and-comers alike. It was the communal gathering place, the perfect spot to swap stories, tell lies, or drown sorrows.

Conner pulled his wallet out of his back pocket and plopped a bill on the bar. "Twenty bucks says it's Silly Putty."

His challenge was met by a chorus of "You're crazy!" and "I'm in!". Conner dutifully recorded the bets on the back of his scorecard.

He didn't have any better use for it. He'd played a miserable practice round, as Fitz ardently kept reminding him. He'd gotten off to a bad start—the brouhaha with Derwood Scott—but usually he could ignore that sort of distraction. Today, his game had gone from worse to worst. Which was bad news in the extreme. Because a score like today's wouldn't get him past the Friday night cut. Hell, a score like today's wouldn't have earned him a PGA card.

This couldn't come at a more improvident time. At the moment, he was sixty-seventh on the money list—hardly a stellar showing. He'd managed to scrape together a living by playing every weekend and occasionally placing, but after three years on the tour, he still hadn't won a tournament, major or minor. Granted, he was only twenty-seven. But golf was not an endeavor in which years of experience were seen as an asset. Golf, like most sports, favored the young. These should be Conner's prime years. Should be—but weren't.

"Can I get a piece of this action?" Harley Tuttle asked quietly.

Conner nodded. Harley was having a great debut year on the tour, but seemed reserved about engaging in the social life. Conner was trying to break him in. "Got it. John, have you met Harley Tuttle yet?"

"Can't say that I've had the pleasure." John shook the man's hand. "But I've been taking a little sabbatical from tournament life this year. How long have you been on the tour?"

"Just since the start of the year."

"Harley's a bit on the shy side," Conner explained.

Harley shrugged awkwardly. "Like my daddy always said, Better to be thought a fool than to open your mouth and remove all doubt."

John grinned, then leaned close and whispered in Harley's ear. "Always bet against Conner. It's the closest you'll ever get to a sure thing."

"All right, this window is closed," Conner said, after he collected all the bets. He reviewed his notes with a practiced eye. He was used to this sort of thing. Golf pros, he had learned, love to bet. "Freddy is in for ten. Barry is in for ten. Harley is in for twenty, and"—he glanced up at his best friend—"John-boy is in for a whopping hundred smackers. You must have a passion for pain, pal."

"It's easy money," John replied, not batting an eye. "Silly Putty. What a ridiculous idea."

"Say, Fitz," Freddy Granger said, shouting across the bar. He had a pronounced Southern accent—a reminder that he was not just a visitor, but a resident of Augusta. "You've been around for a while."

"That would be a nice way of putting it," Fitz said, not looking up from his beer.

"What do you think they put inside golf balls?"

"As I've already told these two coma victims," he answered, gesturing toward Conner and John, "it's rubber. Plain ordinary rubber."

"Rubber?" The five golf pros stared at one another. "Rubber?"

They spoke as one body. "*Naaaah.*" The verdict was echoed by the assembly: "Can't be!" and "No way, Jose!"

Fitz shook his head. "Hopeless. Absolutely hopeless."

"Hey," John said. "Change of topic. Top ten things in golf that sound dirty but aren't."

Freddy leapt to the occasion. "Nuts—my shaft is bent."

Barry joined in. "Look at the size of his putter!"

"Or," Freddy offered, "how 'bout: nice stroke, but your follow-through leaves a lot to be desired."

"I bet you've heard that a lot," Conner suggested.

"You boys are amateurs," John said. "Try: keep your head down and spread your legs a little more."

Conner jabbed him in the ribs. "You are so vulgar."

"Oh, yeah? I haven't heard anything from you yet."

Conner pondered a moment. "How about . . . mind if I join your threesome?"

Everyone at the bar burst out laughing.

"Listen up," Barry said, with the authority of a seasoned pro. "Let's get back to the serious betting. Fifty bucks says they serve roast beef at the champions dinner tomorrow night." As they all knew, by tradition, the defending champion got to dictate the menu—and pick up the tab.

"No way," Freddy answered. "Chicken. Has to be chicken." Dollar bills flew like feathers in the wind.

"How 'bout this," John said. "Let's bet on what corporate client Tiger Woods will do a commercial for this week."

"Nike," Harley said. "Gotta be Nike."

"He wears Nike," Barry said, shaking his head. "I say Ping."

"Ping can't afford him," Conner opined. "What about American Express?"

"Wheaties," Freddy suggested.

"Budweiser," John rejoined.

"Naaah," Conner said. "Might sully Eldrick's squeaky-clean image." That brought a fresh explosion of laughter from all around the table.

Freddy joined in the fun. "I got fifty bucks that says Tom Kite three-putts the eighteenth hole."

Conner liked Freddy, in part because he didn't take himself as seriously as most of the men on the tour, and in part because he was one of few players who ranked even lower on the money list than Conner did. "That's cold, man."

"But intriguing," John said. "How could we verify? He's not likely to tell us."

"We can see it from here," Freddy said, pointing out the northern bay window toward the eighteenth green.

"I got a better proposition," John said, winking. "I got three hundred bucks that says Conner will not win this tournament. And I'm giving five hundred-to-one odds."

The room fell silent. No one took the action.

"Funny," Conner said through thin lips. "Very funny."

"I was just trying to inspire you," John said, slugging his friend's shoulder amiably. "I think it's about time an Oklahoma boy made good at this tournament. Maybe this will be the year."

"Maybe so," Conner echoed, but his heart wasn't in it. Certainly if he continued playing like he had today, it wouldn't be him. And John had not been playing well all year.

Conner watched as John rose from the table and began circulating around the room. John was extremely friendly and well-liked. He was a social marvel. He never forgot a face, and he could instantaneously recall anyone's name, their wife's name, and the names of their kids. Conner was lucky if he could recognize himself in the mirror each morning.

Conner pushed himself away from the bar and joined Fitz at the far table where he was sitting alone. "So," Conner said, inviting himself into an available chair, "am I wasting my life?"

Fitz barely looked up. "Are you referring to your occupation or your wardrobe?"

"Occupation," Conner replied, taking a long swig from his Corona. "Golf."

Fitz shrugged. "You're better than ninety-nine-point-nine percent of all the people on earth who play the game."

"Yeah, yeah, yeah. But I can't hold my own against the top players."

"Correction," Fitz said emphatically. "You *could* hold your own. You choose not to."

"What's that supposed to mean?"

"You know as well as I do. Your pure golf skills are as good as anyone's on the tour. Better than most. I don't know of another player who can drive as long and as hard and as accurately as you can. Hell, you could hit a dime at two hundred yards. These wide-open fairways should give you an edge, just like they did for Tiger Woods in '97 and '01. You've got tons of promise; that's why I agreed to take you on in the first place. Your major problem"—he tapped the side of his head—"is up here."

"My major problem is my putting game," Conner scoffed.

"Because"—Fitz said, not missing a beat—"that's when the mental game takes precedence. It isn't brute force that matters on the putting green. It isn't strategy; it isn't style. It's the mind." Fitz returned to his drink. "So, naturally, your game falls apart."

Conner made a snorting noise. "You're just sore because I don't blindly follow your instructions like some golf robot."

"Listen to me, Conner. I've been around a long time. I go back to the golden years, before television and big money changed everything. I was around for golf's greatest year—1960—when Hogan, Nicklaus, and Palmer made golf the phenomenon it is today. I've caddied for some of the biggest names in the business. Men who understood the importance of courtesy and honor and decorum."

Conner fell back in his chair. "Here we go again . . ."

"Don't check out on me yet, Conner. I've got something to say and I want you to hear it. This is important."

"I know, I know," Conner said, waving his hands. "I need to adjust my swing."

"You don't need to adjust your swing," Fitz shot back. "You need to adjust your attitude."

Conner turned away. "Aw, go soak your head." He pushed out of his chair.

"Don't run away," Fitz said. "Every time I try to tell you something, you either deflect it with some wiseass remark or run away."

"I'm not running away," Conner insisted. "I'm running toward." He jerked his thumb in the direction of an attractive brunette sitting alone at the bar.

Fitz's eyes drooped wearily. "Does this relate to golf?"

Conner winked. "Definitely. I'm going to show her some of my best strokes."

Fitz could only sigh.

SUSSY'S BAR AND Grill was located about thirty miles from the Augusta National Golf Club, following a series of dirt and gravel roads that no Georgia boy in his right mind would travel unless he was in his Jeep Cherokee or, better yet, his mag-wheel pickup. The neon sign in the window with three letters missing (SUS Y'S BA & G ILL) claimed there was a grill on site, but if any food other than beer nuts and pretzels had ever been served there, it was so long ago that no one living had any memory of it. The place was popular with locals; unfortunately, out here in the middle of nowhere, there weren't many locals.

Tonight there were patrons, though—two of them, huddling in a back booth facing one another. The bartender, the only other man on the premises, had never seen them before. And they apparently didn't want to attract any attention. Why else would they choose the most out-of-sight booth in the darkest corner of the bar? They weren't looking for fellowship, and they weren't trying to pick up tail. They wanted to be left alone. So, like any good bartender, he gave them what they wanted.

One of the men was much taller than the other; he seemed to be in command of the discussion. When the two customers finally waved the bartender over to refill their Scotches—neat—he overheard enough to gather that the tall man was making the other fellow some sort of proposition. But exactly what was being proposed he couldn't say. And he didn't ask, either. Because whatever it was, it was clear they didn't want anyone else to know about it.

The bartender returned to his station and pretended to be toweling off glasses. It was only about ten minutes later, when he made a necessary visit to the men's room, that he heard more. Turned out the men's room was the perfect place to eavesdrop on that booth; the sound came in through the air vent just above the sink. He still didn't hear enough to know what they were talking about. But he heard enough to pique his curiosity.

"What if we get caught?" the shorter of the men said. His voice had a tendency to squeak when he was nervous. And at the moment, he sounded very nervous.

"Who's gonna catch us?" the tall man said confidently. "The police? The tournament officials? I don't think so."

"I don't know if I have the stomach for this. I've never had anything to do with—violence."

"Don't be squeamish," the other man said. His voice was reassuring in a way that made the bartender's skin crawl. "I promise you—I've thought of everything. There will be no mistakes."

"Suppose I say yes—what's in it for me?"

The bartender heard the tall man taking something out of his pocket, followed by a fast rippling noise. Money, he reckoned. Lots of it.

"This is just a down payment," the tall man said. "Think of it as earnest money."

The bartender heard another noise, a shuffling sound—as if the bills were being transferred from one hand to another.

"Then you'll do it?" the tall man asked, with a bit of a twinkle.

There was no merriment in the other man's voice when he replied. "I don't have any choice."

3

Tuesday

TUESDAY MORNING CONNER was back on the course, hoping to complete as many practice strokes as possible before the official tournament activities began the next day. Conner tried everything he could think of to improve his score. Nothing worked. He was playing like some duffer who got out twice a year for the Rotary Club scramble, not someone with a PGA card in his back pocket.

"Glad to see you changed your attire," Fitz muttered, as he and Conner and John approached the third tee.

Conner grinned. Today he was wearing black golf shoes, purple calf socks, overalls cut off as shorts, and a Hawaiian shirt with cigars stuffed in the pocket.

"Personally, I like it," John said, suppressing a smile. "Although I miss the Panama hat."

Conner's eyebrows rose. "You thought it brought out the sparkle in my eyes?"

"I thought it covered up your bald spot."

"I do *not* have a bald spot."

John looked at him nonchalantly. "Thinning, then."

"You don't know what you're talking about."

"Fine, fine. Have it your way."

Conner whirled around. "Fitz, am I balding? Or thinning?"

Fitz couldn't have looked less interested. "Relax, Conner. You're still the macho stud of the PGA. A girl in every port—isn't that what the sportswriters say? Women drool when they see your handsome visage."

"But seriously."

"It might be time to start wearing a cap."

Conner bounced back to John. "This is an elaborate joke, right? You two cooked this up in advance. Your idea of sick humor."

John smiled beatifically. "If it makes you feel more secure to believe that, then fine."

Conner folded his arms across his chest. "You guys are just jealous because you can't wear purple calf socks."

"I am not jealous of anything about you, sonny," Fitz retorted, "but I am worried that you're going to be sacked from the tournament before you have a chance to play. Which will not only make you look like a fool, but will reduce my earnings to seven percent of nothing!"

Conner selected a club and approached the tee-off. "Don't be ridiculous."

"I'm not! You think this hasn't happened before? You think you're the first smart aleck who ever made it into the PGA? Think again. The Augusta National tossed out Jack Whitaker for referring to the fans as 'a mob.' They banned Gary McCord for that stupid remark about the fairway being so smooth it looked bikini-waxed. They yanked Freddie Haas for raising his voice! And you're working overtime to see if yours can be the next name on that distinguished list."

"Excuse me," Conner said, stepping aside. "I have a game to play." He took a deep breath of the sweet nandina in the air. "And I'm not going to zombify myself just to please a doddering pack of country-club snobs."

"Even though they follow the official golf rankings, participation at the Masters is by invitation only." Fitz huffed. "You should respect the privilege you've been given."

Conner raised the head of his club beside his ball. "I'd respect it a lot more if I were making more money."

"You'd be making more money if you improved your attitude," Fitz shot back.

"No, I'd be making more money if I could get this stupid dimpled ball to go in that tiny hole." He started to swing.

"Wait!" Fitz shouted.

Conner jerked around in mid-swing. The head of his club drove into the grass. "What?" he said through clenched teeth.

Fitz crouched down and retrieved Conner's ball from its perch on the tee. "What is this you're playing, anyway?"

Conner's expression did not improve. "As I recall, it's a Magfli 6."

"Magfli 6? I thought you were playing a Pro Z1 Titleist. Titleists are the best golf balls in the world. Each one is precision-tested and balanced for premium performance. I bought you a whole box of them."

"Yeah . . ." Conner averted his eyes. "I, uh, gave those to Barry Bennett, actually."

"To Bennett? Why?"

"Well . . . I lost a bet and I, uh, didn't have the cash on hand . . ."

"You're joking."

"See, I bet that Tom Kite would three-putt the eighteenth, but wouldn't you know it, the old shanker ended up pulling it off in two. So . . ."

Fitz's face reddened with fury. "So now you don't have any balls?"

"Of course I have balls. Well, *a* ball, anyway. You're holding it."

Fitz glanced at the palm of his hand. "A Magfli 6? That's a duffer ball. Where'd you buy this thing?"

"Didn't. Found it in a sand trap yesterday."

Fitz slapped his hand against his forehead. "Hopeless. Absolutely hopeless."

Conner continued playing his practice round, but the game didn't improve, not for him or John. Neither of the two pros was in the zone. Conner knocked the ball into the rough so often he wished his bag contained a machete. John had been in the water traps so often he considered investing in scuba gear.

"Damn this stupid game, anyway," John groused, as they marched toward the fifteenth tee. "Who's idea was it to start playing golf?"

"As I recall, it was the only way we could get out of trig with Mr. Imes."

John laughed. "Right, right. Good ol' *Imes-stein.*"

"Just think," Conner said. "If we'd stuck with him, we might be, like, nuclear physicists."

The two men exchanged a long look, then spoke with one voice. "Or not."

After the laughter faded, Conner jabbed his friend in the side. "Look. Up ahead."

Halfway up the fairway, they both spotted another pro on the tour: Abel "Ace" Silverstone. *Ace* was the sobriquet awarded by the sports press after Abel racked up an impressive series of titles his freshman year on the tour. Now, in his fifth year in the PGA, he was still racking them in, creating the biggest buzz in the golf world since Tiger Woods.

"Why is he moving so slowly?" John wondered.

"Over there," Conner answered, pointing just a bit north toward the green. A three-man camera crew was setting up, adjusting lenses and tripods.

"Why are they shooting him?" John asked. "The tournament hasn't even begun yet."

"Probably doing filler spots," Conner guessed. "Getting some pregame background material. Possibly doing a profile. After all, he's favored to win."

Conner turned toward his friend. "You know, I hate people who are favored to win."

"That's just as well. Because as I recall, he hates you."

"That business at Pebble Beach was a total misunderstanding. How was I to know that girl was his daughter?" He glanced back at the camera crew. They looked ready to roll. "Anyway, I don't think this glory hog needs any more exposure. So what are we going to do about it?"

"Don't ask me. I'm just a good ol' boy from Oklahoma." John paused. "I count on you to come up with the evil stuff."

A malevolent grin infected Conner's face. "I was hoping you'd say that." He unzipped a special compartment on the side of his bag and retrieved a single golf ball. "Those camera boys want a show. I say we give them a show."

When they caught up to Ace, he was on the lip of the water trap, barely ten yards from the green. Ideally, he could chip the ball over the water onto the green and then one-putt into the hole. With luck, he might even skip the putt and score with his chip shot.

"Ace, my man. How goes it?" Conner said as he strolled into Ace's face, hand extended. "How lucky to run into you."

The instant Ace saw Conner, his face twisted into a bitter grimace. It was several seconds before he appeared to remember that the cameras were rolling and tried to feign some semblance of cordiality. "Uh, yeah. Lucky." Ace forced up a smile and shook Conner's hand. Even if he hadn't hated Conner's guts, Conner suspected Ace wouldn't be all that thrilled to see someone else invading his spotlight, but there wasn't much he could do about it with the cameras on.

"Looks like you've attracted a bit of attention," Conner said, winking and jabbing the man in the ribs.

"What? Oh, them. Right." Ace shrugged haplessly. "It wasn't my idea. They're from CBS. They wanted some background footage on me, just in case . . . well, you know."

"Of course we do," John said, taking the man by the shoulder. "And we just want you to know we're rooting for you."

Ace blinked. "You are?"

"Course we are. You've always been our favorite. Of the top dogs, I mean."

"Jeez, that's nice to hear. When a man rises to, well, you know, my place on the money list, he starts to worry that there might be some resentment from . . . well . . ."

"The peons?"

"No, no, of course not. I just thank God every morning that he made me one of the winners. We can't all be winners, you know. I learned that back in the first grade, playing dodgeball in gym class. There are winners and losers. It's true on the tour, too. Winners and losers."

"Or," John said, "taking Conner into account, winners and wieners."

Ace laughed. He started to walk on, but John grabbed his shoulder and held him fast. "Say, I've been wondering if you could do something for me—"

Ace's eyes narrowed. "Jeez, I'm really busy right now. After this shoot, I've got a meeting to talk about a cable TV special, then I'm talking to the Ping people about a possible endorsement—"

"This won't take a minute. See, I've been having this trouble with my backswing, and since everyone knows you're the master, I thought maybe . . ." He winked. "Just a few pointers?"

"Oh. *Oh.* Sure." Ace's face brightened. "Well, you know, the key to the backswing is the grip. I know some people say it's the stance, but let me tell you—it's the grip. It's really simple. See, most people hold the club like they're swinging a baseball bat upside down. But what you want to do . . ."

While Ace gassed on about backswing, behind him, Conner surreptitiously replaced Ace's golf ball with the ball he had taken from the compartment in his bag. The cameramen picked up what he was doing, but to Conner's relief, none of them said a word.

". . . then you gotta loosen up, you know? Hold the club firmly, but relaxed. Then carefully bring your club back around and—*pow!*"

John smiled. "*Pow!* That's it, huh?"

Ace gave his familiar aw-shucks shrug. "That's it. Pretty simple, huh?"

"Heck, yeah. I just wish someone had told me before." He shook

Ace's hand with great vigor. "Well, I'll get out of your way so you can hit the ball."

"Thanks," Ace said. "Course, I'd love to chat but—you know." He jerked his head toward the camera crew. "America is waiting."

"Right, right." Smiling and waving, Conner and John backstepped briskly away from him.

"Think he saw me make the switch?" Conner whispered, once they were out of earshot.

"Nah. All he can see is his name in lights."

Back at the water trap, Ace made a great show of addressing the ball. He frowned, crouched down, then gazed studiously at the hole in the center of the green. He placed his club on the ground to check the lie of the course, then brushed some leaves and other debris away. He held his thumb forward, as if measuring the distance, then licked a finger to check the wind.

"Cripes, just hit the ball already," Conner muttered. John jabbed him in the side.

Finally, Ace was ready to swing. With a brow creased by fierce concentration, he took his stance, adjusted his grip, gave his ball a steely-eyed look, then swung . . .

The instant the club hit the ball, it exploded into a cloud of white talc. Ace cried out—something between "Ahhh!" and "Yikes!", Conner and John could never agree—and jumped at least a foot in the air. His club flew backwards out of his hands, narrowly missing Conner's skull. Ace landed off balance and started teetering precariously forward.

"No," Conner whispered silently. "This is just too good to be true."

Ace flailed his arms madly, trying to recover his balance, but it was not to be. With no means to stop himself, he tumbled face first into the water trap, like a diver belly-flopping. After thrashing about in the water for several seconds, he reared his head up, dripping wet, algae around his neck, a lily pad clinging to the side of his head.

And of course, every moment of this performance was recorded for posterity by CBS.

John turned toward Conner. "You think we should help the man out?"

"I think he'd prefer to be alone right now."

"You're so sensitive, Conner. That's what I like about you."

"Yeah." The impulsive grin criss-crossed his face. "Let's see if we can bribe the cameramen for a copy of the tape."

* * *

SHORTLY AFTER DARK, a head appeared in the rough off the fairway for the eighteenth hole. The eyes scanned the surrounding area. Then, when they were sure no one was in sight, an arm emerged and pushed the body out of the ground. He'd made it!

He replaced the manhole cover and quickly ducked behind a tree. It had taken hours of crawling through narrow, claustrophobic tunnels, but eventually, he'd found himself inside the Augusta National compound. And no one was the wiser.

When at last he decided it was safe to move, he stayed low, clinging to the ground. He knew that the Augusta National employed a significant security team, and that their numbers were tripled during the week of the Masters tournament. It was not impossible that someone might be out here, even after dark, even this far from the clubhouse and the cabins.

He scanned the course and, sure enough, a few moments later, he spotted a man cruising the course in a golf cart. He didn't appear to be going anywhere special or doing anything in particular. Definitely security. He waited until the guard was well out of the way, then made a break for a thick patch of trees nearby.

He suppressed a smile, barely able to contain himself. For all he had heard about the much-vaunted ultratight security measures of the Augusta National, he'd made it inside. He wrapped a green flak jacket around his skinny frame, covering his black heavy metal T-shirt. He brushed his long stringy hair away from his face, then checked his pack to make sure he hadn't lost any of his gear. All the essentials still seemed to be in place. Good. Very good.

Slowly, he eased out of the rough, checking in all directions for security. He could probably make it to the clubhouse without being spotted. Course, even if someone did spot him, he would just whip out the false credentials he was carrying. According to his wallet card, he was a member of a CBS film crew. Just out for a walk, he would say. Scouting locations.

As he crested a hill, he spotted for the first time the gleaming white edifice of the Augusta National clubhouse. All the pros would be in there now, he knew, swapping stories, buying drinks. Getting ready for the annual champions dinner later tonight. They would all be there. Including his target.

And after the dinner, they would all move to their cabins. It would be a simple matter of keeping his eyes open and staying out of sight to determine which cabin was John McCree's.

And once he knew that, he would be able to complete his mission with ease.

He smiled, then headed toward the clubhouse. He zipped up his flak jacket, insulating himself. A strong wind was coming out of the west, and he was beginning to feel a chill.

John McCree, he thought silently to himself. Soon, he would be face-to-face with the man.

And there was nothing anyone could do to stop it.

4

CONNER AND JOHN stood just inside the doorway of Butler Cabin and whistled.

"Man," John said, "have you ever seen so many golf pros crammed together? It's like the audition room for the new Titleist commercial."

"Or a meeting of Gamblers Anonymous," Conner suggested.

The large banquet room was packed with golf pros of all ages, from all eras. Scanning from left to right, Conner saw a distinguished pantheon of players, the latest and the greatest, everyone he had worshiped as a kid and everyone he envied as an adult.

The Tuesday night Masters champions' dinner was a huge affair, possibly the most prestigious event on the pro golf social calendar. Founded by Ben Hogan in 1952, it was the greatest event at the greatest of tournaments—small wonder everyone wanted to be there. Beforehand, in accordance with tradition, an autograph session took place in the Champions Locker Room while the past champions enjoyed a predinner cocktail; no autographing was permitted at the formal dinner itself. John, as usual, was immaculately attired in a new sports jacket and tie. Conner was wearing blue jeans with a T-shirt that looked like a tux.

"Over there," John said, pointing toward the dais. "Table One."

Conner followed John's finger toward the long rectangular banquet table at the front of the room. It was Table One, all right. All the giants were there, past and present—Ben Crenshaw, Nick Faldo, Fuzzy Zoeller, Tiger Woods, David Duval, Arnold Palmer, Ray Floyd—just to name a few.

"Check it out," John said, gazing with awestruck amazement. "Jack Nicklaus!"

"Really?" Conner started forward. "I've got a bone to pick with him. He still owes me from the eighteenth hole at St. Andrews."

John grabbed Conner's arm and held him back. "The man is a living legend. Give him some respect."

"It's hard to respect a living legend who welshes on a hundred dollar bet."

"He did not welsh on the bet. There was a difference of opinion about whether your ball moved the first time you swung."

"I never even came close to that ball! It was the wind. You know what those Scottish winds are like!"

"Yeah. So does Jack Nicklaus."

Conner frowned, then relented. There would probably be a better time to try to collect the debt. Like maybe when the Golden Bear was giving a press conference. "I don't suppose we're sitting at Table One."

John glanced at the seating chart. "Not hardly." He pointed toward another table in a recess against the south wall, the table furthest from the dais. "Table Twenty-Four. That's us."

"Swell." Conner made his way toward Table Twenty-Four, John just a few steps behind him. He threaded his way through the labyrinth of tables, pausing to chat with the players he knew, who for the most part were not those wearing green jackets. The green jackets were the exclusive attire of the past champions of the Masters tournament. This was their one night of the year to wear them. And no one was allowed to take them home.

Halfway across the room, Conner saw Ace Silverstone making his way toward them. He grabbed John's arm. "Detour."

They steered hard aport, trying to give Ace the slip. Unfortunately, the press of so many bodies made escape impossible. Within a few moments, Ace had caught up with them.

"Conner! John!" Ace called out behind them. "Wait up!"

As flight was now clearly impossible, Conner turned to face the inevitable.

"Conner!" Ace repeated, as he caught up to them. "I want a few words with you!"

Conner braced himself. "Look, Ace . . . we were just having a bit of fun . . ."

"I want to shake your hand, friend!"

Conner blinked. "You do?"

"Damn straight." Ace grabbed Conner's hand and pumped it like a well handle. "How did you know exactly what I needed?"

Conner's eyes darted to John for help, which was not forthcoming. "I . . . um . . ."

"Those camera boys had been following me all day, but they hadn't gotten a thing they liked. They didn't say it, but I know what they thought—that I was boring. Too conservative. Not camera-worthy. But you changed all that, didn't you?" He laughed heartily. "*Boom!*"

"Uh . . . yeah. I guess I did . . ."

"They loved that bit. Said they got great footage. They're going to use it not just this week, but all year long, as one of those video replays before they cut to a commercial. All year long! I'll get more exposure than I ever could've from some single-play feature piece. I really owe you for this one, buddy." He grabbed Conner's hand again and resumed pumping.

"I truly don't know what to say."

"You don't have to say a word, my man. All is forgotten. And anytime you need something, I'm the one you call. Kapeesh?"

Conner forced his lips into action. "Uh . . . sure. Kapeesh."

Ace slapped him hard on the shoulder. "You've got a friend for life, buddy boy. Excuse me now, okay? Gotta get back to Table One."

Conner and John watched as Ace receded into the crowd. "Well," John said, "congratulations. You've got a friend for life, buddy boy."

Conner nodded. "I liked it better when he hated me."

Conner felt an arm grab him from behind. He turned to find Barry Bennett standing there, fists on his hips. "Hiya Barry. Are you gonna be my friend for life, too?"

Barry ignored him. "Pay up, Conner."

"Pay . . . ?"

"The Tiger Woods bet."

"Oh, right."

"You owe me a hundred smackers. And don't try to pay me off in golf balls, either. This time I want cold hard cash."

"And you'll have it, Barry. But I'm a bit short at the moment . . ."

"Don't give me any excuses, Conner. You owe me!"

Conner wrapped his arm around the big man's shoulder. Getting that close made Conner's eyes water. Barry must've been in the locker room earlier; he had something strong and alcoholic on his breath. "Look, Barry, how about if I gave you something even better than cash?"

"And what would that be?"

Conner's eyes twinkled. "A lien against the Golden Bear."

CONNER AND JOHN finally made it back to their own table. Fitz was seated in a chair just across from Conner; John's wife, Jodie, was facing him.

Conner made eye contact with Jodie and smiled. "I hope you won't think me forward if I say that you look radiant tonight."

Jodie pressed her hand against one cheek. "Conner Cross. You old flatterer, you."

Conner jerked his head toward John. "You know, this clown really doesn't deserve you."

"I know," Jodie answered. "But someone had to save him from his life of sin and degradation."

"When was that?" Conner asked.

"When he was hanging around with you."

Conner smiled. He had known Jodie even longer than he had known John. The three of them had all lived near Watonga. They had spent many a late hour together, chugging beers at Roman Nose State Park, or checking out the flicks at the Liberty Theatre. The Three Musketeers, some of the locals called them. Others favored The Three Stooges. Jodie had originally been Conner's girl, way back when, and there was a time when he thought . . .

But it was best to put that out of his mind. She was John's now, and she had a gigantic diamond ring on her finger to prove it.

"Jodie," Conner said, "why don't you dump this chump and run away with me?"

She blushed. "I'd like that, Conner. Really. But to tell you the truth—I've kinda grown to like Georgia. I've even started to speak Georgian. Listen." She adopted an exaggerated Southern accent—sort of like Scarlett O'Hara on steroids. "Somebody puh-lese bring me mah grits!"

"That's all that's keeping you with this man? A bad accent?" Conner glanced at John; he was barely listening. He was accustomed to Conner and Jodie's banter; he'd been hearing it for most of his life. "That's not enough."

"Well, there's also the tiny matter of money. I hate to admit it, Conner, but I've become a wee bit fond of being rich."

"What am I, chopped liver? I'll get you anything—"

"You still living in that trailer park, Conner?"

Conner stopped a beat. "Well . . ."

"Still gambling away most of your spare dough?"

"Only when I feel lucky."

"Still trying to pick up every chick who wanders into the bar?"

"Well . . ." He squirmed. "Certainly not every chick."

She patted her husband's hand. "I think I'll stick with my Johnny."

After the salad course was served, Derwood Scott rose to the podium. Conner tried not to snarl. "I can't believe that pissant stuck me with a three-stroke penalty."

"It was only two," Fitz hissed back. "You brought the third one on yourself. Actually, you brought them all on yourself."

Conner frowned. "Have I told you to go soak your head?"

"Not in the last half hour."

"Then go soak your head."

Derwood began the proceedings, which of course started with the introduction of every man in the audience wearing a green jacket. Champions running as far back as the 1950s rose and recaptured a brief moment of the limelight. After the roll of champions was completed, Derwood started thanking all the "little people" who made this tournament possible.

"Where does he think he is?" Conner whispered. "The Oscars?"

The thank yous continued for at least ten more minutes. Then Derwood began a panegyric on the "special ambience" of the Masters tournament. "There are many golf tournaments," he proclaimed, "but there is only one Masters. Here, beneath the shady reaches of the spreading magnolias, men from all walks of life can come together to remember a simpler time, a better time, and to engage in the sport of gentlemen throughout the world."

"I don't know how much more of this I can take," Conner said, sotto voce. John jabbed him in the stomach.

"What is this thing, this grand endeavor we call golf?" Derwood continued. "Yes, it's a game, but somehow, in the hands of the men in this room, it becomes something much more. It's an exhibition of excellence, a playing field where men of good cheer can come together in the name of brotherhood."

"Brotherhood?" Conner said, not quite as quietly as before. "Hell, I'm just trying to make a few bucks." Fitz and Jodie and John all gave him harsh looks.

While Derwood droned on, the waiters began serving dinner. When Conner's plate was placed before him, he eyed the mashed potatoes, peas, and asparagus spears encircling a modest pink clump.

"What is this?" Conner said, staring at his plate. "Spam?"

John gave him another *shaddup already* glare. "It isn't Spam. It's baked ham."

"Looks like Spam to me," Conner said, oblivious to the distraction he was creating. "You know where Spam comes from?"

John tried to ignore him. "Shhh."

"It was invented by a guy up in Winnetka. Roy was his name, I think."

John stopped, obviously torn between his desire to tell Conner to hush and the irresistible impulse to correct another Conneresque line of bull. "It was invented during World War II as a way of preserving and shipping meat for soldiers."

"No," Conner insisted, "I read a magazine article about this. It was definitely a guy called Roy. Roy Spam, I believe."

John rolled his eyes. "Spam is short for spiced ham. You don't know what you're talking about."

"I most certainly do. It was invented by Roy Spam."

"I'm sure. And you probably think he made it from Silly Putty."

"I'm telling you, I read about this in some scholarly journal."

"Like what? *The National Enquirer?*"

With each rejoinder, their voices grew louder. Eventually, there were more people listening to the Spam debate than listening to Derwood.

"I'm telling you, this is something I *know.*"

"Right," John said. "I remember in the third grade, you *knew* that babies came from overeating."

"It was Roy Spam!"

"Baloney!"

Conner scooped up a spoonful of mashed potatoes and flung it across the table at John.

John's eyes went wide. "You sorry little—" He grabbed his own spoon and retaliated, sending a clump of potatoes back across the table. Conner fired again, and soon the mashed potatoes were criss-crossing the field of battle. When he ran out of potatoes, John flung his Spam/ham. A big saucy piece slapped Conner on the side of his face.

Enraged, Conner began flinging peas. A few of them veered off and hit Jodie, who then picked up her own spoon and began slinging away. Before long, all of Table Twenty-Four had joined in the warfare. A full-fledged food fight ensued.

At this point, Derwood was no longer able to ignore the disruption in the back of the room. "Excuse me," he said, pounding his gavel. "If I could have your attention."

Derwood didn't get anyone's attention. Conner was under the table, ducking his head to avoid food fire from both directions.

"Excuse me!" Derwood said, pounding even louder than before. "Please come to order."

From Conner's vantage point, half the room appeared to be in culinary combat. Young and old alike crouched beneath their tables, flinging asparagus spears and mushy peas halfway across the room. Someone found the Jell-o dish that was going to be served for dessert, and then the battle really got messy.

Conner looked back at John, who had an asparagus spear in each nostril. "Now this is an exhibition of excellence."

John nodded. "In the name of brotherhood."

"Naturally." Conner removed the ladle from the gravy boat. "Now watch this."

"*People!*" Derwood shouted, desperately trying to regain control. "We can't do this! This is the Masters. The *Masters!* We must—"

He had more that he wanted to say, but what it was no one ever knew, because he stopped talking for good after the fistful of gravy splatted him in the face.

5

CONNER WAS NOT entirely surprised when he received his summons to the chairman's office. Given the way Derwood had stomped out of the champions' dinner, some attempt at reciprocity seemed inevitable. The only questions in Conner's brain were when and how. *When* turned out to be that very night. *How* turned out to be a command performance in the vice-principal's office.

It was impossible for Conner to predict what would happen next, because the Masters—and its powers-that-be—were like no other. The Masters was neither connected with, nor accountable to, any professional association or organized league. It was administered by a private fraternity—virtually a secret society—of well-heeled, conservative duffers. They did not discuss the inner workings of the Club; what had been described as the Augusta National *omerta* was always maintained. And at the Masters, their word was the law.

Two tournament officials escorted Conner back to the clubhouse. Without even allowing him to pause at the bar, they led him downstairs, past the public areas into the inner catacombs of the building. Conner trailed them down a long hallway where the staff offices were located. The hallway seemed enormous; Conner wondered why they hadn't installed an airport people-mover. Only as they approached the end of the dimly lit corridor did Conner realize there were doors there. Two dark mahogany, magnificently carved doors.

As they approached, the doors swung open, as if moved by a higher power.

"Please come in."

Following the instructions of the voice from within, Conner and his two escorts stepped inside.

The office was magnificent, every corner filled with golf memorabilia and curios. One entire wall appeared to be covered with photos and awards relating to Bobby Jones and Cliff Roberts (always referred to by Club members as Bob Jones and Mr. Roberts), the founders of the Augusta National who oversaw the construction of the golf course (designed by Dr. Alister MacKenzie, M.D.) and carved it out of 365 acres that were once an indigo plantation. The walls were all rich, dark wood, floor-to-ceiling. The furniture reflected the dark motif, right down to the plush upholstered chairs. But the most magnificent piece was the desk—as immense as some conference tables. Behind the desk, leaning back in the chair with his fingers steepled, was a distinguished white-haired gentleman Conner knew all too well: Artemus Tenniel—chairman of the Augusta National Golf Club.

Conner nodded politely. "Evening, Artemus."

Conner could see the man burn at the casual use of his first name, which of course was exactly why Conner had done it. "You will address your remarks to Mr. Spenser."

"Ah. Forgive me." Apparently being summoned by the chairman was akin to having an audience with the queen. You could only speak when spoken to, and then only through an intermediary.

Conner pivoted slightly, enough to take in the middle-aged, middleweight figure of Andrew Spenser, the Masters tournament director. And cowering behind him, his associate Derwood Scott.

"Let me ask you a question," Spenser said, in a slow, deep Southern accent. He paced around the room, slowly encircling Conner. "You are Conner Cross. A three-year member of the PGA tour."

"Guilty."

Spenser continued his slow circles, as if he were trying to recreate the torture and brainwash scene from *The Manchurian Candidate.* "What do you think the Masters tournament is?"

"A chance to make some really big buckos?"

"No. The Masters tournament is about much more than big . . . buckos." He gave a mock shiver. "The Masters tournament is a celebration of mankind's finest qualities. When the tournament was established in 1937, it was perceived as the pinnacle of—"

"I've read the brochure," Conner said.

"The Masters tournament represents the best of all mankind—"

"If it represents the best of all mankind, how come the Masters didn't have any African-American players until 1975? How come the Augusta National didn't have any black members until 1990?"

Spenser studiously ignored him. "Over the years, this tournament has come to represent much more than simply a sports competition. At the Masters, we try to establish an exemplar for athleticism, ethics . . . and behavior."

Conner had the distinct feeling that *behavior* was the exemplar they were going to be discussing tonight. "Aren't you guys taking this all a wee bit too seriously? I mean, we're talking about a golf tournament here, not the end of Western civilization."

Spenser drew in his chin. "What we are trying to do is set a standard—"

"No, what we are trying to do is knock a silly white ball into a tiny hole in the ground. It ain't international diplomacy."

Spenser raised a knobbly finger. "Your behavior has been inexcusable."

"I was strafed with Spam. I had to defend myself."

"Tonight's debacle at the champions' dinner was only the culmination of many violations that have come to our attention."

"Such as what?"

"Destruction of tournament property."

"I said I'd pay for the tee marker."

"Use of foul and offensive language."

"You try talking to Derwood without—"

"Disorderly conduct."

"Well, maybe a little . . ."

"Violation of the tournament dress code."

"The tournament hasn't even started yet!"

"Need we remind you, Mr. Cross, that a strict code of dress and conduct applies to the entire PGA tour?" This came from someone behind him. Conner turned to face a man who was altogether too familiar to him.

"Richard Peregino," Conner said, exhaling. "The PGA morals cop."

"Vice president of Decorum and Image, thank you."

"But it isn't even a PGA tournament!"

"As the on-site representative of the PGA," Peregino continued, "I must tell you that we take these charges very seriously." Peregino wore a suit that was too small, too old, and was tacky even when it was new. Perched in the midst of this high-class office, he was like a walking-talking What's Wrong With This Picture? "We've had you under close observation for some time now because we've suspected you of improper conduct."

"Is that why you've been watching me everywhere I go? And here I thought you had a crush on me."

Peregino's jaw tightened. "You know perfectly well that the PGA demands that its members uphold high moral and ethical standards. Our regulations prohibit illegal or offensive behavior, improper or insufficient attire, sexual misconduct, profanity. We carefully screen all entrants to prevent any rogue bull from tarnishing the PGA image."

"Someone must've been snoozing when I got my card," Conner muttered.

"That mistake can be easily corrected," Peregino replied, drawing himself up to his full height, which was still about six inches lower than Conner's. "And believe me, if your conduct doesn't change, it will be. You won't finish the tour."

"You won't finish this tournament," Spenser chimed in. "Here in Augusta, we have rules. And if those rules are not observed, you will be excused from the competition."

"Wait a minute," Conner protested. "I was personally invited to participate. You can't toss me out now."

"I can and I will," Spenser shot back. "I've done it before and I'll do it again. One more disruption or violation, and you will be escorted off the property."

Conner remembered what Fitz had told him earlier about Haas and the others. When the Augusta National wanted someone gone, he was gone. Which would definitely put a crimp in Conner's plan to win big and pay off his trailer home.

Conner paused a moment before speaking. "I'll try to behave myself."

Spenser preened triumphantly. "See that you do."

Derwood stepped out of the shadows. "And your attire?"

"Whatever."

That wasn't good enough for Derwood. "I will be at the first tee tomorrow morning to personally inspect your clothing. If you're not dressed in compliance with our standards, I won't let you on the course."

Conner frowned. "Does this mean that Easter bunny suit I was planning to wear is out of the question?"

His remark was met by a room full of stony expressions.

"Damn," Conner muttered. "I'm gonna lose my deposit."

LATER THAT NIGHT, a different conversation took place in another office in the clubhouse. The office was dark except for the illuminated glow radiating from a single desktop Tiffany lamp. The low lighting silhouetted the two figures standing on opposite sides of a desk. The expressions on their faces and the tone of their voices revealed that the discussion was anything but amicable.

"I want an explanation for this!"

"I'm afraid . . . I have none to give." The man standing behind the desk had a slight catch in his voice. "Perhaps if you could give me some time . . ."

"Your time is up."

"If you could just give me a week. A day, even."

"I want an explanation now. Because if this means what I think it means—"

"Please." The man behind the desk began to fidget with a paperweight. "I promise you. It's not what it seems."

"Then what is it?"

"It—It—It's just a terrible misunderstanding."

"Oh, I think I understand. I think I understand perfectly."

"But—don't—" His head fell into his hands. "If you could just give me some more time."

"I'll give you until tomorrow morning."

"But that's not nearly enough—"

"Tomorrow morning. And if you can't clear this up by then, I'll go public."

"*No!*"

"Yes. Then you can make your explanations to everyone." He turned and started toward the door.

"Please wait—" But it was too late. Before the man behind the desk could finish his sentence, his companion had left the office.

He collapsed into his chair. How had he gotten himself into this mess? It had all seemed so innocent at first, so harmless. And now—

But there was no point in wallowing in those ruminations. He had to do something. To do something quick. But what?

There was no way he could rectify this mess before morning. If the other man was as good as his threats, he would be ruined. Absolutely ruined.

His only hope was that the other man didn't go public, that he kept his mouth shut. Not just tomorrow morning, but forever. Something had to happen. Something had to change his mind. Or something had to make it impossible for him to tell what he knew.

An idea flickered in the corner of his brain. A wild idea—a crazy one.

But just possibly the only one he had left.

He pressed his fingers against his temples, trying to fight back the throbbing inside his head. He had no hope unless John McCree kept his mouth shut. Permanently.

6

CONNER GAZED OUT at the vast stretch of darkness surrounding him. The sky blanketed the horizon, creating an inky satin backdrop interrupted only by dim moonlight reflected by the white-columned clubhouse. Looked as though the stars could use a little help tonight, he thought to himself. Glad to oblige. He swung his club back, and the glistening white ball soared out across the driving range, adding, however briefly, another reflective speck to the sky.

The ball etched a perfect parabola before cascading down in front of the 300 marker—exactly where Conner wanted it. It was a beautiful stroke. The only problems were (1) strokes on the driving range don't count toward your score and (2) there was no one around to appreciate it. Why the hell couldn't he have done that today on the course?

There was no point in berating himself with that question. If he knew the answer, he would have acted on it long before now. He had barely snuck onto the tour three years ago, had a so-so first year, and had gone downhill since. Sure, he was still playing well enough to keep his card, even well enough to make a few bucks here and there. But he couldn't shake the feeling that he was falling short of his potential. He couldn't shake it because Fitz kept hammering it into his brain at every opportunity.

He checked his watch. Where was John, anyway? Conner had expected him to show up more than an hour ago. It was a tradition with them, knocking the balls around in the moonlight the night before a tournament began. They were the only ones he knew who did it, although everyone on the tour had some tradition, some good luck ritual. Perhaps because golf skills were so unpredictable, because the causes for the constant fluctuations in quality of performance were so elusive, golf pros tended to be a superstitious lot. On the night before a tournament began . . . Freddy Granger washed his lucky red socks . . . Ace Silverstone read from the Bible . . . Barry Bennett got drunk . . . Tiger Woods called home. As far as Conner knew, he and John were the only players who actually practiced, which was considered a radical idea in some quarters.

Truth was, knocking the balls down the driving range was not so much about practicing as relaxing. In the still of the night, hidden away under the cover of darkness, Conner and John shared some of their closest moments. It was one of the rare times when the superficialities disappeared and the two men could talk like they did when they were kids. It was these quiet moments, much more than the public carousing and debauchery, that kept their close-knit friendship going.

Or used to, anyway. Where the hell was he? This was totally unlike John. He was theoretically the reliable one. If Conner was late to arrive, no one would think anything of it, except perhaps to put in a call to the local hospitals and whorehouses. But when John was late, that was something else.

Conner heard a rustling on the patio directly behind him. Someone was moving his way. About time. "What happened? Jodie demand a quickie? Or did your—"

He stopped abruptly. The silhouette moving toward him was too short, too wide. Whoever it was, it wasn't John.

"How's it hangin', Conner?"

How's it hangin'? Wait a minute . . .

Conner strained his eyes, peering through the darkness. Freddy Granger.

"I'm fine, Freddy. Just trying to get in some practice strokes."

Freddy nodded. "I heard about your score today. I don't blame you."

Conner tried to remind himself that he actually liked Freddy. "So what are you doing out here? Shouldn't you be in your room chanting your mantra? Or maybe in the locker room, hexing the other players' clubs?"

"I've made a discovery," Freddy announced, in his thick Southern drawl.

"A discovery? What kind of discovery?"

Freddy's eyebrows danced up and down. "The best kind."

"Meaning—?"

"The raunchy kind."

Conner felt his lips involuntarily curving into a grin. He was reminded of why he liked Freddy: he didn't take himself too seriously, which was a refreshing change after being lectured about how golf was the cornerstone of Western civilization. And Freddy was an actual member of this "bastion of tradition," as was John, for that matter. Apparently it was possible to join the Augusta National and still not think of yourself as the "exemplar of excellence."

Conner slid his club into his golf bag. "Well, lead on."

Freddy led Conner off the driving range. A few minutes later, they were inside the clubhouse, heading down the central staircase toward the men's locker room.

"I don't want to disillusion you," Conner said as he followed along, "but I've seen the locker room before. Smelled it, too."

"I'll bet you haven't seen this." Freddy led him past the lockers, past the stalls, past the showers, almost to the door that exited near the first tee. They jogged sharply to the left, where Conner saw a group of pros pressed against the tile-covered wall. Barry Bennett was there, as well as a few of the other PGA stalwarts. The wall was bare; as far as Conner could tell, they were all staring at nothing but blue bathroom tile.

"Didn't there used to be a mirror there?" Conner asked.

"Yup," Freddy agreed. "Carefully placed by some reprobate to hide the treasure that lay beyond. Till I had the sense to move it."

"And you discovered—mildewed tile?"

"No. A peephole."

Conner's lips parted. Suddenly, all those pros pressing their faces against the wall took on an entirely new perspective.

"We think it was drilled for a phone line or something," Freddy explained. "But you can see straight through to the ladies' locker room!"

Conner rolled his eyes. "What a pack of juvenile delinquents you guys are. Get a life already!"

"When did you become such a stick-in-the-mud?" Freddy asked. "I thought you were the 'gonzo player of the PGA.'"

"This isn't gonzo. This is *Porky's II*."

"Yeah, yeah, yeah. So you disapprove. I'll note that on the record." Freddy winked. "Wanna take a look?"

"Well, if you insist." Conner pushed the other pros aside and pressed his left eye against the tiny hole in the wall. "I'm having a hard time seeing anything . . ." He blinked and refocused, trying to let his eye relax. "Wait. I'm getting something. It's . . . It's . . ." He drew in his breath. "It's the puke green doors to the women's stalls! Be still my heart!"

Freddy jerked him away from the wall. "If you're gonna be sarcastic, just leave."

"Sarcastic? I'm serious. I saw the inside of the girl's bathroom! Now I can die happy."

"Yeah," Freddy shot back, "you're playin' the wiseass now. But wait till some women show up. Then you'll be beggin' for a chance to peer through my peephole."

"It's going to be a long wait."

"Whaddaya mean?"

Conner patted Freddy on the shoulder. "No women in the Masters tournament, remember? I think they give that locker room to the caddies."

Freddy was crushed.

JOHN PACED AROUND the green of the eighteenth hole. A damn fool place to be in the middle of the night. Conner must think he fell off the edge of the earth by now. He should have just said no and left it at that. Hadn't he had enough aggravation for one night? And there was still that puzzling sight from yesterday to ponder. The last thing he needed was to be marching around the golf course after hours. Still, the note said it was urgent . . .

He turned around in a small circle, scanning the horizon, all 360 degrees. Why did it have to be such a dark night? The moon was mostly hidden behind the clouds. That could be a bad sign. Rain could really mess up a golf tournament, especially one as tightly scheduled as the Masters.

The thought brought a chuckle to his lips. What was he thinking? They couldn't have rain at the Masters. The board of directors would never allow it. There were undoubtedly several regulations expressly forbidding it.

He heard a soft footfall several yards behind him. Or thought he did . . .

He whirled around. Was something moving? Or was it just the clouds behind the trees, creating the illusion of movement? It was so difficult to tell.

John suddenly realized he didn't like being here and didn't want to be here any longer. He should have known better than to come. The whole thing was starting to give him the creeps. He was going inside. Right now.

He started marching down the fairway. Maybe it still wasn't too late to catch up to Conner, although odds were by now he'd picked up some floozy and fed her that song-and-dance about how he'd "waited all his life for a woman who could make him forget golf and dedicate his life to medical science . . ."

"Leaving so soon?"

John froze in his tracks. The voice came from somewhere behind him.

"Seems a shame. We haven't even had a chance to chat."

Slowly, John turned to face the person speaking to him. Why was he suddenly so damn scared? There was a trembling in his knees that he didn't seem to be able to stop. It had been a mistake coming out here. A stupid, stupid mistake—

"So it's you," John said, when he saw who had joined him.

"Indeed it is. And we have the fairway to ourselves."

"How lovely." John pursed his lips, trying to mask his growing panic behind a shroud of anger. "What's the point of all this, anyway? Why did you drag me out here?"

"I was hoping we could talk."

"I suspect we have nothing to talk about."

"I'm sorry to hear that."

"I'll bet you are," John replied. He strained his eyes, trying to get a better look. The person standing only a few feet away from him was holding something. Something that glistened faintly. "But I don't think talking would accomplish anything."

"Surely we can come to . . . some sort of arrangement."

"I don't think so."

"Is there nothing that would tempt you?"

"Not in the way that you mean." John drew up his shoulders. "Look, if it's just the same to you, I'd like to get out of here—"

"Please don't rush. I've only just arrived. And it's such a long walk back to the clubhouse."

"All the more reason to start now."

"Please—give me one more chance."

John didn't have to pretend any longer. His fear really was starting to be replaced by anger. This had gone on too long already. "One more chance for what?"

"To help you understand. To see things from my perspective."

"That, my friend, is never going to happen."

"You're certain about that?"

"Absolutely certain."

A sigh. "Then I guess there really is nothing more to say."

John started to turn away. "Glad you're starting to see things my way."

"But there is one more thing I must do."

The glistening shape rose up so quickly John didn't know what was happening. He heard a sudden slicing sound, like someone was swinging a scythe through the air just beside his head.

And after that, John heard nothing at all.

7

Wednesday

A FTER TEN MINUTES of frustration and futility, Fitz tired of pounding on the door.

"I'm coming in! Like it or not!" Fortunately, Conner had failed to lock the door to his cabin. Fitz shoved the door open and pushed inside.

He was not particularly surprised to find that Conner's cabin was a mess. Conner had, after all, been lodged here for over twenty-four hours. Coffee tables were overturned; chairs were upended. The floor was littered with dirty clothes, open pizza boxes, spilled beer cans.

Fitz kicked the pile of clothes nearest him. It capsized, spilling out a shirt, three socks, a belt, soiled boxers, a muddy golf shoe, and a bra.

A bra?

Fitz picked up the frilly black lace undergarment and let it dangle from his fingertip. He was beginning to understand why Conner hadn't shown up in the locker room to collect his clubs.

Fitz stomped over to the closed bedroom door and pounded. "Conner! Are you there?"

A strained, barely audible voice responded on the other side of the door. "No."

"Conner, get out here!"

"Don' wanna."

"Then I'm coming in."

"You can't. I'm not decent."

"What else is new?" Fitz shoved the door open and kicked through the clothes and debris to the double bed. There were no heads visible, just two lumps under the top sheet—Conner, and a more petite lump to which Fitz didn't believe he'd been formally introduced. "Conner, get your butt out of bed."

"Don' wanna," the larger lump replied. "What time is it—five?"

"Five! It's nine-thirty, you lunkhead! You've already missed the players' roll call. And if you're not on the first tee in twenty minutes, you'll be disqualified from the par-three tournament."

Suddenly, the larger lump sat bolt upright. Conner's bronzed face and hairy chest poked out from the covers. "Twenty minutes?" He glanced at the lump on the other side of the covers, then ducked back under the sheet. "Sorry, sweetie." Fitz heard a kissing noise. "Gotta go."

"You're leaving?" a softer voice under the covers squealed. "But you said I was the one who could make you forget golf and devote your life to medical science."

"And you believed him?" Fitz shook his head. "The closest he's ever gotten to medical science was when he bought a box of Band-Aids. He faints at the sight of blood. And when he has to get a shot—"

"That's about enough of that," Conner said, diving out from under the covers. He made a beeline for the bathroom and disappeared. "Give me ten minutes."

"Ten?" Fitz raised his eyebrows. "To get ready? Normally only takes you two."

Conner's head reappeared in the bathroom doorway. "Today's a special day. I want to look my best."

TWELVE MINUTES LATER, Conner emerged from the bathroom. Fitz almost didn't recognize him.

"Wow," Fitz said with admiration. He let out a slow whistle. "I'm impressed."

"You should be." Conner was wearing traditional golf attire—cotton Polo shirt, khaki pants, golf shoes. Even a sporty red baseball cap. "Took me two precious minutes to iron this stuff."

Fitz pulled a face. "Yeah, right."

"Okay, it took me two precious minutes to find this stuff. Happy now?"

"I heard you got called to the woodshed last night. I see they made an impression."

"Yeah," Conner mumbled. "They definitely made an impression." He checked his watch, then followed Fitz out of the cabin toward the clubhouse. "We don't have much time. Have you gotten my clubs out of the locker room?"

"You left them on the driving range last night, you nincompoop."

Conner slapped his forehead. "Damn. I was practicing, then Freddy lured me down to the locker room. Then on the way back up, I bumped into this coed golf groupie from Emory and one thing led to another . . ."

"I'll bet." Fitz offered his best disapproving look. "Don't worry. I always check on your clubs before I turn in at night. When I saw they weren't in the locker, I started looking around. I know you like to drive the night before a tournament, so they weren't hard to track down. Once again, I pulled your butt out of the frying pan."

Conner pushed through the clubhouse door and exited onto the walkway that led to the first tee. "That's why I pay you the big money."

Fitz grimaced. "Believe me, kid—seven percent of your winnings is not big money."

Conner approached the first tee marker, which was flanked by officials anxiously looking at their watches. "Sorry to disappoint you, gentlemen, but I've made it, just in time. Now if you'll excuse me—"

Conner inched forward, but the officials didn't budge.

"Pardon me, boys," Conner said, retaining his sunny demeanor. "See, I'm a player. Except it's hard to play if you won't let me on the course. So am-scray."

The officials didn't move. They looked distinctly uncomfortable.

"They don't move till I say so."

Conner's face fell. "Derwood. How miserable to see you again. Why are you here?"

"I told you last night. You don't play unless I say so. These officials have been instructed that you are not to approach the first tee until you are authorized to do so. By me."

"Derwood, you are experiencing serious delusions of grandeur. A Napoleonic complex. But you have nothing in common with Napoleon, except of course your height."

Derwood's teeth clenched together. "Laugh all you want, clown boy. But you don't play till you pass my inspection."

"Fine. Inspect away, Little Corporal."

Derwood did a slow circle around Conner, taking him in head-to-toe. "Shirt is regulation, slacks are regulation," he muttered as he passed. "Shoes are tattered and tacky, but regulation. Even the cap is regulation." He nodded officiously. "Very well, gentlemen. This entrant is authorized to participate in today's tournament."

The officials appeared keenly relieved.

Before he moved away, Derwood pressed close to Conner and smirked. "I knew we could whip your gonzo-ass into line," he whispered.

Conner didn't reply. He pivoted silently, took the club proffered by Fitz, passed through the gauntlet of officials, and approached the first tee. He placed his ball on a tee, pulled on his right-hand glove and, almost as an afterthought, removed his cap.

Gasps sounded in the spectators' gallery.

Derwood's eyes went wide. "He's shaved his head!"

Indeed he had. Not only buzzed it to the scalp, but created a discernable zigzag pattern across the back, sort of like an Iroquois on speed.

"That is *not* acceptable!" Derwood shouted. "Someone stop him—"

Too late. Conner swung, and the white dimpled ball flew down the fairway. An instant later, Conner and Fitz had entered the course in pursuit.

Derwood threw his hat down and stomped on it. "You won't get away with this!" he shouted. "You haven't heard the last of me." But in fact, Conner had heard the last of him, at least for the moment, because he was already well out of earshot.

SAFELY ENSCONCED ON the third tee, Conner thought he could slow down and engage in a bit of conversation. "Where's John, anyway?" he asked Fitz. "Aren't we playing together?"

Fitz shook his head. "He drew an earlier tee time. Problem is, he didn't show up."

"Didn't show up? That's not like John." He paused. "Come to think of it, he never showed up last night."

"I searched all over the grounds. Couldn't find him. Even checked his cabin. His wife said she hadn't seen him since last night."

"You mean he didn't come back to the cabin last night? *John?* That doesn't make any sense. Why didn't you tell me sooner?"

"Like when? During that languorous stretch between when you got out of bed with your coed and when you appeared at the first tee?"

"Well, sometime." Conner dug the head of his club into the ground. "This is totally unlike John. I'm concerned."

"There's nothing you can do about it now."

"Yeah, but still—"

"Concentrate on your game. We'll find John later."

Conner frowned. "I suppose." He scanned the fairway. "I don't think I need the wood for this. Hand me my nine-iron."

"Are you joking? That hole is four hundred and fifty yards away. Plus there's a water trap. Plus the dogleg left."

"I like the nine-iron. It's my best club."

"You're making a mistake—"

"Fitz. I've made my decision. Pass me the club."

"Your wish is my command, sire." Fitz passed the requested club.

Conner shielded his eyes and gazed at the distant green, mentally recalculating the distance. There was a water trap about two thirds of the way up the fairway, but if he hit hard, shot over it, avoided the rough . . .

He turned to his caddie. "Fitz, how do I get to the green in one?"

"Practice."

"But seriously."

"You don't. Especially with a nine-iron. Lay up."

Conner groaned. "I hate that cheesy play-it-safe crap. I think I can make it to the green in one. I'm going for it."

"Conner, don't be a fool. It's a sucker pin." Meaning the pin had been placed such that only a sucker would try to get close to it.

Conner held a finger against his lips. "Please. A master is at work." Conner shook himself down, adjusted his stance, brought back his club, and fired.

The golf ball flew into the air, taking a tremendous lift and forming a beautiful line right down the center of the fairway . . . then took a sudden veer to the right, crashing to earth deep in the rough.

"Damn!" Conner swore. "What happened?"

"You swung," Fitz answered.

The two men tracked down the ball, killing a good ten minutes of course time.

"I could still make the green in two," Conner opined. "I'm going to blast it out of here."

"With the nine-iron?"

"It's my best club."

"That's what you said—"

Before Fitz could finish his commentary, Conner had swung. Once again, the ball took off beautifully . . . and once again, it took a sudden and dramatic turn to the right.

"A fatal slice," Fitz commented, under his breath. "Fatal for you."

Conner tried again, on the fourth hole, the fifth, the sixth, and the seventh. Each time, the story was the same. Beautiful launch, followed by a sudden slice to the right.

"What's going on?" Conner said, as he searched for his ball in the rough off the seventh fairway. "My drive used to be the best part of my game. You said I could hit a dime at two hundred yards."

"That's what you get for listening to me."

"I'm serious. You're my caddie. You're supposed to help me out when I'm in trouble."

Fitz shrugged. "Sorry, Conner. If I could help, I would. But I'm as mystified as you. This is just weird."

"Thank you, Harvey Penick."

"Look, this is going to require some study. After you finish, we'll go out on the driving range and take a look at what you're doing. Maybe I can figure something out."

Conner reluctantly agreed. By that time he was already seven over par. During the next ten holes, he managed to make some improvement, but not nearly enough. As he approached the eighteenth tee, he was four over par, and he knew perfectly well that wasn't good enough to finish in the money in a par-three tournament.

"Fitz, I'm going to try the nine-iron again."

Fitz closed his eyes. "You know, I was just thinking, 'How could this boy possibly make things worse than they already are?' And presto—right on cue—you answered the question. You must be psychic."

"Yeah, yeah, yeah." Conner snatched the club from his bag. "Don't give me any crap or I'll dock your day's pay."

Fitz snorted. "As if there's going to be any pay after this performance!"

Conner ignored him. He placed the ball on the tee, rocked himself into position, and swung. The ball rose into the air and, once again, swerved right, descending into a deep and wide sand trap.

"Goddamn it!" Conner shouted.

"Stop swearing!" Fitz commanded. "Officials are everywhere."

Conner silently trudged down the fairway, finally finding his ball buried in the sand.

"I know better than to imagine that you might consult your caddie on how to get out of this tough scrape," Fitz said. "So I'll ask you. What's your plan?"

"Thought I'd use a wedge. If I pop it high enough, it might go all the way to the green."

"Do you see the sheer wall of this trap, Conner? There's no way—"

"Don't tell me what I can't do."

"It would be smarter to just get yourself out of the trap. Get to the green on your third."

"You always want to play it safe. It's like golfing with my grandmother." Conner addressed the nearly buried ball, crouching slightly for his scoop shot. He swung the wedge. The ball bounced up against the high wall of the trap and ricocheted back into the sand.

"God*damn* it!" Conner shouted, then looked sheepishly at Fitz. "No one heard me," he grunted.

"I did."

"I meant no one who would report me."

Fitz arched an eyebrow. "Oh?"

Conner squared himself once more before the ball half-buried in the sand. He took a deep breath, said a silent prayer to the patron saint of golfers, whoever that was, and swung. The club ground out in the sand before it hit the ball.

"Did the ball move?" Fitz asked, inching forward from his safe berth outside the trap. "If the ball moved, you have to take a stroke, even if your club didn't hit the ball."

"The ball didn't move," Conner said. There was an eerie quiet to his voice. "But something else did." Conner poked the tip of his club into the sand. There was something down there, just below the surface of the sand. Something . . . blue.

He crouched down for a closer look. Using the handle of his club as a probe, he dug around, brushing the sand off the surface. The blue-something was a piece of fabric. A shirt, he realized. A shirt sleeve, to be precise.

Conner shot up in the air, his face stricken.

"What?" Fitz asked, moving forward quickly. "What is it?"

Conner found he couldn't speak. He could barely manage to point down toward the sand.

There was an arm in the shirt sleeve.

A horrible sensation coursed through Conner's body. His brain was beginning to put two and two together, and he didn't like the sum. Taking a deep breath, he bent down and began brushing away the sand surrounding the tattered shirt sleeve.

The shirt was attached to a body, all buried beneath the sand. Grabbing it with both hands, Conner pulled the body out and rolled it over to get a look at the face.

Conner heard Fitz drawing in his breath, just behind him. He was finding it hard to speak himself.

His worst fears were confirmed. It was his best friend, John McCree, with his mouth filled with sand. And a fist-sized bloody gash on the side of his head.

The Gentleman's Game

◆ ◆ ◆

At the Masters, falling out of favor with the powers-that-be can be fatal. After finishing second, Frank Stranahan looked forward to going for the win. But the next year, he had an unfortunate contretemps with Cliff Roberts and was thrown out of the tournament before it had even started. Herman Keiser's upset victory endeared him to many, but Cliff Roberts disliked him so intensely that he accused Keiser of stealing his championship green jacket.

Jimmy Demaret won the Masters three times, but that wasn't enough to impress Bobby Jones or Cliff Roberts. Demaret had told a slightly off-color joke on the grounds one day that resulted in a written reprimand from Jones. And the Augusta National, as many others learned before and after Demaret, had a long memory. Unlike Augusta favorites Gene Sarazen or Ben Hogan (neither of whom won three times), no bridges, ponds, or cabins were named for Jimmy Demaret. "I can't even get an outhouse named for me," Demaret commented.

8

"MY GOD," FITZ whispered under his breath. "What happened?"

Conner found his tongue frozen and his brain almost equally paralyzed. His eyes were locked on the bloody, sand-encrusted figure buried beneath the surface of the trap. A million thoughts raced through his brain, and almost as many emotions as well. John. *John!*

He heard Fitz rustling behind him. "We should . . . do something."

Conner heard the words and knew them to be correct, but he was far too immobilized to act upon them. He didn't know what all he was experiencing—part shock, part grief, part panic. *John!*

"We can't just leave him here," Fitz muttered. "Other players will be along soon."

All true, but at the moment, the tournament was the furthest thing from Conner's mind. He kept staring at John's blood-streaked face, while his brain leap-frogged through the conjoined life the two of them had shared. This is the boy who turned me onto golf, he thought. This is the kid who got me through high school. This is the man who helped me break onto the tour. Everything I am, I am because of this man.

This man whose corpse was buried in the sand trap on the eighteenth hole.

Conner pushed himself up to his feet, drinking in air, hoping the sudden rush of oxygen would clear the cobwebs in his brain. *We have to do something,* Fitz said again, or perhaps Conner was only hearing an echo in the nether reaches of his brain. At any rate, the statement was true. Very true.

Conner stumbled back to his golf bag and pulled out a cell phone. He flipped it open and then, with concentrated effort, punched 9-1-1.

ABOUT AN HOUR after the police finally arrived, the crime scene was secure. Tournament play had been halted; the entire sand bunker and surrounding area was cordoned off with orange warning cones and yellow tape. A man in a suit was videotaping, recording the position of the body and the surrounding area. Three technicians in coveralls were cautiously searching for trace evidence—hair, fiber, blood. Another man was dusting for fingerprints; yet another was on his hands and knees, pressing his nose against the fairway, searching for the imprint of a footprint that might be recordable.

A Sergeant Turnbull from the Augusta police department had responded to Conner's call. He was a short, stocky pit bull of a man in a tacky suit. They'd been over Conner's testimony about a thousand times, or so it seemed to Conner. What was there to tell? They were playing the course, his club went down in the sand, and he found . . . John. All Conner had done was brush some of the surface sand away from his head and shoulders and flip over the body, which wasn't buried all that deeply. If Conner hadn't discovered him, someone else would've, and soon.

Conner could tell Turnbull wasn't satisfied, but didn't know what to do about it. Or perhaps he just had other priorities at the moment. "Don't leave town," he said curtly.

"Of course not," Conner mumbled. The whole thing seemed unreal to him, like a bizarre dream from which he couldn't wake himself.

John was dead. This had to be a dream—a nightmare.

"Who did this?" Conner said suddenly, not really expecting an answer.

To his surprise, Turnbull offered one. "That's what we're trying to find out. Unfortunately, the perp doesn't seem to have left many clues."

"Clues?"

"Right. They're always helpful when you're trying to track a killer."

"A—" Conner eyes widened. "Then you think it's—"

"Murder? Course it is. You thought maybe he beat himself to death on the side of his head? And then buried himself in a sand trap? I don't think so."

"But—who—?"

"We were hoping you might have some thoughts on that subject. Know anyone who had a grudge against McCree?"

Conner racked his barely functioning brain. "I can't think of anyone."

"We're not finding any hair or fibers, although it would be a miracle if we could recover trace evidence from a sand trap. This fairway is cut so short it can't hold onto anything, much less a footprint or a stray hair. No fingerprints on the body. Basically, we're at square one. A very unpromising investigation. Glad it isn't my problem."

"It isn't?"

"Nah. I'm just a lowly sergeant. I was just the highest rank in the office when your call came in. They'll assign this to a lieutenant— Lieutenant O'Brien, probably. I expect you'll get to tell your story all over again. Probably several times."

Great, Conner thought silently. I can hardly wait.

"Y'know, if there's . . . anything else you might know about this mess, I'd sure be obliged if you told me."

Conner cocked one eyebrow.

"Maybe right now it seems best to clam up, but let me tell you from experience—the truth always comes out eventually, and it'll go easier for you if you come clean."

"I didn't kill him," Conner said, almost choking on his words. "He was my best friend."

"Oh, I'm sure, I'm sure. But you know how these things happen. One thing leads to another. Situation gets out of control. First thing you know, someone does something they regret later. It's no one's fault, really. It just happens."

"I did not kill my friend."

"Now, if you were to give me the straight skivvy, I would be extremely grateful. I'd make sure you got every break in the book. It would mean a lot to me."

"Like maybe a promotion to lieutenant?"

Turnbull seemed unperturbed. "God knows I put in enough time to deserve it. So whaddaya say, Cross?"

Conner's expression was as sheer as a cliff wall. "I say I didn't kill my friend. Get your promotion from someone else's misery."

Conner pushed his way out of the circle of investigation and, to his surprise, Turnbull allowed him to go. He supposed the cops had no reason to keep him under lock and key, no matter what they thought. He wouldn't be hard to find when they wanted him.

Conner paced the length of the eighteenth hole, then made a bee-line for the clubhouse. He should just head back to his cabin, he thought to himself. He really wanted to be alone right now. At the same time, he also felt a serious need to partake of an adult beverage. Maybe several.

Conner found a table in the corner by himself and ordered multiple martinis. Somehow, he had to get a grip on himself, to try to make some sense out of the day. How could this have happened? What was John doing out there?

And why the hell did Conner have to be the one who found him?

He downed the first martini in a single swallow, then bit down on the olive. He was trying to shock his system back to life, trying to shift his body back into first gear. But it didn't work. No matter what he tried, his mind's eye kept revolving back to the same grisly image.

His best friend, buried in white sand. His face streaked with blood.

John, he thought, and the word throbbed like someone was pounding a hammer against the inside of his skull. *John!*

CONNER WAS NURSING his fourth martini when he saw Jodie McCree rush into the clubhouse.

Jodie! he thought. Here he'd been swilling and feeling sorry for himself, and Jodie hadn't even crossed his mind. He considered running after her, trying to comfort her. If he could just get his legs working again . . .

As it turned out, the decision was made for him. As soon as Jodie entered the clubhouse, she made a quick visual sweep of the bar area, spotted Conner, then burned a path in the carpet toward him. As she neared, Conner saw her red-blotched face, streaked and wet. Her hands were trembling. She stared at him, as if willing words she could not speak.

"How—" she said, in a voice that sounded like rusty hinges. "How—"

Conner could only shake his head. He certainly couldn't respond to the unspoken question; he had no answers to give. There was only one thing he could give, and so he did. He stood up, put his arms around her, and hugged her tight.

"I don't know," he whispered. He felt her tears spilling onto his shoulder. "I don't know."

NEARLY AN HOUR later, Conner and Jodie were seated in a small lounge adjacent to the clubhouse bar. There had been no healing; there hadn't been nearly sufficient time for that. But there had at least been acceptance. They had both come face-to-face with the horrible truth, and were beginning to try to figure out how they could possibly go on with their lives.

"I—I just don't understand it," Jodie said. Her voice was still raw from crying. "Everyone loved John."

Conner agreed. It didn't make any sense.

"Have you heard anyone complain about John? Anyone nursing a grudge?"

"Never," Conner said firmly. "Not in three years on the tour."

Jodie's hands clenched. "Then who could have done it? And why?"

"I don't know," Conner replied, trying to be comforting. "But the police are working on it . . ."

Jodie frowned. "I talked to Sergeant Turnbull. I gather you did, too?"

Conner nodded.

"So, Mr. Oddsmaker, what would you say is the likelihood that he'll be able to find John's killer?"

Conner shrugged his shoulders. He didn't want to distress her unnecessarily, but . . .

"That's what I thought," Jodie said firmly. For the first time, Conner realized that she was not simply devastated—she was angry. "About zip. The golf world is so insular, so closed-door. Unless the murderer has an attack of conscience and confesses, we're never gonna know."

Conner wanted to argue with her, to give her some comfort. But the truth was, he agreed with her conclusion.

All at once, Jodie reached over and grabbed Conner's hand. "Conner, I want you to try to find out who killed John."

"Me? Are you kidding?"

"I wouldn't kid about this, Conner. This is serious."

"I agree. Which is why I shouldn't have anything to do with it."

"We have to know—"

"Look, Jodie, if you don't trust the cops, fine. Hire a private investigator."

"A private investigator wouldn't be allowed through the front gates at the Augusta National."

"Still—"

"You, on the other hand, are already on the grounds. You have access to all the players and staff. You're an invited guest. Everyone will expect you to hobnob with the players and participate in all the activities."

"Surely you don't think I'm going to continue the tournament after this!"

"You have to," Jodie implored. "It's the only way." She squeezed his hand. "You're John's oldest and best friend. You knew him better than anyone."

"Maybe so, but—"

"You know you owe him."

"I'm well aware of that, Jodie. I owe John for almost everything of any value in my whole life. But what you're talking about—"

"He would've done it for you."

Conner stopped short.

"If the situation were reversed, I mean. John wouldn't have slept till he found out who killed you. That's how much he loved you, Conner."

Conner didn't reply.

"Conner," she said softly, "I realize I haven't seen as much of you as I once did, since John and I moved to Georgia. But I remember a time . . ."

She didn't say anything more. She didn't have to. They both knew what she was talking about. She was forcing his mind to turn back the calendar pages to a time past—a time when Conner and Jodie had been sweethearts. He had been crazy for her—his first love. In fact, he had introduced her to John—a gesture he later regretted. It all seemed a million years ago now. Still, when he peered into her sea-blue eyes, it was hard to forget how much he had once loved her. Impossible, really, because a few of those sparks still lingered.

"Please," she whispered. "Please."

"All right," Conner said. "I think this is a big mistake. But I'll do what I can."

"Thank you." Her lips turned up in the first smile he had seen on her face all day. "Thank you so much."

Conner brushed a tear from her cheek. "How could I say no to a beautiful face like that?" He sat up straight. "Fitz told me John didn't come back last night?"

"It's true. That's so unlike him. I was worried sick. Still, I thought he would turn up, and I didn't want to generate a lot of bad publicity for no reason. I couldn't figure out—" She drew in her breath. "Of course, now I understand. He must have been killed last night."

"Seems likely," Conner agreed. "When did you see him last?"

"Around nine or so, I'd guess. Just after dark. He left our cabin."

"Did he say where he was going?"

"No, and I didn't ask. I assumed he was going out to the driving range to knock the balls around. Like you guys usually did."

"Did he do anything . . . unusual? Say anything out of the ordinary?"

Jodie's eyebrows knitted together. "Now that you mention it, he did say something. Something strange. I didn't recall it until you said that." Her eyes focused on a spot on the floor.

"What was it?"

"I can't remember. But it was something odd. Odd enough to capture my attention, at least for a moment." She clenched her fist. "My short-term memory is going to hell."

Conner placed a hand gently on her shoulder. "It'll come to you later. When you're not trying to think about it. When it does, tell me, okay?"

"Of course." She took his hand in both of hers. "Thank you, Conner. I really appreciate this."

"No need. It's the least I can do—"

He stopped short, but they both knew what he was going to say, and once again, Conner saw unbidden tears crease the flushed mounds of her cheeks.

It was the least he could do, they both thought. For John.

9

THE WEDNESDAY PRESS conference in Butler Cabin was a distinguished Masters tournament tradition, but this year, it was nothing short of bizarre. As tournament director, Andrew Spenser led the proceedings, ably assisted by his lapdog Derwood Scott. The first deviation from tradition came in the timing; instead of being held in the morning, the conference was delayed until late evening. The second deviation was the subject matter. Spenser dutifully tried to drum up excitement about the par-three and the main tournament yet to come, offering up trivia and tidbits about the players' lives, statistics about the players' standings, their performance to date on the tour, their scores in previous Masters tournaments.

No one cared.

"Can you give us more information about what happened to John McCree?"

"Have you got any leads?"

"Is it true the police suspect one of the other pros?"

"What if the killer strikes again?"

Standing in the back of the cabin, Conner watched Spenser wipe his brow. That prim, proper gentleman wasn't accustomed to fielding questions from a pack of vultures like the one assembled in Butler Cabin today. He could almost sympathize with the man, if he hadn't been such a jerk to Conner the day before.

Spenser gripped the podium and stared out into the sea of reporters. "Please. This is not police headquarters. This is the Augusta National Golf Club, home of the Masters tournament, the most important—"

"Is the corpse at the coroner's office?"

"How many times was he hit?"

"Was there a lot of blood? Will you have to replace the sand bunker?"

Conner could feel Spenser's tension clear across the room. It was a relief when Spenser excused himself and Derwood stepped up to the podium—probably the first time in history anyone was glad to see Derwood arrive, Conner mused.

"Please," Derwood began, "we've told you everything we know about John McCree's death. Let's discuss the tournament—"

"Can you confirm that McCree is dead?" one of the reporters shouted from the rear.

Derwood sighed. "Yes. I'm afraid we're certain about that."

"And that he was murdered?"

Derwood began to hedge. "I have no information regarding the cause of death. There are many possibilities. I find it very difficult to believe that anyone at the Augusta National could be capable of—"

"Someone hit him, right?" This voice came from a female reporter near the front. "I heard he was hit on the head. Possibly several times."

"Again, I have no information regarding the cause—"

"You're not suggesting he did that to himself, are you?"

"Well . . . no. Perhaps an unfortunate accident . . ."

"In a sand trap?"

Derwood tugged at his collar. "As I've already said, we are unaware of the details—"

"How can you proceed with the tournament when one of the most prominent players has been murdered? Isn't that more than a bit callous?"

Derwood drew in his breath. He was prepared for this one. "This is of course a difficult question with ramifications that go far beyond the competition itself. We called an emergency meeting of the board of directors and our chairman, Artemus Tenniel, to determine the proper course of action. We also consulted with John McCree's widow, Jodie McCree. After giving the matter close and careful attention, all parties involved agreed that the best course of action was to proceed with the tournament as scheduled. Now, however, the tournament will be held in John's McCree's honor. This endeavor is dedicated to his memory."

Conner tried to stifle his sneer. Given how jam-packed the tournament schedule was these days, it would probably be impossible to reschedule the Masters for a later date. It was now or never. Proceeding with the tournament but dedicating it to John's memory probably appeared to the board to be the best way of preserving their cash cow without seeming incredibly insensitive. Conner wondered how this cover-your-ass smokescreen fit in with "the exemplar of excellence."

Still, he thought, it was just as well. He knew Jodie wanted the tournament to proceed. She wanted to keep all the suspects on the premises as long as possible. Once the tournament ended, and all the players and staff departed, any investigation would be greatly complicated. Realistically, if he was going to have any hope of determining who killed John, he would have to do it before everyone left Sunday night.

Up at the podium, Derwood was still fending off questions about the murder.

"Why was the body buried in a sand trap?"

"Really," Derwood insisted, "I have no way of knowing." All at once, his eyes lit upon Conner in the back of the room. Conner felt a chill race through his body.

"If you must inquire about these unsavory matters," Derwood continued, "why don't you ask Conner Cross? He's the one who found the body."

That was a tidbit they hadn't heard before. As one, the sea of reporters whipped around to face Conner. They began to press in his direction.

Conner felt like a fox who'd been treed by the circling hounds. He broke for the front doors, but two men bearing minicams blocked his path. Before he could take off in a different direction, he was surrounded by reporters, many of them shoving microphones under his nose.

"So," Conner said, clearing his throat, "I guess you folks want to ask me about my spiffy new haircut, huh?"

IT TOOK CONNER more than an hour to extricate himself from the reporters. It was amazing—especially since he'd told them everything he knew in the first minute and a half. Normally, a few minutes of Conner's trademark obnoxiousness would be sufficient to drive anyone away. But the reporters weren't even fazed; if anything, they seemed to like it.

The whole experience was ironic, Conner thought, as he trudged back to the clubhouse. Most of the pros on the tour spent half their spare time trying to rustle up some publicity. Conner had just gotten a ton—and he didn't want it. Not under these circumstances.

Conner passed through the clubhouse doors, wove his way to the bar, ordered a martini, and found a seat at an empty table in the corner. Most of the other pros were there, too, but the mood had altered radically. There was none of the madcap revelry—no betting, no joking, no carousing. John's death had hit everyone hard. The room was permeated by somber, sullen depression. Conner realized he should probably circulate, try to find out what if anything the others knew, but he just wasn't in the proper frame of mind.

About ten minutes later, Freddy Granger ambled over. "Hi there, Conner."

Conner didn't even look up, but Freddy's deep Southern accent was a dead giveaway. "If you've found another peephole, I'm not interested."

Freddy looked embarrassed. "Nah, I—" He pointed to the empty chair on the opposite end of Conner's table. "Mind if I sit?"

Conner shrugged. "Suit yourself."

Freddy took a seat. "I just wanted to tell you how sorry I am, Conner. We all feel terrible. We all miss John. But I know you were closer to him than any of us. I've always considered you a friend and—I'm sorry this had to happen. If there's anything I could possibly ever do—all you have to do is ask."

Conner nodded. "Thanks, Freddy. I appreciate that." Conner meant it, too. Sometimes he felt like the pariah of the tour; his status as PGA bad boy caused him to be ostracized by those who considered themselves the class acts of the tour. It was nice to hear that he had at least one friend. Other than the one he'd lost. "How'd you do in the tournament?"

"No improvement."

Conner knew what that meant. Freddy's career had been in the dumper of late. Not only was he lower on the money list than Conner; he barely qualified for an invitation to the Masters.

"I had delusions of restarting my game here," Freddy said. "You know. Winning the tournament in a dramatic surprise upset. Or at least placing. Now I'm afraid I won't even make the Friday cut."

Conner nodded appreciatively. "I've had similar concerns myself."

"Aww, the hell with it, anyway." He laughed quietly. "I shouldn't even be thinking about this stupid game. My daughter's gettin' married."

"I heard something about that. Congratulations. You must be very happy."

Freddy beamed. "We are. We truly are. This isn't the first time my baby girl's tied the knot, but last time she ran off with some loser and we didn't get to have a real wedding. This time we're throwin' her the party she deserves. We're gonna do it up right. Havin' a great big gala affair. And you're invited. All the pros are. It's Friday night, down at the Magnolia Glade Country Club."

Conner raised an eyebrow. "Not at the Augusta National?"

"Couldn't get in," Freddy said. "It's all booked up with some stupid golf tournament."

"Right, right. I hear those big weddings are a lot of trouble. You must be drowning under all the details."

"Hell no," Freddy said. "The womenfolk never let me near any of the details. The only time I see them is when they drop by to tell me how much to make the check for." He smiled, but Conner thought the smile had an edge to it. "And there's been a hell of a lot of checks, believe you me."

Conner eyed Freddy carefully. He seemed uneasy, almost jumpy. But he supposed the man had been unnerved by John's death. Weren't they all.

"Anyway," Freddy said, pushing himself to his feet. "I meant what I said. You need anything, just call me."

"Appreciate that, Freddy."

"See you Friday night, if not before."

Conner nodded, but he thought it unlikely in the extreme that he would want to attend a gala wedding anytime in the near future.

A few minutes later, the empty space at Conner's table was taken by yet another pro, Harley Tuttle. Conner glanced up from his martini. "I hope you're not here to complain about that Tom Kite bet."

Harley half-smiled. "Nah. Forgot all about it. I—just wanted to offer my condolences."

"Thanks, Harley."

"I didn't know John well, of course. Hadn't met him till you introduced us. And now I suppose I never will."

"You would've liked him," Conner said. "Everyone did."

"That's what I hear. That's what I hear." Harley nervously fingered the edge of the tablecloth. Conner could tell there was something on his mind. "Conner . . . how long have you known John's wife? Jodie, is it?"

"As long as I've known John. Longer, actually."

"Really? Wow. Well, look. I don't know the woman at all, but I know she must be going through a rough patch."

"She is," Conner said. "But Jodie's tough. She'll pull through."

"That's good. Would you tell her something for me?"

"Sure. What?"

"She probably doesn't need it but—well, I know how complicated things were when I lost my mother. And expensive. And John hadn't been playing so well lately and—oh, hell. Just tell her if there's anything she needs, all she has to do is ask. And I mean anything, including money. Just let me know."

"Okay."

Harley would be the one to call, too. He'd only started on the tour this year, but he'd already lined up an impressive list of finishes. He hadn't won a tournament yet, but he'd placed in the top five in every single tournament this year except Pebble Beach, which he didn't play. Conner would've preferred to hate the man, but unfortunately, he was just too damn nice. "I'll pass the word along."

"Thanks, Conner. And the same goes for you. I can imagine how you must feel. Like my daddy used to say, 'You don't know what you've got till it's gone'."

"I thought that was Joni Mitchell."

Harley gave him a shy smile. "All the greats stole from my daddy." He wandered off, and Conner was relieved. He knew these people were trying to be kind. But he didn't want to be *on* at the moment. He wanted to be alone. He wanted to stew in his juices and wallow in his martinis. He wanted to remember John the way he was, not the way he'd found him in that sand trap.

A flood of memories surged through Conner's brain. Growing up poor as dirt, wondering what it might be like to get out of town, make some real money. Junior high, high school. Golf at Watonga's Dusty Duffer. Everything John had done for him. All the times he cared, when it seemed no one else did.

Conner's reverie was interrupted, not just once, but repeatedly, by boisterous activity behind him. What insensitive jerk—? Conner forced his muddy brain out of the past and focused on the source of the disturbance.

It was Barry Bennett, that stupid blowhard. He'd obviously been drinking again. He was standing at the bar, talking to no one in particular, but doing it in a voice everyone could hear.

"Sure, I'm sssorry he's dead," Barry said, slurring the words so badly they were nearly incomprehensible. "But I haven't got amnesia. I hated that ssson-of-a-bitch."

Conner whirled around, staring at the man with wide-eyed amazement. He was actually trashing John. John hadn't been dead twenty-four hours, and the creep was dissing him in public. He'd always thought Barry was an asshole, but this was beyond the pale.

"Course I kept quiet about it," Barry droned on. "I was a good boy. But I didn't forget. Hell no. I didn't forget. And I never will." He hiccuped. "Ssson-of-a-bitch."

Conner felt his bile rising. Barry's behavior was inexcusable, and Conner wasn't going to sit still for it. He'd ram those words down that sorry drunk's throat—

"Kind of a jerk, isn't he?"

Conner peered across the table and saw a kid wearing a green flak jacket, soiled T-shirt, and torn blue jeans. His first question was how someone looking like that ever managed to be admitted onto the Augusta National grounds. His second question was why someone who looked like that was talking to him.

"Bennett has a problem with alcohol," the kid said. "Everyone on the tour knows it."

Conner cocked an eyebrow. Was that a fact?

The kid brushed his long straggly black hair out of his face. "You're Conner Cross, aren't you? I recognize you from your pictures. Everyone knows you were John McCree's best friend. And here I am, face-to-face with you. Wow."

Conner's eyes narrowed. He was getting the distinct impression this kid was not part of the Augusta National staff. "Who are you?"

The kid slapped himself on the forehead. "Didn't I say? Oh, wow. Duh." He held out his hand. "I'm Ed Frohike. President of the John McCree Fan Club."

The light began to dawn in Conner's eyes. A golf groupie. "I see . . ."

"I came here to meet John. I've corresponded with him by e-mail—even talked to him on the phone. But I never met him. So I blew my life savings—everything I made working at Taco Bell for six months—to come out here and meet him. But before I could—"

"I'm sorry, kid. That's rough."

"Yeah. Tougher on you, though. I mean, you actually knew him. Knew him well."

"Yeah. That I did. That I did." He glanced back at Ed. "So how'd you get in here, kid? The Augusta National prides itself on its security."

Ed grinned, like a kid caught dipping a girl's pigtails in the inkwell. "Can you keep a secret?"

"In theory."

Ed leaned across the table and whispered. "I snuck in underground. Through the sewer system tunnels. Came up through a manhole just off the eighteenth fairway. Late at night."

"I didn't know there were tunnels under the course."

"Only part of it. Apparently the Augusta National makes some heavy demands on the water system. Keeping all those greens green, you know."

"And how did you find out about that?"

Ed waved him away. "Oh, man, I know everything."

"You do?"

"Oh, yeah." He shifted to his reciting voice. "Conner C. Cross, from Watonga, Oklahoma. Six foot one, two hundred and five pounds. Third year in the PGA. Best power drive on the tour. Worst putting game on the tour."

Conner gave him a withering look. "I guess you do know everything."

"Everything about golf, anyway. I eat and breathe golf."

"Really. What's your handicap?"

"Oh, I don't play the game. I . . . merely worship it."

"Excuse me?"

"You know what I mean. I'm into it, big time. It's my favorite thing. I follow all the players, all the tournaments. Heck, I've even got your trading card."

"Really? I'm sure *that's* in great demand!" Conner said with heavy irony.

"It's . . . um . . . well . . . you know. It's . . . hotter than a Freddy Granger." Ed looked away. "But I always thought John was the greatest, you know? That's why I started the fan club. He was just so cool, so suave and sophisticated. Like, just the opposite of you."

"I can see where that would be in his favor."

"No—I didn't mean—I mean—"

"Calm down, Ed. Take a breath."

"I just meant that he was so classy. Had a style all his own. You've got a style, too."

"That would be one way of putting it."

Ed's eyes darted around the room. "I can't believe I'm actually at the Masters! This is so awesome! I started going crazy the second I stepped onto the course." His chest deflated. "But then I heard what happened to John. Man, what a bummer. I went to so much trouble to meet him. All that planning, all that money and time. And then—this."

Conner peered into the kid's eyes. "It's tough."

"I was so close!" Out of nowhere, Ed's fists rose up and pounded down on the table. "I saw him, you know. Tuesday night. But he was heading somewhere in a hurry and I didn't want to bother him. I thought—no, Ed, wait. You've got all week." He slumped down in his chair. "Except I didn't have all week. That was my last chance. And I blew it."

"Are you saying you saw John alive Tuesday night?"

"Right. Around nine-thirty."

Nine-thirty! That would be after he left the cabin, after Jodie last saw him alive. "Do you have any idea where he was going?"

"Sure. It was obvious. I saw him pass through the door."

Conner's eyebrows knitted together. "The door? What door?"

Ed's eyes widened. "Didn't you know? He was going to see Andrew Spenser."

10

ONCE AGAIN, CONNER was not entirely surprised when he received his summons to appear in the chairman's office. He'd been expecting it since he saw Derwood stomp off earlier that morning, and it probably would've come sooner, had the tournament officials not had some rather more pressing business. When the call came, he didn't resist. It was just as well—he'd finished his last martini. And this time, he had questions he wanted to pose to Mr. Spenser.

Conner knew the way to Tenniel's office now, so he took the lead, letting the Augusta National Nazis trail nervously in his wake. He walked briskly down the dimly lit corridor till he reached Tenniel's office, then flung the double doors open and stepped inside.

Derwood was there, as he expected, hovering in the background like a vulture waiting for his daily dose of carrion. Tenniel sat behind his desk, impassive as ever.

Spenser stepped forward from the recesses of the office. It appeared that, once again, he was going to take the leading role in Conner's Trip to the Woodshed, Part Two.

"First of all," Spenser said, "let me express our deepest sympathies to you. We know what a loss you've suffered. Believe me when I say you have our most sincere condolences." Spenser held out his arms, as if he actually thought for a moment he was going to embrace Conner. Conner did a quick sidestep to avoid that possibility. "We know you and John were close, and we understand that you must be suffering the most profound grief."

Conner remained unmoved. "Why do I feel you're coming to a *but?*"

Spenser's stoic resolve wavered, if only for an instant. "We know these are troubling times, and if we can assist you in any way, please do not hesitate to tell us."

"Yeah, yeah, yeah," Conner said impatiently. "If that was all you had to say, you could've sent a Hallmark. What's the real purpose of this meeting?"

Spenser cleared his throat. "We realize that this tragedy may affect your . . . powers of judgment, and that a certain lack of rationality may be inevitable . . ."

"Lack of rationality?"

"I'm sure you've heard that we intend to continue with this tournament. That decision being made, it is crucial that we maintain our standards . . ."

"Spenser, just cut to the chase."

Spenser drew himself up. "We have wondered if it wouldn't be best if you dropped out of the tournament. No one could fault you for that. No one would suspect that there was any . . . controversy. People will simply assume that you are overcome with grief due to the loss of your friend."

Conner felt his teeth locking together. "Let me see if I've got this straight. You want to use John's death as an excuse to get me the hell out of Dodge."

"I was only considering your welfare. Surely you're not in any condition to play a major golf tournament. Proceeding with this could only lead to . . . severe embarrassment."

"And what is that supposed to mean?"

"I've seen the scores from the par three, Mr. Cross. Your performance was hardly . . . Masters caliber, and we can't realistically expect it to improve after all you've been through today. I think the wisest course would be for you to excuse yourself from the competition."

Conner had so many emotions racing through him he couldn't identify them all. A few hours ago, before he talked to Jodie, he was certain he would drop out of the tournament, exactly as Spenser wished. But now, after hearing Spenser use John's death as a tawdry excuse to get what he wanted, he'd sooner die first. Besides, he made Jodie a promise. "No."

Artemus Tenniel leaned forward, his hands clasped on his desk. "You don't have to answer now. Give it some thought. Sleep on it."

"I'm not dropping out."

"Don't force us to become antagonistic," Spenser said. "I'm sure it's clear to you by now that . . . we don't want you here. You're just . . . not the Masters type."

"The Masters type? What is that?"

"We have remarked previously on your unacceptable behavior."

"Now wait just a minute. I did as you asked. I dressed in your silly Sears clothes."

From the back corner, Derwood made a loud throat-clearing noise. He jerked his head toward Conner's.

Spenser took the cue. "There's still the matter of your, um, hair style."

"I read the PGA rules and the Augusta National regulations. None of them prohibit a shaved head."

"It's hardly orthodox."

"Says who? Lots of the pros are bald."

"It's not the same thing."

"You can't toss me out. I didn't break a rule."

"The haircut is simply one example. Your attitude is what we find offensive."

"What are you—the attitude police? What makes you think you can tell me what attitude to have? If I haven't broken a rule, you haven't got anything on me."

"We've given you a graceful out. Show some sense for a change. Take it."

"I will not quit the tournament. And you won't throw me out, either."

"You think we can't?" Tenniel said, a tiny edge to his voice. "You think you're invulnerable? That's what Frank Stranahan thought, too, back in 1947. We ousted him for arguing with a greenskeeper."

Conner raised a finger. "If you try to shaft me after my best friend was murdered in your sand trap, I will raise a stink like you've never seen in your life!"

"Think of what you're saying!" Spenser implored. "You would dishonor John's memory."

"Is that a fact?" Conner shot back. "Speaking of John's memory, why was he in your office just before he was killed?"

Spenser looked as if someone had slugged him with a tire iron. "Why—John—*what?*"

"You heard me. He was in your office, late at night. He was meeting you, wasn't he?"

"I—He—"

"Spit it out, Spenser. Why did you meet John? Were the two of you having a disagreement, perhaps? Maybe you were trying to push John around, too? And maybe he didn't like it?"

Spenser took a step backward. "I'm afraid I don't know what you're talking about."

"You deny it?"

"I certainly do. John McCree was not in my office last night. Neither was I, for that matter." Spenser's eyes darted from one end of the room to the other, as if checking to make sure his colleagues believed him. "It's all a lie. Something this scoundrel cooked up to confuse the issues."

Conner stared back at the man, puzzled. Fanboy Ed had definitely said he saw John go into Spenser's office. Either Spenser was lying, or Ed was.

And what possible reason could Ed have to lie?

11

Thursday

THURSDAY WAS THE first day of the actual Masters tournament. Conner was always amazed at the amount of rigmarole that attended the opening. From all the buzz and excitement, all the attention and interest, one might think the president was about to declare war, or aliens had just landed on the seventh green.

As always, the press was present in force. Reporters were everywhere, looking for inside tips, news, and gossip about the players and the game. Conner spotted three different CBS minicams. The official network commentators were safely tucked away in their high-rise booth, specially constructed for tournament coverage. There were even a couple of helicopters buzzing around overhead, providing aerial photography.

And of what? A golf tournament. Conner shook his head in amazement. If the police department could summon this much talent and energy for its investigation, John's murder would've been solved yesterday.

It was a beautiful morning; the azaleas were in bloom and the air was thick with the scent of tea olive. The greens were bright and vibrant—trimmed to perfection. Even the roughs were—well, not very rough. Just "second cut" once a year. This really was, Conner grudgingly admitted, the best-kept golf course on earth. If a leaf fell on the fairway, he suspected, an alarm sounded in the groundskeeper's bunker and a golf cart was dispatched to remove the offending item.

Conner showed up early for the opening ceremony; he wasn't going to give anyone an excuse to toss him out on some obscure technicality. Before the tournament began, all the pros gathered to watch the first tee-off, which was traditionally shared by the three senior members invited to play. Since all former Masters champions are invited back, regardless of their current standing, that meant that the three oldest former champions shared the stage. Each of the three seniors knocked off one token swing, then retired to the clubhouse to watch the real contenders.

After that ceremony was completed, an assistant tournament director assigned numbers to each of the players. Last year's champion was always 1; Jack Nicklaus was always 86, commemorating the year he won the last and most extraordinary of his six Masters titles.

Fitz brought Conner the news that he had been assigned number 51. "I assume that was chosen to commemorate your I.Q."

"Ha ha," Conner replied.

Conner was matched for play with Barry Bennett, who appeared somewhat soberer than he had the night before. Ace Silverstone and Freddy Granger were the twosome just behind them.

"Glad we got to tee-off early," Freddy said, as the group gathered. "I got a million things to do. This weddin' is drivin' me crazy."

Conner tried to be sympathetic. "Are the in-laws in town yet?"

"Oh, yeah. They've been here for days. They're not so bad. I'd rather be with them than with that nimrod my daughter's marryin'."

"I thought you were happy about the marriage."

"I'm happy about the fact of a marriage. I think my new son-in-law is worthless. Never played a round of golf in his life—can you believe it? Doesn't know a bogey from a booger."

"Fate plays cruel tricks sometimes," Conner said sympathetically.

Freddy continued to rattle on about the cost of the wedding, the caterers, the country club, the wedding gown. Conner grabbed Ace's arm and tugged him toward the tee. Normally, Conner wouldn't be able to stand anyone who played so much better than himself, but given the alternative of spending time with Barry, the man who badmouthed his late friend, or Freddy, who was babbling about crudités and tiered cakes, he chose Ace.

"How'd the feature spot turn out?" Conner asked as they approached the tee.

"Fabulous, fabulous. Didn't you see it? Oh—" He covered his hand with his mouth. "Of course not. You weren't watching television last night. Look, I'm sorry—"

"It's all right. Really. Think it'll run again?"

"Oh, yeah. Probably all week. And they're going to shoot some more footage as well. In fact, we're talking about me doing my own show for ESPN. Not just a special, but a regular weekly program. Kind of a golf instruction thing."

"Sounds great," Conner muttered.

"Course, it'll be hard to squeeze in with my usual color commentary gigs, but I think I can make it work. Especially now that I have a new plane."

Conner did a double take. "You have your own plane?"

"Sure. Don't you? I thought everyone did."

"Uh, no."

"You really should, Conner. Get yourself a little Lear, like I did. It'll vastly improve the quality of your life."

"No doubt." Conner pulled a tee and ball out of his golf bag.

"Did I tell you about the chain stores?"

"Uh, no." Conner was beginning to think he'd made the wrong choice. As a conversational gambit, the wedding of the century was infinitely preferable to Ace's grandiose career plans.

"Oh, yeah. We're going to go national. Ace's Place, that's what we'll call them. We'll specialize in custom-made golf equipment."

Conner cautiously selected his nine-iron. "Sounds like a winner."

"I'd like to start my own tournament."

Conner pounded his club against the ground. Would this never end?

"I've got sponsors lined up. All I need is a weekend."

"Excuse me?"

"You know how jam-packed the tournament schedule is. There's no opening for another tournament, unless one of the current tournaments disappears."

"Well, that's something to hope for, anyway. Whaddaya say we play some golf?"

Conner took a deep breath and tried to concentrate on the game. He still couldn't believe he was playing golf the day after he found his best friend dead. But—Jodie was right. The killer probably was someone at the tournament, and he was more likely to figure out who that was if he remained involved.

He felt a tugging at his sleeve. It was Fitz.

"You're not really going to use that, are you?"

"Who are you—my safe sex counselor?"

"I'm reminding you that your nine-iron play was disastrous yesterday. And we never had a chance to figure out what was causing it."

"Well, I've slept since then. I think it'll be all right."

"Don't be nuts. Use the three-wood."

"The nine-iron's my best club."

"Not yesterday, it wasn't."

Conner frowned. "Maybe you're right." Reluctantly, he accepted the wood from Fitz.

The first nine holes went reasonably well for Conner, although he was handicapped by not being able to use his nine-iron on the shorter shots, and he still had a nasty tendency to choke on his putting game. Still, he finished the first nine only two over par; not as good as Ace played, but a respectable showing.

Unfortunately, at the Masters it's the back nine that make all the difference. The eleventh, twelfth, and thirteenth holes are traditionally referred to as "Amen Corner"—the famous holes where water can turn the tournament upside-down. Conner weathered the eleventh, overshooting with a three-wood but still managing to make par.

The twelfth hole was a par three with a tiny green. Conner stood at the tee and gazed out at the smooth sheer green horizon. "Perfect hole for a nine-iron," he commented.

"For someone else maybe," Fitz replied. "Not for you." He held out a club. "Here. Use this."

Conner hesistated.

Fitz's face fell. "Oh, damn."

"What?"

"I can tell by the expression on your face. You're about to do something stupid."

Conner put his hands on his hips. "I beg your pardon?"

"You will. I know it." Fitz shook his head back and forth. "You're not going to use the wood, are you?"

Conner gazed once again at the fairway. "You have to admit, it's a perfect hole for a nine-iron."

"Not when your ball slices every time you use it!"

Conner pursed his lips thoughtfully. "I'm going to give it a try."

Fitz slapped his forehead in despair. "No, no, *no*! Conner—you're playing a good game. Don't screw it up."

"I can't avoid the nine-iron forever." He snatched the club from his bag. "Besides, when a man falls off his horse, he's got to get right back on again."

"Spare me the cowboy philosophizing."

"Stand back, Fitz. I'm going to make this one count." Conner took his position, carefully concentrating on his stance, his grip, his destination. He took a deep breath, held it . . . then let it fly.

The ball soared beautifully up into the air . . . and then, as predictably as a heart attack, took a severe turn to the right. The slice cut sideways across the fairway, just short of the green, and rolled into a water trap.

Conner cursed and threw the club back at Fitz. "I'm never using the damn thing again."

"That's it," Barry said, chuckling. "Blame the club." Barry seemed to be a good deal merrier than he had been when they started the round. Come to notice, Conner thought, his nose seemed a bit redder, too. Did the man have some hooch hidden in his golf bag, or what?

The thirteenth was not much of an improvement. It was a dogleg left, with dogwood, a creek running down one side of the fairway and trees running down the other. The narrow water trap in front of the green was invisible from the crook in the fairway where the players traditionally lay up for their second shot.

Conner used the wood to hit a perfect drive into the sweet spot. He was relieved; that was supposed to be his specialty, after all. He selected his pitching wedge to pop the ball onto the green.

As he took his stance, he felt Fitz lay a hand on his shoulder. "Envision the water trap. Locate it in your mind."

"How can I locate it in my mind? I can't even see it."

"That's the point, Conner. You can't see it with your eyes, so don't try. Close your eyes and see it with your mind's eye. You know where it is, where it must be. Picture it, and drive the ball across it. Don't think, do."

"Thanks, Yoda." Conner closed his eyes and swung . . . and the ball plopped down into the water trap.

"May the frigging Force be with you," Conner grumbled.

The rest of the course went uneventfully, but after the debacle of Amen Corner, Conner was way behind Ace. After they completed the seventeenth hole, they headed for the locker room. By agreement, the pros were playing only seventeen holes; the eighteenth was still roped off by the police.

Before they reached the locker room, Conner and the rest encountered a group of reporters huddled under the giant oak tree just outside the entrance to the clubhouse. Conner knew that was one of only two places on the grounds where the media was allowed to talk to players—the other being Butler Cabin. It was standard procedure; they were all used to it. Today's questioning, however, was anything but standard:

"What can you tell us about John McCree's murder?"

"Is it true the eighteenth green is still smeared with blood?"

"Do you think the killer might strike again?"

Before Conner could get himself out of the way, one of the reporters had thrust a microphone under his nose. He saw the red light on the minicam blinking and realized that he was on. "Conner, how are you dealing with the loss of your best friend John McCree?"

What Conner really wanted was tell these people exactly what he thought of this vulturous picking away at John's death. But he knew it would be fruitless; they'd edit the footage so that he sounded ridiculous, then make a fool of him on the evening news.

Conner tried to stammer out a coherent response. "I've known John since I was eight," he said haltingly. "All that time, I've considered him my best friend. Obviously, his death has hit me . . . very hard."

The man holding the microphone smirked. "But not so hard you couldn't play the tournament, right?"

Conner's head felt as if it were about to boil. He grabbed the man's shirt and jerked him forward. "Look, you sorry son-of-a—"

Conner froze. The red light was still blinking. This was all being recorded. The man had baited him, and now Conner was giving him exactly what he wanted.

Conner released the reporter. "John McCree's dream was that one of us Oklahoma boys might one day make good at the Masters tournament. I can't very well make that dream come true by quitting, can I?"

Conner turned before the reporter could respond and quickly moved out of camera-shot. Behind him, he heard the mob surround Ace, looking for fresh meat.

As always, the mediagenic Ace rose to the occasion. "Although I didn't know John long or well, I sensed that in his chest beat a heart of purest gold . . ."

Conner had to stifle his gagging reflex.

". . . but now, there's an empty place in the locker room where John McCree's blue-and-white bag used to be." Ace looked as if he might burst out in tears at any moment. "One thing is certain—from this day forward, pro golf will never be the same. He will be missed."

Conner turned, shaking his head, and made his way down to the locker room. He found Barry was already there, changing out of his golf clothes. Somehow, the man had managed to elude the fourth estate wolf pack altogether. That must've been tricky. And totally unlike a PGA golf pro.

A thought occurred to Conner. He strode over to Barry, who was lacing up his street shoes. "Barry, I want a word with you."

"I've got nothing to say to you."

No doubt about it; there was something strong and alcoholic on the man's breath. Perhaps one reason he didn't care to be interviewed. "You had plenty enough to say last night when you were in your cups."

"I don't know what you're talking about."

"Don't bother denying it. I'm not the only one who was in the bar last night. You made your feelings known to everyone within earshot."

Barry glared at him. "You'd be better off just leaving me alone, Cross."

"Why have you got such a chip on your shoulder about John?"

"That's between him and me."

"The police might feel differently."

Barry's eyes narrowed. "What's that supposed to mean?"

"It means, if you had some kind of grudge against John, I want to hear about it."

Barry finished tying his shoes, grabbed his gym bag, and stood up. "Maybe you should ask Jodie." And on that note, he pivoted quickly and stomped out of the locker room.

12

ONCE HE'D CHANGED, Conner made his way to the eighteenth green. A hundred-yard area surrounding the sand trap
was roped off. Homicide technicians were still combing the
crime scene, some of them crawling on hands and knees, searching for
clues. Some of them were using tweezers, and they were all wearing yellow coveralls. What they could possibly find this long after the fact
Conner couldn't imagine, but he was gratified that they were trying.

An idea sparked in Conner's brain. Wouldn't Derwood be impressed
if Conner showed up at the first tee tomorrow in one of those snappy
yellow coveralls? He wondered if they came in his size.

He approached a few of the technicians, but they either refused to
talk or claimed they didn't know anything. No one would tell him anything of value, like whether the police had a suspect, or even a good
lead for that matter. Their blank faces reinforced in his mind the fear
Jodie had expressed—that John's murder would never be solved.

How had he let her talk him into this? As if he knew anything about
conducting a crime investigation. They were just kidding themselves,
imagining that he might discover something the cops couldn't. He
needed to find Jodie and tell her this was a mistake. She was probably in
the clubhouse. Maybe he should just wander over there . . .

Conner glanced toward the clubhouse, but his eyes lit upon a much
closer scenic wonder. A tall red-haired woman made him do a double-
take. She was standing at a distance, staring in his direction.

He grinned. Probably another golf groupie, one of those women
who follow the tour around the country and will do anything imaginable to get close to a real live golf pro.

Conner sauntered a few steps in her direction. "Hi," he said, flashing his best smile. "I'm Conner Cross."

The woman barely turned her head. "I'm glad for you."

Conner laughed. "No, seriously. I'm Conner Cross."

"You're not going to ask me for money, are you?"

Conner frowned. "Uh . . . aren't you here to watch the tournament?"

"Get real." She had a lilting accent, slow and deliberate. Definitely a local. "You think I have nothing better to do than watch a bunch of clowns in pastel Polos knock a little ball around?"

Conner's grin faded fast. This wasn't going to be quite as easy as he had imagined. "Well, then . . . why are you here?"

She whipped out a leather wallet and revealed a shiny silver badge. "Lieutenant Nikki O'Brien, Augusta PD."

Conner's face flattened. "You—you're investigating the murder?"

"You *are* a quick study, aren't you?"

Well, as long as he was here, maybe he could get a little information. "So, uh . . . how's the investigation going?"

"We're just getting started."

"Got any leads? Suspects?"

"I'm afraid I'm not at liberty to discuss it right now."

"Oh, of course, of course." Okay, then back to Plan A. The pick-up. "You're really truly a cop?"

Her lips turned down at the edges. "Who did you say you were?"

"Conner Cross."

"That sounds familiar. What do you do?"

"Me?" Conner pressed a hand against his chest. "I . . . well . . ."

"Is this a hard question?"

"No, I just . . ." His eyes scanned the horizon. Think, man, think! "I'm a horticulturist."

Lieutenant O'Brien blinked. "Excuse me?"

"You know. Plants, grass. That sort of thing."

"And you're here because . . ."

"Because I'm helping care for the grounds. You see, the Augusta National uses a very special, very rare kind of grass, imported from South America. Somewhere south of the Amazon."

"South of the Amazon."

"Right. Makes for an excellent course. But it's very temperamental. Hard to care for. Requires a specialist."

"A specialist."

"Right. That's me."

"So you tend golf courses. That must be incredibly rewarding."

"Well, this isn't what I normally do." Still not impressed. Keep the wheels turning . . . "This is only one week a year, during the Masters tournament. I just do it to finance my . . . real work."

"Which is?"

"Tending to rare South American . . . plants. And things."

"Plants? And things?"

"Did you know that hundreds of plant species become extinct every day? It's a horror what's going on in the rain forests these days. An absolute horror. Who knows what some of those plants might yield? They might hold the key to curing cancer, and yet we plow them under and bury them to make room for more cattle so McDonald's can make more burgers. It's criminal. I'm doing everything I can to stop it."

O'Brien's face softened a bit. "Well, that does sound like important work." She paused and scrutinized Conner intensely. "Mr. Cross, you'll have to excuse me. I'm on duty."

"Oh—right, right. The cop thing."

"Yeah, that."

"Are you—absolutely *sure* you're a police officer?"

"Welcome to the New South, Mr. Cross." With an enigmatic smile, she turned on her heel and walked away without giving him so much as a backward glance.

Conner sighed as he watched her shimmering figure fade from view. Maybe I didn't handle that as well as I might've . . .

13

CONNER HEADED BACK to the clubhouse. Some of the pros were hanging about; some were probably still out on the course. He searched from one end of the building to the other, but couldn't find any trace of Jodie. They needed to have a serious conversation.

There were only a handful of people in the bar. The bartender was idle; he had one eye on the television beside the cash register, watching a Braves game. A sport other than golf? Conner mused. Now there's a novel concept.

A thought occurred. Weren't bartenders supposed to know more or less . . . everything? Mouth shut and ears open, weren't they supposed to pick up all the best gossip? John had been a member of the Club, after all. And Vic, the man currently on duty, had been tending bar here forever—or at least as long as Conner had been on the tour. He might be an ideal person to have a chat with . . .

Conner sidled up to the bar. Vic smiled. He was a big man, mostly bald, with a rugged complexion and a drooping mustache. "What's your poison, Conner?"

"Ginger ale." If he was going to be any use to Jodie, he needed to keep a clear head.

The bartender stared at him briefly, then dutifully fixed the drink. Conner knew what he must be thinking. Man, this death has hit Conner harder than anyone realized.

Conner did his utmost to seem nonchalant. "Have you seen Jodie?"

Vic shook his head. "Not for an hour or so. I don't think she's gone far."

"Probably just wanted some time alone."

"No one could blame her for that."

"How well did you know John?"

Vic eyed him carefully. He seemed surprised by the question. "Not as well as you. Why?"

"Just wondered. I thought I knew him well. But the police keep asking me who might've done this and—I don't have a clue. It's embarrassing. I feel more like a fraud than a friend."

"Don't blame yourself." Vic picked up a towel and began absently wiping the bar. "You can never tell what might be going on in someone else's life. Some of the things I hear in the bar . . . well, you just wouldn't believe it. Someone could've held a big grudge against John and—maybe his own wife didn't know about it. Maybe John himself didn't know."

Conner nodded. If that were true, Conner concluded, it would make tracking down this murderer all but impossible. "Did you hear anything about John? Anything that might constitute . . . a motive?"

" 'Fraid not. Far as I knew, everyone loved John to pieces."

Something about the way Vic said that didn't ring quite true to Conner. "How about you? Did you like John? Was he a generous tipper?"

Vic averted his eyes. "I . . . probably wouldn't have called him . . . generous, no."

"Did John seem different to you lately?"

"Now that you mention it, I did think he seemed a little down of late. Depressed, maybe."

Conner was surprised. John was depressed? He hadn't noticed anything.

"But I didn't think much about it. John's been having a bad year. He made a big flash when he started out on the tour, but it's been—what?—two years since he placed in a tournament? This year he hadn't played at all."

Conner considered this. It was true, but he had never seen any signs that it was wearing John down. Was that because it wasn't—or because Conner was too wrapped up in his own performance to notice anyone else's problems?

"And of course, John was serving on the board of directors here at the Club."

Conner glanced up. That was true. He'd forgotten all about that.

"And I think that'd be enough to depress anyone." Vic made a sort of snorting sound that was not so much laughter as cynicism.

"What was his position on the board?"

"You're asking the wrong man. I think he led some kind of finance committee. But I really don't know."

Hmm. If Vic didn't know, Conner knew someone who would. "And you can't think of any other reason why John would be depressed?"

"Sorry. No."

"Pardon me, Vic. I need a word with Mr. Cross."

Conner turned and, to his great distress and disappointment, found himself face-to-face with Richard Peregino, the PGA morality cop.

"Just what I need," Conner said. "What ill wind blew you in?"

"Don't give me any crap, Cross." In his right hand, Peregino held a baggie filled with sunflower seeds, which he popped in one after another whenever his mouth wasn't busy talking. "I'm here to deliver a warning. And it's the last one you'll get."

"Did Derwood send you? Or Spenser?"

"I don't have anything to do with them, Cross. The PGA pays me to uphold the honor and integrity of the tour, and that's what I intend to do."

"And maintaining honor and integrity includes hounding me for no good reason?"

"We have standards to maintain."

"I know all about the PGA's standards. They didn't delete the Caucasians-only clause from the PGA Constitution until 1961!"

Conner watched as Peregino pulled two empty sunflower seed shells out of his mouth and shoved them into his pocket. "Don't try to confuse matters. I'm here to enforce the rules and regulations of the PGA. I've got a file folder on you an inch thick. You're skating on thin ice. You're at the end of your tether."

Conner paused to see if any more clichés would be forthcoming. "Just leave me alone. In case you haven't heard, my best friend died."

"Oh, I heard all right. And despite million-to-one odds, you're the person who found his body. Quite a coincidence, I'd say."

Conner felt his teeth clench. "What the hell is that supposed to mean?"

"I just think it's very suspicious, that's all. I wonder if maybe you and John were having a little disagreement."

Conner grabbed the man by his collar. "Look, you son-of-a-bitch. You don't know what the hell you're talking about, and if I hear you spreading this kind of bull around—"

"You'll what? Sue?"

"I'll knock your stupid empty head into the next county."

Peregino made a tsking noise. "Violent tendencies. Explosive temper. I think the police will be interested to hear about this. By the way, assaulting a PGA official is a serious rules infraction. One more page for your ever-expanding file."

Conner pushed him away. "Just leave me alone, you two-bit gestapo-wannabe. You haven't got anything on me."

"Your behavior. Your dress. Your stylish new haricut."

"You can't toss me out of the PGA for those things."

"That isn't true, strictly speaking. Don't forget the image clause."

"The what?"

"Your agreement with the PGA contains an image clause, just like everyone else's. If you evince behavior unbecoming to the reputation or image of the PGA, I have the authority to yank your card."

"That's a crock of—"

"That's a fact. And frankly, what I'm observing at the present time is hardly what I'd call model behavior."

Conner came very close to exhibiting behavior considerably less model on Peregino's face, but he managed to restrain himself.

"Remember, Cross—this is your last warning. I'll be watching you."

"You watch all you want, you sorry little—" In the corner of his eye, Conner saw Jodie passing in the corridor. "I'll finish with you later, asshole."

He raced through the door and met Jodie outside. "Jodie, we need to—"

"Conner! There you are!" Jodie ran up, threw her arms around him, and hugged tightly. She planted a kiss on the side of his cheek. The touch of her lips sent an electric charge down Conner's spine. "I can't tell you how grateful to you I am."

"You are? For what?"

"For—you know. Agreeing to look into what happened to John."

Conner squirmed. "Jodie—about that—"

"I was so distraught after I found out what happened. So directionless. I even thought about—" She paused. "But never mind. The point is—I'm past that now. Thanks to you."

"Jodie . . . I think you may have too much confidence in me. I think—"

She pressed her fingers against his lips. "Shhh. Don't. I'm not expecting miracles. Just knowing you're out there trying . . . well, I can't explain it. But somehow—it gives me the strength to keep going."

Conner drew in his breath, then slowly released it. So much for trying to back out of this. "The press is giving me grief about continuing in the tournament."

"I heard. But they won't anymore."

"How can you—"

"I just released a formal statement. That's where I've been the last hour or so." She reached into her purse and produced a sheet of paper. "Among other things, I told them that I begged you to continue playing the tournament in John's memory, and that you reluctantly agreed. So you're off the hook."

Conner quickly scanned the press statement. It was just as she said, if not better. "Thanks, Jodie."

She smiled, then took his hand and squeezed it. "Least I can do." She pulled him into the nearest lounge, then closed the outer door. "Have you learned anything?"

Conner shrugged. "Not really. The police don't have a suspect or, by all indications, any strong leads."

"I'm not surprised."

"I have heard someone say they thought John seemed depressed. Did you notice anything like that?"

"Depression? John? No. If he were depressed, I would've known."

"That's what I figured."

"I've never known a less depressed person than John in my entire life. Now—*angry*—that's a different matter."

"John seemed angry?"

"That last night. He definitely had a bug up his nose about something."

"Did you ask him what it was?"

"Never got the chance. Figured I'd ask him when he returned. But of course . . . he never did."

"Another thing . . . Why is Barry Bennett so down on John?"

Jodie turned her eyes away. "Why would you ask me?"

"Because Barry told me to."

"It was all so long ago. But you might know—Barry is exactly the kind of person who would never forget."

"Forget what?"

Jodie drew up her shoulders and sighed. It was obvious she didn't want to proceed, but Conner was gratified that she did anyway. "Several years ago, after John made the PGA but before I married him, I dated Barry."

"I never heard anything about this."

"It was before you joined the tour."

"Barry? And *you*?"

"It seems incredible now. What can I say? I was young and, frankly, stupid. Didn't know diddly about men."

"Evidently not."

"Let's give Barry some credit. He's made a success of himself, despite extremely humble beginnings. And he can be kind and thoughtful and generous. Of course, he can also be domineering and possessive and insanely jealous."

"I'm beginning to see where this is going."

Jodie nodded. "It was never serious—except in Barry's mind. John was the one I loved—I just had to be with someone else for a while to realize that. But every time I suggested to Barry that we ought to see less of each other, he'd fly off the handle. He scared me, Conner, he really did. I finally told him I didn't want to see him any more—but I did it over the phone. Cowardly, I know—but I was seriously afraid he might lose control and—well, take it out on me. He drank too much, even back then, though nothing like he does now. The booze made him unpredictable."

"You did the right thing."

"But I still feel guilty about it. At any rate, about four months later, John and I were married. Barry apparently transferred all his anger from me to John. Blaming him for coming between us. It was never like that at all, but try telling Barry that."

"Try telling Barry anything," Conner groused.

Jodie nodded. "Especially something he doesn't want to hear."

A stray thought returned to Conner. "Did you ever remember what it was John said when he left that last night? The strange remark that puzzled you?"

"No, I haven't. I'm sorry." She shrugged apologetically. "I'm not much help, am I?"

Conner gave her shoulder a squeeze. "I think you're very brave, Jodie. Brave and . . . wonderful."

She gave him a broken, lopsided smile. "Not bad for an Oklahoma girl, anyway?"

Conner pulled her close. "Not bad at all."

14

CONNER RETURNED TO the bar and found it considerably more crowded. Barry was downing Scotches like nobody's business, complaining to anyone foolish enough to listen. Ace was waxing on about his plans for "the greatest golf tournament this world has ever seen." Freddy was nowhere in sight; probably at the other country club making last-minute purchases for his daughter's wedding, Conner mused.

He saw Fanboy Ed sitting at a table by himself, wearing the same clothes he had worn the night before. Probably the only clothes he had smuggled in.

"Still here, kid?"

Ed barely grunted in reply.

"Where did you stay last night?"

"Found a dark place in the back of the greenskeeper's storage shed."

"And food?"

He shrugged. "Leftovers. And the breakfast buffet. When no one's looking."

Ed did not look happy. Had the full impact of his disappointment finally settled in? Or was it something more?

Conner tried to offer sympathy. "I know how you must be feeling, Ed. This has hit us all very hard."

"I know," Ed said. His eyes were moist. "But at least you had a chance to know John. I never even met him. All my life, as far back as I can remember, I've had only one ambition. To be John McCree's caddie at the Masters tournament. And now—now—" He couldn't finish the sentence.

"I didn't know you caddied," Conner said softly.

"Well, I never have. I didn't want to be anyone else's caddie. I wanted to be John McCree's caddie."

"Ed, being a caddie for a pro requires experience and knowledge and—"

"That's why I came early. So I could seek John out and offer my services. I wouldn't have charged him or anything. I wanted to show him what I could do, to be close to him for a little while. And now—"

Once again, Ed's voice dissolved. Conner decided to leave the kid to his grief. There was nothing he could do for him now.

A group of pros were huddled at the bar, preparing to make a toast. Conner wormed his way into the group. "What are we toasting?"

One of them chuckled. "Since when did you need an excuse to have a drink, Cross?"

Conner tried to laugh. "I thought we were celebrating something."

One of the men pushed Harley Tuttle forward. "Harley's the man of the hour!" someone shouted.

"Really!" Conner was glad to see Harley breaking into the social life on the tour. "What have you done?"

Harley looked keenly uncomfortable about all the attention. "Oh, it's really no big deal."

"Don't be so modest," Conner said. "What?"

Harley hesitated. "I'm in fourth place going into Friday."

"That's spectacular. Congratulations."

Harley shrugged shyly. "Like my daddy used to say, Every dog has his day."

"Your daddy was quite the philosopher."

Harley smiled. "Poet laureate of Muellenburg County."

Conner hadn't even thought to look at the postings. He wondered what place he was in. Happily, he didn't have to wonder long. A familiar voice sounded behind him. "Forty-seventh. In a field of sixty."

Conner closed his eyes. "Thanks, Fitz. I was wondering. I'm sure everyone else here was, too."

"I don't know why you should be disappointed," Fitz snapped. "You should be relieved."

"Relieved?"

"After a performance like the one you gave on the course today, you should've placed in the three-digit numbers."

"There are only sixty players in the tournament."

"Like I said." Fitz leaned into Conner's ear. "I don't know where your head is, Conner, but if you don't get it on this game, you're not going to make the Friday night cut!" With that, Fitz stomped out of the bar.

Harsh words but, alas, true ones. Conner knew he was right, and he knew that dimpled ball didn't care what all Conner had been through. If his performance didn't improve, he'd never make it to Saturday—the ultimate embarrassment.

As if his thoughts weren't gloomy enough already, Fitz spotted Derwood headed his way. Derwood planted himself in front of Conner and spoke but a single word. "Come."

Conner looked at him wryly. "This is becoming an every night thing." He took Derwood's hand and squeezed it. "Aren't you afraid people will talk?"

"You're a sick man, Cross."

"I love it when you're mean to me." Conner leaned forward and kissed Derwood on the cheek.

Derwood grimaced and bolted away, wiping his cheek. "You sick— *sick*—" He turned and ran out of the bar amidst a chorus of hoots and hollers.

IN THE CHAIRMAN'S office, Conner found the usual cast of characters in their usual places. He began to wonder if these people choreographed these meetings before he arrived.

"I'm sure you know why we've called you here," Spenser said in somber tones.

"As a matter of fact, I'm clueless. I thought I'd been a good boy today."

Spenser glanced at a piece of paper in his right hand. It was some kind of report—no doubt prepared by Derwood. "I understand you've been bothering people on our premises. Hounding them with questions about John McCree."

Conner's eyebrows knitted. Who would've told Derwood that?

"I also understand that you behaved in a belligerent manner to certain members of the press." He looked up from the paper. "It seems incredible but apparently you actually assaulted a reporter."

"He had it coming," Conner grumbled. "And then some."

Spenser appeared flabbergasted. "You mean you don't deny it?"

"No, I don't deny it. He was hassling me, making nasty insinuations. Using John's death to boost his ratings."

Spenser drew himself up. "Well, then. Since you make no attempt to deny these charges, let me make myself absolutely clear. We will not tolerate any improper behavior toward the journalistic community. If you have a complaint about someone, you should give it to Derwood."

"I'd sooner die."

"But under no circumstances should you ever behave in a hostile, unprofessional manner. Much less actually strike someone!"

"Oh, all I did was shake him around a little. And believe me, he deserved it."

"You think you're the first pro who ever got hassled by a reporter? We depend on the press. Those big purses only exist because television reporters are interested in what you're doing. If the reporters go away, so does the big money."

"This is not about money."

"On that, we are agreed," Spenser said firmly. "It's about decorum, a quality you are sadly lacking!"

Conner's eyes narrowed. "Was that John's problem?"

Spenser took a step back. "What? I don't know what you mean."

"Did he lack decorum as well? Did he, for instance, have trouble keeping his mouth shut?"

Spenser looked wild-eyed at the others. "Cross is a madman. An absolute madman."

"I know John was disturbed about something the night he was killed, and I can't think of anyone who could disturb someone more than you."

"You're insane!"

"Stop playing games, Spenser. I know John headed up the finance committee."

"But—so?" Spenser sputtered. Conner was relieved. He'd taken a wild shot, but judging by Spenser's reaction, he wasn't far from the target. "You don't know what you're talking about."

"I think John knew something. Maybe he had something on you. Something you didn't want to get out. What was it, Spenser?"

"This is an outrage!" Spenser threw up his hands. "I want this man out of here! *Now!*"

Conner took a step toward the door, pleased with the knowledge that he'd definitely gotten under Spenser's skin. More than ever, he was convinced the man was hiding something. But what?

Conner saw the others in the room glancing at one another, exchanging looks. What were they thinking? Were they marking this down as another of Conner's gonzo behavior spasms? Or were they beginning to wonder what Spenser was hiding, too?

"I'll go," Conner said quietly. "But I'll be back. And when I am, I'll expect an answer to my question." Conner marched toward the door and, before Spenser had a chance to sputter another word, left the office.

Friday

Friday morning, bright and early, Conner dressed and headed for the coffee shop. He had a relatively late tee time, but he still wanted to be up and around with his eyes wide open. As he rounded the corner, he saw Lieutenant O'Brien standing just outside the coffee shop. As soon as she saw him, she moved forward. She was obviously waiting for him.

"Lieutenant O'Brien," he said, grinning. "So nice to see you."

"And so nice to see you," O'Brien said, with her slow Georgia drawl.

Had he really told this vision he was a horticulturist? A sudden wave of guilt overcame him. He laid his hand on her shoulder. "Look, I can't stand keeping secrets from a beautiful woman like you. Maybe I should come clean."

"That would be very welcome." She took his hand and, with a smooth sudden motion, spun Conner around, pinning his arm behind his back. "You're under arrest for the murder of John McCree."

15

"HEY, WATCH IT!" Conner shouted.

"You have the right to remain silent," O'Brien said, shoving her knee into the small of his back. "Anything you say can and will be used against you."

"What the hell is going on?"

O'Brien shoved him up against the wall. "You have the right to an attorney. If you can't afford an attorney, one will be appointed for you." She slid the cuffs over his wrists and clamped them shut.

Conner bellowed, as best he was able with his face pressed against the wall. "Would you stop with the Mirandizing and tell me what's going on?"

"I already did. You're under arrest for murder."

"Murder? You think I killed John?"

"No wonder you were lurking around the sand trap yesterday. The perp always returns to the scene of the crime." She whipped Conner around to face her, then shoved him back against the wall.

"Would you stop already? That hurts."

At that moment, Ace Silverstone happened by, apparently on his way to the coffee shop. He took one look at Conner, then the cuffs, then rolled his eyes. "Conner, keep the kinky stuff in your room, okay? We have an image to maintain." He shook his head, then walked on toward breakfast.

O'Brien grabbed Conner's wrist and jerked him forward. "C'mon dirtbag. I'm taking you to the station."

"Look, lady, you're making a big mistake."

"Tell it to the judge." She jerked his wrists all the harder.

"*Ow!* Cool it, will you? Do you get off on this rough stuff?"

"Just shut up and walk." She marched him toward the front doors. "In case you haven't heard, murder is a serious charge."

"How can you possibly think I murdered John?" Conner asked. "He was my best friend."

"That's no big surprise. Most murder victims are killed by someone they know."

"But I had no reason to kill him."

"No? Then why the masquerade? Why'd you give me that song and dance about being a horticulturist?"

Conner flushed. "Is that what this is about? I was just having some fun. Trying to make a good impression on you."

"By lying?"

"I got the distinct impression you weren't nuts about golf pros."

"You got that right."

"So I made up a harmless story. You can't haul me down to the station for that."

"I'm not."

"Then what possible reason could you have?"

O'Brien paused just outside the front door. "We found the murder weapon."

Conner's eyes widened. "Where?"

"In the rough beside the eighteenth fairway. It's been buried since Tuesday night, but not very deep."

"Did you run tests?"

"Of course I ran tests. Who do you think I am, Deputy Fife? She glared at him. "And guess whose fingerprints we found."

"No way!"

"That's why you're wearing those pretty silver bracelets."

"There must be some mistake."

O'Brien's lip curled. "My only mistake was not locking you up the second I laid eyes on you."

"But—" Conner paused, trying to gather his thoughts. "I haven't been near any weapons. What was it, a knife? A blunt instrument?"

O'Brien looked at him levelly. "A golf club."

If Conner's eyes were wide before, they were twin balloons now. "A golf club?"

"What are you, a parrot? Yes, a golf club. A golf club with traces of blood and hair embedded in the indentations on the metal base. *Your golf club.*"

"How can you be sure?"

"You play with Excalibur clubs, don't you?"

How did she know that? "I'm not the only player in the PGA to use Excaliburs."

"Damn near. But at any rate, we traced the serial number on the base of the club. You made the mistake of buying direct from the dealer. They have your name in their files." She leaned close to his ear. "Word of advice. Next time you're buying a murder weapon, go retail."

As O'Brien continued dragging him toward her car, Conner tried to process all this new information. If the serial numbers matched, then it had to be his club. But how could that be? He hadn't killed John. And his club hadn't been buried since Tuesday night, either. He'd had all his clubs with him during the par three Wednesday, and yesterday, too. Unless . . .

"Lieutenant O'Brien . . ." He stopped just outside the red Tercel that appeared to be her unmarked vehicle. "What club did you find buried in the rough?"

"The boys in the office tell me it's a nine-iron. Why?"

"Of course . . ." he murmured. Why hadn't he figured it out himself? He hadn't hit a decent shot with his nine-iron since Tuesday. Why?

Because it wasn't his nine-iron.

"O'Brien," he said slowly, "there's been a horrible mistake."

"Yeah. Yours."

"No, I mean it. I think someone switched the clubs."

"Do I look like I've got grits for brains?"

"I'm serious. I've been framed."

"Cross, we've already confirmed that it's your club."

"The killer must've taken my club and planted a look-alike in my bag so I wouldn't notice it was gone."

O'Brien placed one hand on her hip. "And I suppose you can prove this cockamamie story?"

"Well . . ."

"Tell me this, Fantasy Man. How could this purported killer get to your clubs?"

"I don't know," Conner said, biting down on his lower lip. "We need to talk to Fitz."

* * *

ON THEIR WAY back to the clubhouse, Conner explained that, as his
caddie, Fitz was the official Keeper of the Clubs. It was his job to make
sure they were always where they were supposed to be. He made sure
they were polished, clean, and ready to play. Golf pros and their caddies
were notoriously—and understandably—protective about the clubs.
They locked them up in the locker room before going to sleep. Conner
also explained that Fitz was a man of honor, a man of his word. He
wouldn't lie for anyone—least of all Conner.

They found Fitz in the coffee shop enjoying a light breakfast of toast
and a poached egg. At least, until they showed up.

"Hiya, Fitz," Conner said amiably. His attempt at nonchalance was
pretty feeble, considering he was being shoved forward by a police officer and had his hands cuffed behind his back. "How are the eggs this
morning?"

"A bit runny, but I don't like to complain." His eyes lighted on the
handcuffs, then on the woman close behind him. "A new paramour,
Conner?"

"A new homicide detective. Lieutenant O'Brien. I'm under arrest."

"What a novel idea. I wish I'd thought of that." He smiled at
O'Brien. "Would there be any possibility of a gag?"

Conner frowned. "I need you to explain to her about golf clubs."

"Is the lieutenant thinking of taking up the game?"

"Hardly," she snarled.

Conner quickly summarized what O'Brien had told him about the
clubs, and what he had managed to deduce. "Fitz, I think someone
must've taken my nine-iron and planted a ringer."

Fitz nodded thoughtfully. "A distinct possibility. It would explain a
great deal." He wiped his mouth with his napkin and rose to his feet.
"Let's go find out."

FITZ LED THEM to the locker room, and the special row of lockers
designed to hold the players' golf bags. "As you can see, there's room for
an entire set of clubs."

"And you've been using these lockers?" O'Brien asked.

"Absolutely. Without exception. If his clubs weren't in play or in my possession, they were in locker 42. During the day, there's a security guard posted outside, and at night the door is locked and bolted."

"Then it wouldn't be possible for someone to make a switch."

"Unless," Conner interjected, "Fitz did it."

"Very astute of you," Fitz said through thin lips.

"Fitz has been rather cranky lately. Perhaps the combination of bad temper and advanced years caused some sort of breakdown . . ."

"Very droll. But seriously—"

"Seriously," O'Brien said. "I don't see how any switch could have been made if the security on these clubs is so tight." She grabbed Conner's bracelets. "You're coming downtown."

"Wait," Fitz said. "We're forgetting something."

"And what would that be?" O'Brien asked.

"Tuesday night."

Conner shook his head. "Believe me, Fitz, Tuesday night is indelibly stamped on my brain."

"You're forgetting the driving range."

Conner's lips parted. "Oh, my—"

"The driving range?" O'Brien said.

"Tuesday night Conner took out his clubs so he could hit a few balls on the driving range," Fitz explained. "It's something he and John do— did—before the first day of every tournament."

"John never showed up," Conner continued.

"And I guess now we know why," Fitz added.

"So I started hitting the balls myself. Then Freddy lured me to the locker room so I could peep through his—" He shot a quick glance at O'Brien.

"You were saying?" she inquired.

"—his . . . stock portfolio."

She looked at him levelly. "He wanted you to peep through his stock portfolio?"

"Right. Had some new company he was promoting that's invented a better . . . um . . . better battery."

"A better battery?"

"For video cameras and stuff. A battery that doesn't have a memory so you don't have to worry about draining it completely before recharging."

"But why—"

"Anyway," Conner said hurriedly, "I left the driving range with

Freddy. Afterwards, I met someone in the bar and we got to talking and—"

O'Brien took out her notebook. "Who did you meet?"

Conner stopped. "A . . . an old friend."

"And your friend's name?"

Conner glanced at Fitz, who shook his head, then back at O'Brien. What was that student's name? "I don't remember."

"You don't remember your old friend's name?"

Fitz cut in. "It's the brain seizures, ma'am. They strike without warning. Some mornings he can't even remember where he is."

"Brain seizures?"

"It's a tragedy. Especially with a man so young."

"Brain seizures?"

"Well, of course." Fitz leaned close to her ear and whispered. "How else could you explain the way he dresses?"

"Good point."

"Anyway," Fitz said, forging ahead, "the gist of it is, this maroon left his clubs on the driving range. I found them, maybe an hour or so after he left, and I locked them up for the night. But before that anyone could've gotten to his clubs." Fitz put the key in the lock, opened the door, and pulled out Conner's bag.

O'Brien peered over his shoulder. "Which one of these is the nine-iron?"

"This one," Fitz said, pulling the club out of the bag. "And if I'm not mistaken . . ." He pulled one of the other irons out and held the two next to one another. "See for yourself. The nine-iron is shorter than the other."

"What does that mean?"

"It means it's not Conner's club." Fitz laid the suspect nine-iron on the changing bench. "See that? It's bent, too. Just a bit, in the middle."

O'Brien crouched down beside him. "Sure enough."

"That explains why your game went to hell in a handbasket whenever you used the nine," Fitz said. "The shaft's too short for you and it's bent to boot. Small wonder your drives sliced."

"Damn," Conner said. "Why didn't I think of that?"

"Why didn't *I* think of it, is the question." Fitz folded his arms angrily across his chest. "It's my job."

"You couldn't possibly have known. It looks like the other clubs."

"It's my job to know. I should've suspected the second your game went off. If it had happened to Arnold Palmer, I'd have realized immediately it must be the club. But when it's you, I just assumed—"

Conner arched an eyebrow. "Ye-es . . . ?"

"I just assumed—" Fitz drew in his breath. "Well, never mind what I assumed. I'm sorry, Conner. I should've been on top of this." He addressed himself to Lieutenant O'Brien. "So you see what really happened, ma'am. Conner isn't the murderer. Someone pulled a switch."

O'Brien frowned. "I'm not entirely convinced. His fingerprints were all over the murder weapon."

"Course they were. It's his club. The killer probably used gloves."

"The fact that the clubs were switched doesn't prove he didn't commit the murder. He might've switched the clubs just to throw us off his trail."

"Could you both stop referring to me in third person?" Conner asked.

Fitz gave O'Brien a penetrating gaze. "Do you really think this man is capable of thinking of something that smart?"

"Now wait a minute—"

O'Brien nodded. "Good point. I suppose I have to release him—that is, *you*, Cross. For the moment, anyway." She withdrew the key from her pocket and popped open the cuffs. "Mind you, you're still under suspicion. So don't leave town."

"Can't. Got a tournament to play."

"There's no point in arresting you and initiating a preliminary hearing unless I can make the charge stick. I need to be able to answer some of these questions about the murder weapon." She snapped her fingers. "Wait a minute. Maybe if we traced this club—" She picked up the nine-iron resting on the changing bench and examined the metal base. "Blast. The serial number has been scraped off."

"What more proof do you need?" Conner said. "Obviously, that club originally belonged to the killer. He scraped off the serial number so you couldn't trace him. Then he switched it for mine and used mine to kill John."

"Maybe so," O'Brien said, deep in thought. "But if that's so—someone was intentionally trying to frame you."

"She's right," Fitz concurred.

"But who would want to see you in trouble?"

Fitz answered for Conner. "Who wouldn't?"

CHAPTER

16

O'BRIEN SMILED THINLY. "I heard you were doing a little investigating on your own yesterday. I assumed you were just covering yourself. Diverting suspicion."

"You were wrong," Conner said firmly. "I want to know who murdered John. And if you can't figure it out—I will."

"Bold words from a man who makes his living knocking a little white ball around." O'Brien clipped her cuffs to the back of her belt. "Well, if you have any sudden brainstorms, or remember anything new, I expect you to call immediately."

"I will," Conner promised. "And Lieutenant—"

"Yeah?"

"I swear I didn't kill John."

"That remains to be seen."

"You know, there's one thing I haven't heard yet. You say the murder weapon was a golf club. How exactly was John killed?"

The corners of O'Brien's mouth turned up, as if a playful thought was tossing around in her brain and she just couldn't decide whether to go for it or not. "You really want to know?" she said finally.

"That's why I asked."

She pondered a moment. "I suppose it might be useful to have someone around who understands this silly game." She nodded. "Okay, come with me."

CONNER BLEW AIR through the holes in the top of his face mask. "This isn't what I had in mind."

Merry crinkles outlined O'Brien's eyes. "You said you wanted to do some investigating."

"Yeah, at the golf course. Not the county morgue."

Before he'd had a decent chance to protest, O'Brien had shoved him into her car and driven him ten minutes downtown to the coroner's office where, Conner was delighted to learn, the autopsy of his best friend's remains was still in progress. She'd issued him a face mask and rubbed some Mentholatum under his nose. It was supposed to kill the smell of formaldehyde and . . . whatever else might be in the air.

It didn't.

"Look at it this way, Cross," O'Brien drawled. "You've missed the preliminary examination. Dr. Jarrett is already well into the actual postmortem."

"What's the difference?"

"Well, basically, the preliminary examination involves the skillful violation of each and every bodily orifice."

"Sounds like the sort of thing you'd enjoy."

"Whereas the postmortem involves the actual slivering and dismembering of bodily tissue."

"Delightful."

"With a few other tests and examinations along the way, just to keep things lively. C'mon—let's go inside."

Together, they stepped into the operating theater. There was one table in the room, and one body on the table, partially draped by a sheet. Even in this deteriorated condition, Conner had no trouble making an identification.

It was John McCree. His best friend. What was left of him.

In life, John had always had a wonderful tan. The miracle tan, the press called it, since it seemed to stay with him even during the off-season. But today, his complexion was a sickly ochre, complementing the puke green paint on the operating-room walls.

His face was much as it had been when Conner had last seen it. There was still a pronounced gash on the side of his skull, but now the blood had dried and coagulated. Conner suspected some of it had been removed; it had seemed much messier when he first rolled the body over in the sand trap. His jaw seemed loose, perhaps even disconnected. From the murder? Conner wondered. Or had the decomposition already begun?

"Let me introduce you to Dr. Jarrett," O'Brien said. "Dr. Jarrett, this is Conner Cross, the world-famous golfer."

Dr. Jarrett made a grunting noise that may have been a greeting but sounded more as if he were in gastric distress. He never looked up from his work.

"Is he always this friendly?" Conner asked.

"This is a good day for him," O'Brien answered. "He hasn't tried to evict you or started throwing stilettos."

"Stilettos?"

"Surgical stilettos. The man is deadly with them. Could probably get work with the circus. As you'll likely see when I start asking him questions."

Conner made a mental note to keep a close watch on the man's throwing arm. What surprised him most about Dr. Jarrett was his age— or lack thereof. The good doctor appeared to be in his early thirties, maybe even younger. Conner wasn't sure why that surprised him. Somehow he had always imagined coroners as aged, grizzled men, hunched over the autopsy table, finding perverse pleasure and strange satisfaction in filleting corpses. With his broad shoulders and long blond hair (currently tucked into a hairnet), Dr. Jarrett looked more like he should be down at the beach with Gidget and Moondoggie than in the autopsy room.

"Dr. Jarrett's only been with us for two years," O'Brien explained, as if reading Conner's mind, which he didn't rule out. "But he's greatly distinguished himself in that time. He's considered the top forensic man in the county."

Goody, Conner thought. That explains everything. Except why I'm here.

"Dr. Jarrett," O'Brien said, projecting her voice across the operating table, "have you had a chance to run any time analysis?"

Conner found Jarrett's grunt incomprehensible, but O'Brien obviously took it as an affirmative reply. Conner wasn't sure if this was a sign of greater comprehension or simply greater optimism.

"Can you estimate the time of death?"

At last, Dr. Jarrett took a break from his slicing and dicing. He drew himself up and squinted at O'Brien, as if he were having a hard time focusing. "Estimates are difficult, given the time that expired before the corpse was discovered. But based on an analysis of relative body temperatures, correlated with an analysis of the stomach contents, I'd say the victim died Tuesday night. Between ten and midnight."

Conner nodded. "Shortly after he left his cabin. After Jodie saw him last. That explains why he never showed up at the driving range."

"What was the cause of death?" O'Brien asked.

Dr. Jarrett didn't look up. His reply was barely audible. "That is what I am endeavoring to discover."

"C'mon, doctor. Give me a break."

"Gladly," he replied, holding up a ball-peen hammer. "Where would you like it?"

O'Brien smiled thinly. "I know the drill. You haven't finished all your tests and the lab work isn't in and you haven't filed a report. When you do, I'll read it and I'm sure I'll be riveted by every word. But in the meantime . . . give me something to go on, okay?"

Dr. Jarrett's lips pursed, considering. Conner wasn't sure if he was considering whether to talk or whether to cause bodily injury.

At last, Jarrett spoke. "See this?"

He pulled down a goose-necked lamp and shone it directly on the side of John's head. Conner winced. Under the harsh light, John's face seemed scarred by a translucent blue-green spider web. Conner looked away.

"You going to be all right?" O'Brien asked.

"Yeah," Conner said, barely above a whisper.

"Close your eyes and think of Pebble Beach." She turned back toward Jarrett. "All right, doctor. What's the point?"

"Death was, in all likelihood, caused by a sharp blow by a metal object."

"Like a golf club?"

"That would be consistent with all the external evidence." He paused. "There may have been two or three blows, but no more than that, I think. And if there were multiple blows, they were delivered with considerable skill and accuracy to the same region of the head to such an extent that I can't be certain. At least not yet."

O'Brien arched an eyebrow. "Hear that, Cross? You got any suspects who are good with a golf club?"

"Yeah," Conner grunted. "All of them."

"The blow or blows ruptured the meningeal artery," Dr. Jarrett continued, "and caused an immediate brain hemorrhage. After that, death would have soon followed."

"Would he—" Conner drew in his breath and tried again. "Would he have felt much . . . pain?"

For once, Dr. Jarrett's face softened a bit. "It's impossible to know with any certainty. Death would have come quickly. But how quickly . . . well, I just can't say. I'm sorry." He looked down abruptly and returned to his work.

O'Brien tried another question. "What can you tell us about the place of death, doctor? Are we dealing with a DRT? Or was the body moved?"

A state of extreme irritation blanketed the doctor's face. "If you don't mind, Lieutenant, I'm working."

"So am I. What about it?"

Conner saw Jarrett's eyes flicker toward his instruments' table. Was this when target practice would begin? He took a step toward the door, just in case. "If the body was moved, it wasn't moved much. Probably just pushed into the sand trap and buried."

"Then John was already out on the course," Conner said, thinking aloud. "Either that, or he was lured there by the killer."

"Maybe he was forced out there," O'Brien offered. "Like at gunpoint."

"I find that hard to believe. Too risky. John was strong and smart—he'd have figured a way out. And what if they'd been seen? No, he must've had a reason to go out there. Someone must've persuaded him to go." Conner's face suddenly went white.

"What?" O'Brien said, staring at him. "What is it?"

"Don't you see? Security has been at its peak since before the tournament began. I know at least one person who slipped in, sure, but the fact remains—security is tight. But someone still got to John. Someone lured him onto the eighteenth green and killed him."

"So?"

"So," Conner said slowly, "all the evidence points to one conclusion. The killer must've been someone John knew." He paused. "Probably someone connected to the tournament."

17

AS SOON AS he could escape the morgue, Conner hitched a ride back to the Augusta National, where Fitz was anxiously awaiting him at the first tee. He still couldn't believe he was actually going to play golf, after all that had happened. It didn't seem right, even after everything Jodie had said, and all he had promised her. On the other hand, given the most recent developments, he was lucky he wasn't in prison. And playing golf was definitely preferable to prison.

For once, Fitz didn't appear to be in his attack-dog mode, perhaps because he knew where Conner had been and what he must have been through. "How was it?" he said, not quite looking Conner in the eye.

" 'Bout like you'd expect," Conner replied. He preferred to avoid details that he'd rather forget.

"Learn anything?"

"Not really." Conner paused. "Well, one thing. I'm pretty certain John's killer must be someone here at the tournament."

Fitz nodded. "Stands to reason." He laid a hand on Conner's shoulder. "Think you can play golf?"

"Think I'd better." Conner shook himself, trying to rouse himself out of his stupor. "Don't want to disappoint my groupies."

Fitz led Conner toward the first tee-off, where he already had Conner's clubs ready to play. Once again, Conner had been paired with Barry and Ace, but today Harley Tuttle joined their little group as well.

"Big crowd, isn't it?" Harley said, gazing at the large collection of fans gathered behind the ropes beside the first tee.

"Yeah," Conner agreed. "Biggest I've seen in a long while." He would've liked to have believed the legions were gathered to see him play, but a quick reality check told him they were more likely assembled to observe Ace. "That bother you?"

Harley shrugged. "I don't much like the razzmatazz. I usually try to stay away from the superstars. All this attention blows things out of proportion. You know what my daddy used to say?"

"I have a hunch I'm about to."

"You can't hang pumpkins on a morning glory."

Conner nodded thoughtfully. "Harley, what the hell does that mean?"

"Beats me. Guess I should've asked daddy."

Conner gave him a slap on the shoulder. "You'll get used to the crowds." He tried to be reassuring, although in truth, he sympathized with Harley. Normally he loved attention, but this morning, he wasn't in the mood. For someone who tended to be reserved and reclusive like Harley, and who was new on the tour, he could see how having an entourage could ruin his game. "Block them out of your mind. Pretend they're not there."

"Easy to say." Harley wandered off toward his golf bag and took a few practice swings.

Ace emerged from the clubhouse, and the instant the crowd saw him, a tremendous cheer went up. Hats flew into the air, people pumped their fists, and a group in the rear began chanting: "Ace! Ace! Ace!"

"Is he running for something?" Conner inquired.

"As opposed to you," Fitz replied, "who are usually running *from* something."

Ace waved to the gallery, bowing his head in feigned humility. The crowd cheered again. Ace flashed a perfect dentally-enhanced smile, then strolled over to Conner. "Did you see that? Did you hear it?"

"We saw it," Conner replied. "We heard it."

"Man, those people love me. They just . . . *love* me!"

Conner nodded. "But will they respect you in the morning?"

"I've got to get myself a tournament," Ace said, pounding a fist against his open hand. "Can you imagine? With this following? It'd be the biggest event of the season! There's got to be some way to open up a weekend on the schedule."

"Maybe if the Augusta National was buried by a volcano," Conner suggested.

Ace nodded grimly. If he perceived that Conner was making a joke, he didn't let it show. "That's something to hope for, anyway."

Conner brushed past Barry on his way to the first tee. Barry didn't look at him, and he didn't look at Barry. Didn't speak, either. Conner supposed he should feel slightly less hostile toward the man now that he knew what his grudge was all about—but he didn't. Besides, Barry looked as if he'd been drinking already, and a pungent whiff of alcoholic afterbreath was probably all Conner needed to send him to the vomitorium.

Fitz tugged at his sleeve. "Look, before you start, let's go over a few things."

"Nah," Conner said. "Let's just do it."

"Do it? Do what? Do what you did yesterday?" Ah, now this was more like the Fitz Conner had grown to know and . . . tolerate. "I realize you're playing under adverse circumstances. But the fact remains—you are playing. Your reputation is at stake, as well as your record. If you play another game like yesterday's, you won't make the cut tonight. You won't even get to finish the tournament."

"Fitz, you know I don't take well to scoldings. Let's just play."

"If you play like you did yesterday—"

"Yesterday I was playing with a nine-iron that wasn't mine. Today I'm not. That should make a difference, don't you think?" Conner drew a wood from his bag. "Besides, for some reason, I feel good about my game right at the moment. I'm ready. So clear out of the way and let me play."

Fitz screwed his lips together and, after transmitting a few stony glares, stomped away. Apparently even he knew when persistence was futile.

True to Conner's prediction, he did play better. In fact, the first nine holes went like a dream. Now that he had expunged all the too-short clubs with dents in the side, he was back on track. His putting was still the weakest part of his game, but he compensated for it with consistent power drives. He managed to finish the first nine four under par. And he traversed Amen Corner without picking up too many strokes. But on the fifteenth, he ran into trouble.

"Now be careful," Fitz said, bending Conner's ear whether he liked it or not. "The embankment in front of the green just over the water has been cut so short that any ball that lands in front of the green from a distance will roll back and get wet. Trust me on this—I've already seen it happen to three players this morning. Hell, Johnnie Walgreen's ball landed *on* the green—but it still rolled down into the trap. You need to lay up."

"Lay up?" Conner repeated, appalled. *Laying up* meant he would hit the ball part of the way down the fairway, then chip the ball onto the green with his second shot. "That's not my style. I hate laying up."

"I know you do. But we aren't on the playground and this isn't the time to show what a macho stud you are."

"Only wussies and sissies lay up."

"Sissies like Arnold Palmer? Wussies like Jack Nicklaus? Champions lay up, Conner. Strategy is part of the game. That means knowing when to go for it—and when not to go for it."

"If being a champion means being a sissy, I'd just as soon not."

"Conner, don't be such a damned juvenile. Lay up!"

"I don't like playing it safe. Doesn't seem right."

"Do it anyway."

"Mmm . . . nah."

"Conner! This is not about proving how big your club is."

"Thank you, Bagger Vance. I'm going for it."

Fitz looked as if he might start tearing his hair out at any moment. *"Conner—!"*

"I've made up my mind. Give me some room, okay?" Conner snatched a driver and squared himself before the tee. If he could get the ball all the way to the far side of the green, surely that would be enough. How long could the ball roll?

Conner took a deep breath, focused on the ball, focused on the target, and swung. The ball flew into the air, rocketing upward like a comet.

Gasps emerged from the peanut gallery. The ball was halfway down the fairway and still flying fast. The only question was how close it would get to the green.

The ball started its downward spiral, finally plopping impressively close to the green. Unfortunately, it didn't stop there. There was a little bounce as the ball touched down . . . and then it began inexorably rolling downhill. It moved slowly at first, but to Conner's horror, instead of running out of steam, it picked up speed the more it rolled. The grass was simply too sheer, and his ball had come down too hard . . .

A groan from the spectators followed the little plopping noise that told Conner his ball was in the water. Enraged, Conner whipped off his cap, threw it down on the ground and began stomping on it.

"Don't take it out on the cap," Fitz said sharply. "It wanted you to lay up."

Gritting his teeth, Conner saw that Barry was laughing his head off, bracing himself against a ball washer. "Your balls have been in the water so much," Barry said, between bursts of hysterical laughter, "you ought to buy them scuba gear!"

No, there was no ambiguity about it now, Conner thought silently. He definitely didn't like Barry. Definitely.

BY THE TIME they reached the seventeenth hole, relations between Conner and Fitz were even more strained. Conner had lost three strokes on the debacle of the fifteenth hole, then two more on the sixteenth. He was over par now, and his chances of making the cut were getting slimmer with every stroke.

The seventeenth hole was a par-five, but Conner knew it was doable in three, possibly even two, if he pushed the ball to the max and didn't drive into one of the pot bunkers on the fairway.

Given the importance of the matter at hand, Fitz apparently found himself unable to remain quiet any longer. "Use the seven-iron. Go for four. Five, even."

Conner shook his head. "I need to make up some strokes."

Fitz clutched his forehead. "Please tell me you're not going to try to get to the green in two."

"I am."

"Are you nuts? Do you not see those pot bunkers out there?"

"I'm over par."

"What's done is done. You can't make up for past mistakes now. The smartest thing to do is just try to play the rest of the holes right."

"I think I can do this in two." He reached for a wood.

"You're delusional! You're in Fantasyland!"

"Thanks for the vote of confidence," Conner said airily. "I know there's some risk. But I think I can do this. And I'm not a wussie. So I'm going for it."

Fitz jammed the seven-iron back in its slot, and kicked the golf bag for good measure. "Why do you bother to keep me around, anyway?"

"Because you're such a snappy dresser."

Conner stretched, took several deep breaths, then let it fly. To the surprise of no one other than Conner himself, the ball careened into a pot bunker with such unerring precision that it seemed as if it must have some kind of homing mechanism. Conner had to play out sideways, adding two unwanted strokes to his score. Worse, he missed the green with his next shot, putted poorly as usual, and ended up bogeying the hole.

By the time he finished the eighteenth hole, there was no conversation between Conner and Fitz—and no need for it, either. They both knew what had happened. Conner had crashed and burned. This time, he was the one who blew off the reporters huddled under the spreading maple and headed straight for the locker room. He threw his gear in a locker and headed for the showers. By the time he had toweled off and returned, he found Fitz waiting for him.

"What are you doing here? Don't you have some . . . caddie stuff to take care of?"

Conner hoped Fitz didn't wear dentures, because if he did, given the way he was clenching his jaw, they were likely to pop at any moment. "I have something to say, and I want you to listen."

"It's over, Fitz. Let it be."

"I will not let it be, and you will listen!" Fitz grabbed Conner's still damp shoulder and shoved him down on a bench. "What does it take to get through to you? You're killing yourself out there, Conner! Committing sports suicide!"

"It's just a game, Fitz. Don't blow it all out of proportion."

"Don't give me that, 'I'm so cool I don't really care' routine. I know damn well you'd like to be a winner. And I know you could be a winner. But not until you shape up and learn to listen!"

"I listen fine, Fitz. What bothers you is that I don't always obey."

"No, what bothers me is that you keep doing things that are so stupid, stupid, *stupid*!"

"Fitz, take a chill pill."

"You signed up with me for a reason, remember, Conner? Because you knew I could help you. And I can, too—if you'll let me."

"Do you mind if I get dressed? I'm starting to feel a draft."

"What does it take to get you to listen? Do you have any idea how long I've been playing this game? Since 1960, golf's greatest year. I watched the Masters that year on television—Hogan, Palmer, Nicklaus, all playing their best. It was spectacular. I'd never seen anything like it."

"You must've led a very sheltered life."

"Yeah," Fitz shot back. "I didn't live in a thriving metropolis like

Watonga, Oklahoma. For your information, I had a great childhood. But what I saw those men do on television that year—that was magic. I wanted to be a part of their world."

"So you took up golf?"

"Damn straight. I got my first caddie job when I was twelve, at the Riverside Country Club in New Brunswick. I toted bags for some of the best Canada had to offer. Half the time I didn't even get paid—but I did get onto the course free, which was all I really wanted. Before long, I got a rep as a player and as a caddie—someone who knew what he was talking about. By the time I was sixteen, I was caddying on a regular basis for the club pro. He started taking me around, introducing me to the courses, the clubs, the pros, and . . ."

"If you were such a hot player, why did you end up caddying?"

Fitz hesitated. "I was good . . . but I wasn't that good."

"But that's what you always wanted, wasn't it? Deep down, you didn't want to carry bags—you wanted to have bags carried for you."

Fitz gave him an evil eye. "I was realistic enough to know that I wasn't good enough to play the pro circuit. But I still wanted to be a part of the action. To me, golf was sacred. Still is, damn it. So I worked as a caddie. And I've been working ever since. I've worked with some of the great names of the last forty years of golf. That's why it's so frustrating for me to see you playing the way you have been."

Conner grunted. "Yeah, must be a real comedown to be associated with the likes of me."

"Don't you get it, you moron?" He grabbed Conner by the shoulders. "I *chose* you. I had tons of offers, from some of the top men on the money list. But I decided to work with you, because when I first saw you play, I saw something."

"Manly good looks?"

Fitz ignored him. "I saw the same thing I saw in Gary Player and Ben Hogan and Jack Nicklaus and Arnold Palmer. The makings of a champion."

Conner fell silent.

"You have the stuff, Conner. You could be one of the greats—maybe the greatest. If I could just get you to start taking the game seriously and to listen to me. I know every stroke, every course, every club—"

Conner's head jerked up. "Every club?"

"Yeah. Every player, every strategy—"

"Wait a minute. Let's go back to 'every club.' "

"What are you babbling about?"

"Since you're the expert on players and their clubs—who else uses an Excalibur nine-iron?"

Fitz pondered for a moment. "Excalibur clubs are a bit unusual and rarely used—as I'm sure you already know. That's probably why you picked them."

"Yeah, yeah—so who else uses them?"

Fitz answered without missing a beat. "Only three players currently on the tour use Excaliburs. You—assuming you count as a player on the tour—Ernie Korman, who's out sick this week and safely back in Newark—and Freddy Granger."

"Freddy? Freddy uses Excaliburs?"

"Right. Has for years. Quite a coincidence, huh?"

"Yeah. Especially since he was the one who lured me away from my clubs Tuesday night." Conner pressed a finger against his lips. "Where is he, anyway? I haven't seen him all day."

"Freddy played early. Probably took off as soon as he was done. He's got a wedding to get ready for, you know."

"Right, right," Conner said, deep in thought. "I heard all about it yesterday. Big wingding. Costing him an arm and a leg. The best little daughter a daddy ever had. Reception at the Magnolia Glade Country Club."

"You're smarter than you look," Fitz replied. "All the players are invited. Are you going?"

"I wasn't planning to," Conner murmured, as he reached for his clothes. "But now I may change my plans."

18

AFTER HE ESCAPED Fitz and the locker room, Conner made a beeline for the clubhouse where he knew the results of the day's play would be posted. He tried to act as if it didn't matter, tried to tell himself he didn't care. But the sad truth was, it did, and he did. His stomach was churning over the thought that he might not make the cut. That he might suffer the ultimate humiliation—being sent home packing before the real tournament play began.

When he arrived, Conner saw the bar was packed. Practically every pro in the tournament was there, anxiously awaiting the posting of the results. Despite the crowd, the room was deathly silent. A few scattered whispers, nothing more. It was almost as if no one wanted to breathe, at least not until they learned whether they'd made the cut. He also noticed that Vic the bartender was working overtime; lots of booze was circulating—soothing nerves and calming fears while each player's fate remained in limbo.

"Psst." Ace Silverstone waved Conner over to the bar. Conner reluctantly complied, not in small part influenced by the fact that there didn't appear to be an empty seat in the room. "Have you heard anything about Tiger?"

Conner frowned. "Can't say as I have. Why?"

Ace shrugged. "Rumor is he tied my score. Maybe even beat me by a stroke. Just wanted to confirm."

"Relax, Ace. I'm sure you made the cut."

"Well, yes. Obviously. But I want to know if I've got the lead."

"Whether you're first or second, you're going to be sitting pretty for the last two days of the tournament."

"That's not the point. I've got a film crew dogging me, remember? I don't want them to report that I came in second, you know? Too humiliating."

"Oh, right," Conner said. "I'd be devastated."

"I wish they'd get those damn postings up. I can't stand not knowing."

Conner made a tsking sound. "Success is a cruel master."

"You can say that again." A grin crept over his face. "Say, did you hear what Freddy did today?"

Conner's ears perked up. "No. What?"

"Oh, man. He was a disaster out there. A walking comedy of errors. Truly awful."

"Like what exactly?"

"I haven't gotten all the details yet. But I hear he hit every water hole on Amen Corner. Some of them twice."

Conner shrugged. "Anyone can have an off day. God knows I have."

"This was more than an off day. This was more like an off lifetime. Word is he finished ten over par."

Ten? Conner whistled. That had to hurt. "I expect Freddy just has more important things on his mind. His daughter's getting married tonight, you know."

"Yeah. You going to the reception?"

"I'm giving it some serious thought. You?"

"I don't know." Ace glanced over his shoulder. "Film crew, remember? I hate to make a scene—you know, disrupt the reception. But the camera boys thought it might be nice to have some footage of me showing up at a family celebration for one of the other pros. You know, showing that no matter how successful I've become, I still have time for the . . . uh . . . the . . ."

Little people? Conner wondered.

"The better things in life. Family. Friends. And they thought if I came, it might help make the event special. For Freddy and his daughter."

Sort of like the arrival of a visiting dignitary, Conner presumed.

He was distracted by the all too familiar sound of drunken grumbling on the opposite side of the bar. In this mostly quiet room, the raspy words were like a gong sounding at daybreak. Barry Bennett was back on the sauce, and to make matters worse, he'd returned to his favorite subject: why he didn't like John McCree.

"It iss't so much whadde did," Barry said, slurring his words with impunity. "It'ss the way he did it."

Conner bit down on his lower lip. Don't start, Barry. Just don't start.

"Sure," Barry continued, even louder than before, "they say allss fair'n love and war. But some thingsiss right, and some thingsiss wrong."

Conner glanced over his shoulder. As he suspected, everyone in the room was listening. The expressions on their faces covered a wide spectrum from the amused to the appalled.

"Mind you, I don't care 'nymore," Barry said with a hiccup. "I'm over it. Totally over it. But iss hard to have much respect for a man with no honor."

"Barry," Conner said, trying to keep his voice calm and even, "why don't you just shut the hell up?"

"I gotta right to speak my piece," Barry said. Unfortunately, it seemed the booze made him both feisty and stupid. "There's this li'l thing called the First Amendment, see? You can't censor me."

"I can censor you with my fist," Conner said curtly. "And I'm about two seconds from starting."

"Hey, calm down," Ace said, laying a hand on Conner's shoulder.

"Oh, stop playing the peacemaker," Conner shot back. "The cameras aren't on." He turned toward Barry. "Just listen to me for one second, you sorry inebriate. Did it ever occur to you that there might be something screwy about blaming John? Jodie's the one who dumped you. She made the choice, not him."

"It wass't her fault," Barry answered. His eyes wavered so Conner thought he might crumble to the floor at any moment. "He manipulated her. Took advantage of her. Bought her."

"Bought her? Man, you are truly looped."

"He did. With lossa jewelry and fancy cars and a lotta other crap I couldn't begin to afford. He didn't play fair. He jus' bought her—like he did everything else."

Conner was about to follow up when he detected some rapid movement behind him. Craning his neck, he saw his good buddy Andrew Spenser entering the room. He was holding a large spreadsheet. And Conner knew what that meant, as did every other pro in the room.

The postings.

Spenser cleared his throat. "First of all, I want to thank each and every one of you for your participation in our tournament. By your noble efforts and stalwart athleticism, you have once again maintained the high standards of excellence that the Masters—"

"Jesus God," someone in the back of the room groaned. "Just tell us if we made the cut!"

Even Spenser had to smile this time. "As you wish. I'll post the results next to the bar. For those who will proceed, tee times begin tomorrow morning at nine. And to all of you, my heartfelt congratulations. You're all winners."

Conner wondered if that included him; he decided it was probably best not to quiz Spenser on that particular point.

As soon as Spenser had the results thumb-tacked to the bulletin board, the crowd surged forward en masse, pressing forward to see where they stood. Conner stayed at the bar, determined to remain cool, trying to look superior while the other lemmings desperately shoved their way through the throng. It was just a game, for God's sake. The world would go on spinning regardless of who hit their little white ball the best. It didn't matter a hill of beans—

Oh, the hell with it. Conner sprang from the bar and elbowed his way to the bulletin board. The first thing he saw was the top score, which belonged—surprise, surprise—to Ace. He'd shot a 136—a full ten strokes better than Conner.

His heart sank. What chance did he possibly have? His eyes raced down the list. Happily, it was alphabetized and the distance to the Cs was not great. Calley, Carter, Cresswell . . .

Cross. Conner Cross. A quick check for the magic checkmark in the right-hand column . . .

He'd made it. *He'd made it*! Just barely, but praise God he'd made the cut.

Conner quickly checked the scores of his partners. Harley was ranked fourth, but Barry had finished a stroke worse than Conner and consequently came in under the cut. And Freddy hadn't even come close.

Conner staggered away from the postings, feeling as if some guardian angel had just rescued him from the jaws of death. Sure, it didn't matter, and the world wouldn't stop revolving . . . but thank heaven! *He'd made the cut*!

He stumbled into the corridor, so relieved he barely knew what he was doing. He almost collided with Jodie before he'd even realized she was there.

"I'm guessing," Jodie said, "from that pathetic grin on your face that you made the cut."

"Yes." Conner beamed. "*Yes!*" He calmed himself. "I mean, not that it matters."

"Right. John always felt the same way." She smiled, and Conner had no choice but to reflect on what a beautiful smile it was. So sweet it made you feel all warm and fuzzy; so tender it made you want to wrap her in your arms and never let her go. Was that what had first drawn him to her, all those years ago?

"Which reminds me," Jodie said. "I thought of it."

Conner blinked. "Excuse me?"

"I thought of it. What I was trying to remember. What John said on his way out of the cabin. Just before he was killed."

Conner grabbed her by the arms. "What was it?"

"Well, you have to understand up front—I don't know what the context was. I'm not sure there was one, actually, except maybe in John's brain. But I do remember what he said. I would've asked him about it. If I'd ever gotten the chance."

"Jodie, tell already. What did he say?"

She drew in her breath. "Fiji."

"*Pardonnez moi?*"

"You heard me. Fiji."

"As in . . . the islands?"

"Beats hell out of me. But that's definitely what he said. Fiji."

Fiji? *Fiji?* Conner rolled the word through his brain. What could it possibly mean?

"Wait a minute," Conner said, after a moment's reflection. "Didn't you and John go on a cruise through the Pacific not too long ago?"

"That was before my time," Jodie explained. "Before John married me. But he went on an island cruise. I don't know if he went to the Fijis or not."

Conner wasn't sure, either. To be honest, he wasn't even sure where the Fijis were. But it might be worth finding out. Was it possible something had happened to John on the cruise all those years ago—something that eventually led to his death?

"Jodie, are you sure he said *Fiji*? Could it have been something that just sounded like Fiji? Like maybe . . . squeegee? Or Ouija?"

"I suppose it's possible."

"Or maybe he was saying several words, but saying them so fast they kind of ran together."

"Maybe. He didn't realize I was listening."

"Or maybe not words. Maybe . . . letters." If someone said the letters F-E-G very quickly, wouldn't it come out sounding something like . . . Fiji? "I don't know what to make of this, Jodie."

"It may not mean anything," Jodie admitted. "Who knows—maybe he was just humming the words to a song or something. It's just that—well, I wanted to ask him about it. And I never—I never—" Her voice trailed off.

Conner put his arm around her. "I'm sorry, Jodie," he said quietly. "This must be tearing you apart. Maybe we should just let this be."

"No," she said firmly. "I want answers. I want to know what happened to my—my—" She paused, collecting herself. "My Johnny." All at once, tears spilled out of her eyes.

Conner hugged her tightly. "Then we will, honey. We will." As he gazed into her eyes, Conner realized that she really hadn't changed all that much from those days in high school when he'd had such a terrific crush on her. When he'd loved her so much.

Come to mention it, he hadn't changed all that much either.

Conner kissed her gently on the top of her head, then returned to the main lobby. It was starting to get dark now, and if he remembered correctly, the "wedding reception of the century" was scheduled to begin at eight. He picked up the phone.

Seven beeps on a touch-tone later, he was connected to police headquarters.

"Lieutenant O'Brien here."

"Conner Cross here. How would you feel about a wedding?"

"Is this a proposal?"

Conner laughed.

"I've heard of some interesting techniques for getting the cops off your tail, but this one takes the cake." Somehow, her slow Southern drawl gave her sarcasm an extra punch.

"That isn't what I had in mind," Conner explained. "You see, Freddy Granger's daughter is getting married."

"Should I be excited or jealous?"

"Freddy Granger is one of the players on the tour. The reception's going to be a huge affair. At the Magnolia Glade. And get this—he uses the same brand golf clubs I do."

"Is that a fact?" The tone of her voice suggested that her interest level had perhaps increased.

"Yup. And here's another one. Freddy's shorter than I am. Hence, requiring clubs with a shorter shaft."

"Now I'm interested. But why do we need to crash his daughter's wedding reception? I'll just come by tomorrow—"

"Freddy's out of the tournament. And he's planning to take off after the reception and be gone for a good long time."

"Now I'm beginning to get the picture."

"What's more, practically all of the pros and their spouses and caddies will be there. Think of it—all your chief suspects gathered together in one room. It's like something out of Agatha Christie. When should I pick you up?"

"Wait a minute, pardner. You've explained why I might want to go—but why would I want to go with you? Don't let your freedom fool you—you're still my ace suspect."

"Aw, c'mon. You don't want to go alone. You've as much as admitted you don't know word one about golf. You'd be lost."

"Well . . ."

"C'mon, O'Brien. Succumb to my charm."

"Well . . . it might be useful to have someone nearby to translate golfese for me. Tell me who's who." He heard the clicking of her nails on the other end of the line. "All right, Cross, you talked me into it. Have you got a car?"

"A rental."

"Good. Pick me up at the station in half an hour. Wear a tux."

Conner balked. "A tux? I hate those monkey suits. Nobody's gonna wear a tux."

"Didn't you say this was a big gala reception? In the heart of Augusta? At the Magnolia Grove?"

"Yeah. But I still don't want to look like a fool."

"If you don't show up in a tux, you will."

"How can that—"

"Trust me, golf boy. You're in my world now. See you at seven-thirty."

The line disconnected before Conner could so much as sputter in protest.

19

CONNER DIDN'T EVEN have to honk. As soon as he pulled up in front of the police station, Lieutenant O'Brien emerged. Except, this time, she didn't look much like a police lieutenant. As promised, she was dressed to the nines—a pink chiffon gown and a string of pearls.

With some effort, she managed to suppress the natural buoyancy of her gown enough to slide into the front seat of Conner's rented Chrysler LeBaron convertible. "You're late."

"Sorry. I had some trouble finding the station."

"And let me guess: you wouldn't ask for directions."

"Well . . ." Conner decided it was best to change the subject. He gave O'Brien a quick once-over. "Nice dress. Are you a bridesmaid?"

O'Brien smiled wryly. "Believe me, sugar, compared to most of the debs and dilettantes at this gig, I'll look underdressed."

Conner grinned. "I love that accent of yours. We don't get that back in Oklahoma."

"You don't get much of anything back in Oklahoma, do you?"

"Let's not be snobby. It's not still all cowboys and Indians." He arched an eyebrow. "Last year we even got cable."

"Do tell." Conner sensed he was getting a return once-over himself. "So you found a tux. I'm impressed."

"Not easy, either, on short notice. Fortunately, the Augusta National has its own tux rental wardrobe." He fidgeted with his collar. "Hate this silly bow tie, though."

"That's because you don't have it on right." She reached across the seat. "Allow me to adjust."

"Feel free." Conner felt the warm touch of her fingers brushing against his neck. Not an altogether unpleasant sensation. "So . . . have you lived in Augusta all your life?"

"Pretty much so. 'Cept when I went off to college in the big city." She winked. "That would be Atlanta."

"Got family around here?"

"More than you can shake a stick at. My daddy had a little shoe shop downtown that grew into a twelve-store chain. He's seventy-six now, but he still goes in to work five days a week. He'll never retire."

"What about your mom?"

"Still alive and kicking. I've even got a paternal grandmother. We O'Briens live forever."

"I guess so. What do all these relatives think about you being a cop?"

"They're concerned. My female relatives, who are legion, have spent most of my life trying to teach me how to be a proper Southern lady. I've been relentlessly drilled on all the essential rules of Southern living."

"Such as?"

"Never serve pink lemonade at your Junior League committee meetings. Never wear white shoes before Easter or after Labor Day."

"All the essentials."

"You can see now why I went away to college. Except that I joined a sorority house, and it turned out they had even more rules than my family!"

"You were a sorority girl?"

"And what's so incredible about that, may I ask?"

"I just can't quite picture the rough and tough police lieutenant flirting with frat boys and singing secret songs."

"I was a top-level soror, I'll have you know. I pledged Pi Beta Phi— that's Piefie, for short. Just like my mother and grandmother and—well, eleven or so cousins. You get the picture. It was a matter of tradition." She paused, then smoothed a crinkle in her dress. "I try to stay in touch with some of the Piefie girls, but it gets harder as time goes on."

"What caused you to become a cop?"

She shrugged. "I don't know. Just wanted to do something more than pick out silver patterns and layettes, I guess. Gives my poor mother fits, though."

"I can imagine."

"She keeps reassuring her society friends at the Junior League meetings that there's nothing wrong with me. 'Girls are getting married later these days,' she tells them. 'Lots of girls over thirty-five are settling down and having lovely weddings.' "

Conner laughed. "I'll bet your mother thinks you're a pistol, no matter what she says."

O'Brien allowed herself a little smile. "I think maybe she does at that." She pushed her seat back a few notches and relaxed. "So what about you, cowboy? Where are you from?"

"Little town called Watonga. Population 3,234. 3,233 when I'm on tour."

"Do tell. How did you ever get linked up with golf?"

"Lieutenant—was that a pun?"

"Was what a pun?"

"Never mind. We didn't have an Augusta National back in Watonga, but we did have Bobby Ray Barnett's public nine-hole golf course–slash–bait and tackle shop. The Dusty Duffer."

"Sounds magnificent."

"It was—or at least it seemed like it was, when I was a kid. Everyone in town referred to it as "the Club." It was about the only green pretty spot in that whole windy red-dirt town. I fell in love at first sight."

"I've heard that happens to young boys. Except that they usually fall for girls, not landscape."

"Girls came later. When I was just a squirt, all I wanted was to play golf like a pro—to spend the rest of my life on pretty green courses. I wanted it to be my one-way ticket out of town."

"Except that you still live there."

"Funny how things work out, isn't it?" He shifted gears and took a hard right following the billboard that pointed the way to the Magnolia Glade. "John was the one who really made it happen. He had the talent. I had the drive, the determination. But John was a pro from the second he picked up a club. He was always better than me—better than just about anyone. If it weren't for him, I'd be back in Watonga right now, probably scooping balls out of the water trap and washing down golf carts."

"Don't sell yourself short, hotdog. You are on the PGA tour."

"True. But I never would've gotten there without John. In addition to being more talented, he was also a hell of a lot smarter than me. He got a scholarship to Stanford, made the Dean's Honor Roll, and was on the tour before he'd even graduated. Meanwhile, I was back in Norman at OU, rarely attending class but always attending the golf course. It's a miracle I graduated."

"And when you got out?"

"I tried out for the tour. The qualifying school is a bear-and-a-half. To make a long story short—I didn't make the cut."

"But I thought—"

"The first time. I thought I was finished, but John wouldn't leave it at that. He took me under his wing, got me private lessons. I even got instruction from the late great Harvey Penick himself, God rest his soul. And I practiced like a demon. And next year—I made the tour. Got my official membership card and secret decoder ring and everything."

"That's a great story."

Conner blinked. "I wonder if I could get a book deal? Pardon me while I call Random House."

"But you left one part out. What about your real life?"

"Excuse me?"

"You know—off the course. Are you married?"

Conner glanced at her out the corner of his eye. Her eyes darted away. "Nah. Got close once, but—well, she didn't want to spend the whole year traipsing from one golf course to another."

"Fancy that. How long can you keep this up?"

"What do you mean?"

"Surely you don't plan to play golf forever. Don't you ever think about growing up and getting a real job?"

Conner thought it best to let the question remain unanswered. He beeped his horn. "Sorry this is taking so long. I'm stuck behind someone determined to coast at fifteen miles per hour."

"Relax," O'Brien replied. "Down here, a lot of folks learned to drive on a John Deere, and for them, this is the right speed."

"I could live with that, but he's also got his left turn signal blinking."

"Must be a Yankee. Most of the locals don't use turn signals, and ignore those who do."

Conner's lips turned up. "Sorry to disillusion you, Lieutenant, but he's got a Georgia license plate."

"Do tell? Then you may rest assured the signal was on when the vehicle was purchased."

A big sign arching the front drive told him he had arrived at the Magnolia Glade Country Club. He leaned toward the front guard post and identified himself. The gate popped up and Conner eased onto the driveway . . . which stretched into infinity. It was like driving down the Yellow Brick Road. Conner could see no end in sight. It was more than a minute later when the car emerged from a thicket and the clubhouse appeared.

And magnificent it was, too. A huge marble edifice—even larger than the Augusta National clubhouse—with Doric columns flanking the front porch.

"Isn't this where Scarlett O'Hara lives?" Conner asked.

O'Brien laughed. "Was. Nowadays she's got a condo downtown."

One look at that enormous mansion house, with the huge gushing fountain out front, was enough to make Conner glad he'd decided not to wear his Bermuda shorts. He parked in the first available spot—which was still a good ways from the front door—popped out of the car and raced around to the other side to open O'Brien's door for her.

"And who do you think you are?" she said, arching an eyebrow. "Rhett Butler?"

Conner suddenly felt himself flushing pink. "I just thought . . . since you're all gussied up . . ."

"I always appreciate a gentleman."

Conner beamed. "Gee, can I carry you to the front door? Looks like it's about a mile away."

"I bet we don't have to walk." She scanned the horizon. "Yup. Look."

A black stretch limousine pulled up in front of them. The passenger side window lowered. "May I take you to the ballroom?" the driver asked.

"If you insist." O'Brien scampered into the back seat, Conner close behind.

During the short ride, Conner resisted the impulse to play with everything. There were buttons controlling the air, buttons controlling the windows, buttons controlling the music and buttons controlling the dividing glass between the seats. There was even a small television, an electronic stock ticker, and a minibar. For those who couldn't make it to the front door without a quick snort, Conner presumed.

The limo eased beside the front steps. Conner hopped out, again holding the door open for O'Brien.

"Enjoy the reception," the chauffeur said, with a tip of his hat. Then he pulled away in search of other arrivals.

Conner stood next to the fountain. It had an enormous round base, with water spurting up in four different directions at once. Lights at the base made the water change color every few seconds.

O'Brien tugged at his shoulder. "I think we should split up."

"Why? I wore the tux. I used mouthwash."

"We can cover more ground separately. Talk to more people. We'll meet later and compare notes. Make sense?"

"Well . . ." Conner tried to mask his disappointment. "I suppose."

"Besides, I'm starving. I gotta find me a deviled eggs plate."

"What, at a classy soirée like this?"

"You're in the South, Conner. There's always a deviled eggs plate."

CONNER ENTERED THE clubhouse agog. The reception was located in an immense ballroom—seemingly larger than a football field. The decorations were festive and fabulous. There were vines, flowers, and colored lights everywhere he looked. Ivy and other greenery twined the bannister on a central staircase leading upward, and was draped over the tables and walls as well. Silk streamers shimmied down from the ceiling.

The guests in attendance were no less impressive. O'Brien had been right. All the men were strapped into monkey suits, and the gowns worn by some of the women looked as if they had been borrowed from the finalists at the Miss America pageant.

After a brief survey of the ballroom, Conner discovered the wedding cake—which to his great disappointment was still uncut. It was a seven-tiered number with a miniature staircase descending from each layer. Sparklers jutted out all over the cake. On each staircase was a miniature replica of one of the bride's friends or relatives. At the top of the cake, of course, stood the bride and groom, in what appeared to be exact replicas of their wedding attire.

"Not bad, eh?"

Ace, looking as if he had stepped out of a Fred Astaire movie, was leaning over Conner's shoulder. "I assume you're talking about the bride."

"Ding, ding. I wouldn't mind licking off her frosting."

Conner rolled his eyes. "Keep your tongue where it belongs, Ace. You don't want the camera crew to get the wrong idea." He gestured toward the cake. "I notice the bride is wearing white. Isn't this her second marriage?"

"In Georgia, the bride always wears white. Even if it's her eighth time down the aisle."

"I see you decided to come."

"I had my doubts, but eventually I realized that bringing in a camera crew wouldn't disrupt the reception. If anything, it would make it more special. And when you get right down to it, I didn't feel I had the right to make that little girl on the cake's day any less special just because I might be more comfortable staying at home."

Conner nodded. "Must've been agonizing. Wrestling with your conscience like that."

"It was. Hey, you know who else is here? Jodie."

"Jodie McCree?"

"Can you believe it? With her husband not even cold in—" He stopped short.

"Don't worry about it." *Creep,* he added mentally. He wondered why Jodie had come. To make a social appearance like this so soon after John's death—she must have a reason. What could it be? "That does seem strange."

"Hey, I can't fault the little lady. She's precious."

As soon as he was able to extract himself from Ace, Conner made his way to the dining tables that stretched across the center of the ballroom. He grabbed one of the numerous champagne bottles close at hand. He found an empty flute and poured himself a tall, cool one.

He heard a hiccup, and following the sound, spotted Barry Bennett on the opposite side of the table. "Bollinger's 1989. It's the best."

Conner nodded. If anyone would know, it would be Barry. He looked as if he had sampled quite a bit. Why was it every time he turned around, this drunk was sitting opposite him?

Conner found the nearest empty seat and pulled up to the table. Scant seconds after he sat, waiters dressed in white tails appeared out of nowhere. One brought him a glass of sparkling water, another delivered an artfully arranged mixed salad, while another deposited a dinner plate bearing filet mignon, smoked salmon, and caviar.

"What?" Conner said. "No soufflé?"

The senior waiter cleared his throat. "We can have that for you in approximately twenty minutes, sir."

Conner waved his hands. "I was just—oh, never mind." He picked up a crostini and nibbled a bit of the caviar. Generally speaking, Conner preferred corndogs and pork rinds, but hey, if they were going to stick this crap under his nose, he might as well give it a try.

Conner licked his lips. A bit salty, but not at all bad. He wondered how he went about getting seconds.

"Tying on the feed bag, Conner?" It was Harley Tuttle, sliding into the seat to Conner's right.

"That would be one way of putting it," Conner replied. "It's a feed bag fit for a king."

"Freddy told me he planned to spare no expense on his little girl's wedding. I guess he meant it." As soon as Harley was seated, another phalanx of waiters bearing goodies descended upon him.

"I guess so." A crash of cymbals suddenly brought the background music to Conner's attention. "Who's playing the mood music?"

Harley spoke while shoveling in bites of filet mignon. "I believe that would be the Atlanta Symphony Orchestra."

Conner nearly choked on his salmon. "The Atlanta Symphony is the wedding band?"

"One of three, if I'm not mistaken."

"Criminy." Conner sampled the filet steak. A bit underdone for his taste, but he'd probably manage to devour it just the same. "Seems like they'd be better off just getting a record player and some old Jerry Lee Lewis LPs."

"Not our Freddy's style, I think. Might be yours, though."

Conner was distracted by the sudden whooping and gales of laughter from the center table. "Who are all those people?" Conner asked, pointing. "They're awfully chummy."

"I believe that would be the wedding party," Harley explained.

"The wedding party. I thought we were the wedding party."

"You know what I mean. Bridesmaids and groomsmen."

Conner did a quick scan of the table, from one distant end to the other. "Are you kidding? There must be eighty of them!"

"True. I understand Dillard's had to hold a special seminar just to coordinate everyone's wedding outfits. The bride kept all her bridesmaids informed of the wedding's progress by putting out a newsletter."

Conner wiped his eyes. "Am I the only one who thinks this is a little . . . extreme?"

Harley shrugged. "Like my daddy used to say, 'Folks do things differently in the South.'"

Conner grinned. "With the budget for this wedding, they could probably feed a third-world nation."

Conner returned his attention to his plate, managing to finish off his first serving and a magically appearing round of seconds as well. By the time he reached the bottom of the bottle, he had decided this Bollinger's stuff wasn't half bad, either.

"Well," Conner said at last, dropping his napkin on the table, "if you'll excuse me."

Harley cast him a sidewards glance. "You're leaving? Now?"

"Yeah. Is there a problem?"

"You'll miss the fireworks display!"

O'BRIEN HELPED HERSELF to another plate of deviled eggs and a glass of champagne. She supposed she should be abstaining; technically she was still on duty. Then again, this was essentially an undercover operation, and to successfully remain undercover, it was necessary to blend in with the crowd.

Across the ballroom, she saw Conner at one of the banquet tables, wolfing down food like there was no tomorrow. She had to smile. He wasn't nearly as obnoxious as he seemed determined to make people think he was. He was almost cute, in a perverse sort of way. She just hoped he wasn't John McCree's murderer.

She headed to a nearby table where a man was sitting alone. She didn't know who he was, but she noticed no one had sat with him all night long. Given the boisterous fraternizing and revelry surrounding them, that seemed odd.

She took a seat and flashed her best smile. "Hi. My name's Nikki. What's yours?"

"Dick," he replied. "Dick Peregino."

Peregino. O'Brien ran the name through her head. It seemed vaguely familiar. Had Conner mentioned him? "Are you a golfer?"

"No. Well, yes and no. I'm with the tour, at any rate." He smiled, then leaned closer to her than she felt was entirely necessary. "I'm the PGA cop."

"Really." She was tempted to mention that she was a cop of a different stripe herself, but she figured that would not help loosen his tongue. "What does a PGA cop do?"

"Maintains the high standards of the PGA."

"Which are?"

"Clean living. Clean appearance. We think it's important that people believe our golfers are decent human beings. It isn't like boxing, where almost anything goes. We run a tight ship. We have a dress code, prohibit foul language, punish lewd and lascivious behavior. We don't even permit our players to have facial hair."

"It's the road to hell," O'Brien said, nodding. "One day you allow a mustache, the next thing you know they'll be having orgies in the clubhouse."

"I detect sarcasm." Peregino pulled a baggie filled with sunflower seeds out of his pocket and began munching them. "That's all right. I'm used to it."

"I'm sure that's not so."

He waved her remark away. "I'm like the vice principal in the school of golf. I'm Mr. No-Fun." He pulled a couple of sunflower seed shells out of his mouth and put them on the table, in a pre-existing pile of saliva and shells. "Mind you, what I do is important. What I do makes it possible for all those pros to rake in the big bucks. But do they appreciate me?" He shook his head vigorously. "Not in this lifetime."

"Do I sense some resentment?"

"Just stating facts. I've made my peace with the universe. Long ago, I dreamed of being a pro golfer, but I wasn't good enough. So I worked my way up to this position. That way I get to stay in the golf universe. I know what I do is important, even if none of those spoiled overpaid pros appreciate it."

"Mind if I ask why you're here? Especially since the pros don't like you and you don't seem to like them."

"I'm investigating." He leaned across the table, making a point of brushing her arm. "There's been a murder."

O'Brien played along gamely. "Really? You know, I think I heard something about that."

Peregino jabbed his thumb at his chest. "I've got the inside track."

"You do? What is it?"

His voice dropped to a whisper. "Ace Silverstone was not in his cabin at the time of the murder."

"How do you know?"

"Because I went to see him, to remind him of the rules and regulations regarding private camera crews during tournament play." He popped another sunflower seed in his mouth. "Only he wasn't there."

"So you think he's the murderer?"

Peregino pursed his lips. "I think it's pretty damn suspicious, don't you? If he wasn't in his cabin, where was he?"

Who knows, O'Brien thought. Getting a sandwich, maybe? But she played along. "Have you told the police?"

"Not yet. I will in time. I want to see if I can crack this case myself."

"Yourself?"

"Why not? I am a cop, after all. Sort of. And if I pulled that off, the boys would almost have to respect me." He brushed aside the centerpiece and leaned even closer to her. "But enough about these gruesome matters. I'm sure a pretty thing like you doesn't want to talk about some nasty old homicide."

O'Brien resisted rolling her eyes. Here we go, she thought.

"What say you and I go for a stroll outside by the fountain? I know a private spot in the magnolia glade where we could get to know each other much better."

"Thanks, but I'm meeting a friend."

"Yeah, right. We both know you didn't come over to my table by accident, pretty lady. You saw something you wanted. So why don't you just let me give it to you and stop playing hard to get?"

O'Brien suppressed her strong desire to barf. "I don't think so."

He grabbed her arm and gave her a strong jerk. "I'll put something between your legs that'll keep you warm till New Year's."

"I said, *no*." She jerked her hand free.

He didn't back off. "C'mon, you stupid tramp. Let me give you what you need."

"No, let me give you what you need." She picked up her champagne flute and upended it over his head.

The yellow-tinted liquid cascaded down his face and across his chest. "Stupid bitch," he muttered.

"Did I forget the hors d'oeuvre? Damn, I think I forgot the hors d'oeuvre." She picked up a deviled egg and smashed it into his face.

She brushed her hands off, then stood. Peregino's lips parted, but she stopped him with a finger. "One more word, jerkoff, and I'm going for the punch bowl."

Peregino remained mute.

*   *   *

IT WOULD BE nice to find O'Brien, Conner thought, and besides, after that meal, if he didn't move around a bit he was probably going to fall asleep.

From a distance, he spotted Freddy on the opposite side of the ballroom.

Conner's step quickened. I'd like to have a few words with that man, he thought. And not just about the wedding festivities, either.

Conner started moving across the room, pushing his way through streamers and revelry. To his surprise, however, he found that Freddy was moving even faster than he was. A sudden rush for the men's room? No, Freddy passed that by without even blinking. Where was he going? And why was he in such a hurry?

One thing was clear: Freddy was headed toward the central staircase. He hit the first step and started up, fast as was possible without creating a scene. Conner quickened his own pace. He wasn't sure why, but he didn't want to lose him.

Conner hit the staircase and followed, trying not to be spotted. He didn't know what Freddy was rushing toward, but whatever it was, Conner suspected it wouldn't go down if Freddy knew he was watching.

Freddy hit the landing, turned right, and started down a long corridor. Conner did the same, several steps behind. Fortunately, the corridor was dark, with lots of shadows he could duck into if necessary, and the plush carpeting prevented his footsteps from being audible.

They appeared to be passing a series of rooms—probably the administrative offices for the country club. At the end of the corridor was a large mahogany door with an oversized brass doorknob. Freddy quickly opened the door, then slid into the dark room beyond, shutting the door behind him.

Conner tiptoed to the end of the corridor, then pressed his ear to the door. He didn't hear anything. If Freddy was having a secret meeting, they must be communicating in sign language.

Perhaps Freddy just needed to get something. Or get rid of something.

Whatever it was, Conner would never find out standing on this side of the door.

Gently, he laid his hand on the doorknob and turned. There was a tiny creaking noise. Conner froze: had Freddy heard? Or anyone else? He didn't detect any signs of it. Slowly, he pushed the door wider . . .

The room inside was dark; the only light streamed in from the open window, and that wasn't much. As far as Conner could see, it was a bed-room, and a magnificent one at that. Why would they have a bedroom in a country club? he wondered. And why would Freddy be in it? Surely he had more important things he needed to be doing at the moment.

Conner saw a passage at the opposite side of the room. Leading to a bathroom? he speculated. Or another room altogether? He didn't know, and once again, the only way he was going to find out was by creeping over and taking a look-see . . .

Conner had almost made it to the passageway when he heard foot-steps. Fast footsteps, from inside the room. Freddy was returning the way he came.

Conner leapt out of the passage, out of sight. He glanced back at the outer door. It was too far away. He'd never get there in time.

Damn! How'd he let himself get into this mess? How would he ever explain to Freddy why he'd been sneaking around behind him? Worse, if Freddy really was the culprit, this would be a sure tip-off that Conner was onto him.

Conner spotted a closet an arm's reach away. Without even think-ing, he pulled the door open and ducked inside.

It was dark in the closet, no big surprise. Though Conner couldn't see anything, he could feel what he suspected were coats all around him, crowding him. He had to brace himself against the frame to keep from falling against the door and blowing his cover.

Conner heard the footsteps stop, somewhere just beyond the closet. For some reason, Freddy wasn't leaving, wasn't going back to the party. Damn! What if he decided to lie down and read *Gone With the Wind* or something? Conner might never get out of here!

An instant later, Conner heard a familiar creaking noise. Someone was opening the door to the outer corridor. He felt certain it wasn't Freddy, though. Freddy hadn't budged from his spot just outside the closet.

It seemed there was going to be a meeting, after all.

Conner pressed his ear against the door. He could hear voices, two of them, both low and hushed. He thought one of them was Freddy, naturally, but he couldn't make out the other one. And he couldn't understand what they were saying, either. Although, as the conversation continued, it became progressively clear that they were arguing. Their voices gradually rose and became more agitated. After a few minutes, they were loud enough that Conner could pick up some of what was being said.

"Why'd you come here?" He was almost certain that voice was Freddy. Even muted, it had Freddy's distinctive squeal. "Do you want people to know?"

There was a muffled reply from the other person.

"What? Here? Surely you don't think I'm going to do that."

Do what? Conner thought, gritting his teeth. What were they talking about?

A few moments later, he heard Freddy say: "I tell ya, that's not enough. I need more. Much more!"

Conner heard more arguing, then sounds of a scuffle. What was going on? He desperately wanted to break out of the closet and look. But how could he explain what he was doing here? Besides, if he kept quiet, he might actually figure out what they were talking about. Thus far, he couldn't prove anything. Revealing himself would accomplish nothing, except to embarrass himself and tip off the combatants that he was onto them.

Conner heard footsteps rapidly moving away, then more footsteps following close behind. They were leaving—both of them!

As soon as he heard the outer door slam shut, Conner burst out of the closet. The coast was clear. Whoever had been here before was long gone. He raced to the door and slowly opened it. No Freddy—or anyone else. He flung the door open and dashed down the corridor. He winged past the interior offices and hit the landing, then started down the long central staircase. Where could Freddy have gone so quickly? And what happened to the person with whom Freddy was fighting? Surely if he kept running he could catch up to them. How far could they have possibly gone?

Conner hit the bottom of the stairs and kept running. He thought he caught a glimpse of Freddy toward the front doors, although it was difficult to be certain when every man in the immense room was wearing the same black tux. Conner bolted across the room, pushing people aside, knocking over waiters, spilling champagne.

He was almost halfway across the ballroom when he felt a hand grab him by the collar. Propelled by his own momentum, Conner whirled around . . .

. . . to face Barry Bennett, his nose engorged and his breath thick with booze. "Hey," Barry slurred, "you shouldn't be runnin' in here. This'ss a classy place."

Conner tried to remove Barry's hand, but unfortunately, the tottering inebriate had a tight grip. "I'm busy, Barry. Let go."

"Man, did you see those fireworksh?"

Conner felt certain he could break Barry's grip, though possibly not without breaking Barry's arm. "I'm sure it was magnificent, but—"

"Fabuloush. Just fabuloush. Lit up the whole lagoon."

"Barry, let go of me."

"And when the glittery lights spelled out the bride and groom's names—I thought I was gonna cry."

"Barry, I'm giving you one last chance to avoid major surgery. Let *go*."

"Did you know Freddy's girl spells *Karen* with a *C*? I didn't."

"Don't say I didn't warn you." Conner brought up his foot then jabbed the heel down hard on Barry's toes. Barry was apparently too snockered to cry out, but he felt it. His eyes went wide and he dropped his glass. And let go of Conner's collar.

Conner whirled around, searching to see if he could find any trace of Freddy and whoever he had been with. Unfortunately, Freddy was nowhere to be found.

Damn! In just a few precious seconds, he'd lost what little he'd gained.

Cursing himself, he started looking for O'Brien. At the very least, he could tell her what he'd heard. Maybe she could figure out a way—

All at once, the ballroom was split apart by a piercing scream. The shocking sound echoed and reverberated through the hall, rattling the chandeliers. The cry was picked up by others; soon the entire room was shouting and yelling and running every which way at once.

What the hell was going on? Conner wondered. He didn't know, but there was an aching hollow in the pit of his stomach telling him that when he discovered the answer, he probably wasn't going to like it.

A crowd was gathering at the front of the ballroom, swarming toward the front doors. Conner headed in that direction, pushing people out of the way with impunity. "Excuse me," he bellowed. "I need to get outside! Move!"

When he finally made it through the doors, it was immediately clear that everyone's attention was focused in one direction—toward the technicolor fountain in the center of the front patio.

"Let me through!" Conner shouted, shoving past the spectators.

Women were holding their faces in their hands. A few people looked sick. Some were even crying. What the hell was happening?

Finally, he made it to the base of the fountain and peered inside. It didn't take him long to see what all the commotion was about.

Her body was still floating, rocking back and forth with the gentle currents and ripples, and her gown was like a kaleidoscope when illuminated by multicolored lights. A casual observer might suspect that a party guest who'd had one too many had decided to take a dip in the fountain with her clothes on. But Conner knew that wasn't what had happened. He knew, because he saw the steady stream of blood oozing from her throat.

Steeling himself, Conner reached into the water and turned the body over so he could see her face. And when he did, his jaw fell open, gasping.

He released the body but remained where he was. He felt frozen, locked into place. His brain felt paralyzed, too. He was petrified by shock and horror and an utter lack of comprehension. How could this be?

It was his first love, Jodie McCree, just as he had seen her only hours before. Except now there was a deep, bloody gash across the base of her throat.

A fatal slice.

THREE

Swinging in the Dark

◆ ◆ ◆

In 1968, Bob Goalby and Roberto De Vicenzo dueled for the Masters championship. As they approached the final hole, De Vicenzo was ahead by a stroke. Goalby sliced on the tee shot and barely made par. De Vicenzo overshot the green and bogeyed. The score was tied. But De Vicenzo's scorekeeper, Tommy Aaron, had made a tragic error. Aaron gave De Vicenzo a four on the seventeenth hole, even though a worldwide television audience had just watched him do it in three. De Vicenzo didn't catch the error and signed the scorecard. Therefore, the official score showed Goalby winning by a stroke, even though everyone knew better.

At first, the Augusta National powers-that-be didn't know what to do. The Masters is not a USGA or PGA event, so they weren't bound by their rules. Should they abide by the letter of Rule 38, Paragraph 3, or allow equity and justice to prevail? Perhaps there should be a sudden-death playoff, some suggested. They huddled in the clubhouse, meanwhile forbidding the CBS sportscasters from announcing a winner. At last, Bobby Jones himself was called upon to resolve the controversy, while the TV people stalled for time.

"We are the Augusta National Golf Club," Jones ruled, "and we will abide by the rules of golf." De Vincezo had signed the card, and that was that. Goalby was declared the winner.

CHAPTER

20

AFTERWARD, CONNER LOST all sense of time, all notion of where he was and what he was doing. It was as if he'd fallen into a curvature in the time-space continuum; he was aware that the world was proceeding apace, but he wasn't a part of it anymore. Somehow, he'd disconnected himself; the people swarming around him were like actors in a play—a horrible, gruesome play—and he was safely ensconced in the audience. Or so he wanted to believe.

Jodie. With a hideous oozing slash across her throat.

People buzzed all around him, droning on, creating a dull roar at the edge of audibility, like bumblebees swarming in the distance. He heard himself answering their questions, but the answers came from somewhere else, some separate brain, some distinct consciousness. Only when he saw a friendly face did he slowly start coming back to his head.

"Cross? Hey, Cross?" It was Lieutenant O'Brien. "Are you going to be all right?"

Conner blinked several times rapidly. His consciousness attempted to recollect itself. "I'm fine. I'm okay."

"Good. You clowns clear out. Give him some air."

Conner was only vaguely aware of everything that happened after that. They asked him more questions and he tried to answer them. He heard them asking others questions, too, but no one seemed to know anything. There were no leads, no witnesses. Somehow, the killer had managed to murder Jodie in the fountain, or at least deposit her body there, and no one saw it happening. No one who was talking anyway.

All the reception guests were required to stay on the premises until late into the night—even the bride. Despite all the preparations and programming consultants and the investment of monumental wads of cash, Freddy's party was ruined.

Around one in the morning, Conner somehow managed to stumble to his car and drive back to his cabin, where to his infinite relief, he fell into a deep and dreamless sleep.

Saturday

He was awakened by an insistent pounding on the door of his cabin. Given his current state, it felt as if someone were ringing a gong inside his cerebellum. Groaning, Conner rolled out of bed, stumbling against the nightstand in the process. He abruptly realized he wasn't wearing anything. He checked the closet, but couldn't find a robe, so he settled for a towel.

He heard the front door of his cabin pop open. Damn! he thought. Guess I forgot to lock the door again. He heard the footsteps crossing the outer room. A few moments later, the clamourous pounding resumed at the bedroom door, even more insistent than before.

Wrapping the towel around his waist, Conner plodded to the door. "Damn it, Fitz, can't you ever give me—"

He stopped cold. It wasn't his caddie standing on the other side of the door. It was Lieutenant O'Brien.

"Nice outfit," she said, as she marched into the bedroom. "Is it monogrammed?"

Conner clutched the top of the towel. He didn't want any comic accidents. "Good morning, Lieutenant. I knew I'd get you into my bedroom eventually."

"You're a riot, Cross." She stared at the unmade bed, the tangled sheets, the pillows strewn across the floor. "How the hell are you?"

"Not as good as I was a few minutes ago. When I was in bed. I think I'll go back now. You can come, too, if you like."

"I'm here on business."

Conner pressed his fingers against his forehead. "Surely you don't have more questions. Haven't I already answered every question that could possibly be asked? Especially given that I don't know a damn thing."

"I'm assuming you don't know who killed Jodie McCree. But surely you learned something last night."

"Not really."

"I was keeping tabs on you, Cross. You disappeared for a good while. And later, a witness told me you were racing across the room, pushing people out of the way. Heading toward the fountain. As if you knew what had happened. Or was about to happen."

Conner held up his hands. "Hey, now—don't get any crazy ideas."

"It looks pretty damn suspicious."

"I can explain."

"Then you'd better. As quickly as possible."

"Right." He fell onto the edge of the bed. "After I saw Jodie floating in the fountain . . . I guess I forgot all about it." Slowly, dredging up the memories, Conner recounted how he had trailed Freddy up the stairs, how he had overheard a mysterious conversation with an unidentified second person, how he had followed them but lost them.

And then found Jodie instead.

"I don't know what the hell Freddy was talking about, or who the other guy was, but it has to relate to these murders."

"You don't know that."

"What else could it be?"

"How should I know? Maybe he was having an argument with the caterer. Maybe one of the violinists broke a string. Maybe they bet on a golf game. It could've been anything. We can't assume that because there was a murder, every weird conversation beforehand related to it."

Conner appeared unconvinced. "Whatever they were discussing, it was crooked. And very secret. If I were you, I'd arrest Freddy. Before he leaves."

"I don't have grounds to arrest him. And he's been told not to leave town."

"At least bring him in for questioning."

"What would be the point? Do you think he's going to confess to murder? Much better to leave him alone. Let him think no one suspects—but keep a close eye on him."

"I guess that makes sense." Conner pounded his fists together. "But I'd still like to know what Freddy was talking about."

"Did he mention Jodie?"

Conner mentally traced back through the conversation. "I don't think so. Not as such, anyway." He snapped his fingers. "But Ace did." He related their brief conversation at the reception to O'Brien. "He said something about Jodie. That she was sweet or nice or something like that."

O'Brien arched an eyebrow. "Did he say sweet or nice?"

"I don't know." He tried to recall the exact phrasing. "Come to think of it, I think Ace said precious. Yeah, that was it. Precious. Definitely. I think. What difference does it make?"

"A hell of a lot."

"I don't follow you."

"Ace Silverstone is from the South, isn't he?"

"Yeah . . . so?"

"Well, down South we have our own vocabulary. If he said she was precious—that's a compliment. But if he said she was sweet—that's the kiss of death. And if he said she was nice—that's the kiss of death with the coffin sealed."

"I'll try to keep that in mind." Conner glanced at the clock radio beside the bed. "Look, I hate to break up this fascinating etymological discussion, but see, I'm in this golf tournament thingie. And I'm not even dressed."

"You can get dressed. But you're not going anywhere near the golf course."

"Excuse me?"

"Don't worry. You've been given a late tee time. For a reason."

Conner tapped his foot impatiently. "And that would be . . . ?"

O'Brien looked at him gravely. "Sorry. I got distracted. There's been another development in the case."

Conner felt his blood go cold. "And that would be?"

"Get dressed. You can see for yourself."

O'BRIEN LED CONNER into the office of the club chairman. But sometime between his last visit and the present, the entire room had been transformed. People were scrambling all over the place—mostly men in black suits and white shirts and thin black ties. He spotted a reel-to-reel recorder and some high-tech communication equipment. And he couldn't miss the stiff-necked men with solemn expressions lining the wall closest to the door. Security officers, he surmised.

"This doesn't seem like Tenniel's usual decorating style," Conner remarked. "What's going on?"

"Mr. Tenniel's office has become FBI Headquarters South."

"Because of the murders?"

O'Brien shook her head. "There's more to it than that. Let me introduce you to someone."

She waved a hand in the air. A few moments later, a woman about O'Brien's age walked toward them.

"This is Special Agent Liponsky," O'Brien explained. Liponsky was wearing a close-fitting gray suit with a scarf tie. To Conner's disappointment, she looked nothing like Scully on *The X-Files*. "She's one of the FeeBees in charge. We're liaisoning."

Conner looked at the two women. "Is that legal in Georgia?"

O'Brien gave him a wry grin. "I'm her local contact."

"Contact on what? Isn't someone going to tell me what's going on?"

O'Brien glanced at Liponsky, who returned a curt nod. O'Brien retrieved a piece of paper from a nearby desk, then passed it to Conner.

"Mr. Tenniel received this fax about two this morning. It was sent from a local convenience store. The clerk doesn't remember the sender, who was probably wearing a disguise anyway, and the security camera wasn't working, so don't bother asking."

Conner quickly scanned the one-page fax. It was typewritten, all in block capital letters. The fax copy was dim; he couldn't make out all the words. But it didn't much matter; he could get the gist of it. He scanned the note quickly, drinking in the salient facts—and the big number at the bottom.

The author of the fax claimed to have killed John McCree and his wife. He—or she—further stipulated that unless the tournament officials paid one million dollars in unmarked bills—there would be more murders.

"This can't be real," Conner said, clutching the paper in his hands. "Must be a copycat. Someone trying to cash in on the murders."

"We considered that." Agent Liponsky's voice was flat and direct. "But as you'll see when you read the letter, so did the killer. He's provided numerous details about the first killing—how John McCree was killed, what was the weapon, where on the body it struck. None of this information has been released to the public. No, we don't think there's much doubt. Whoever wrote this letter is the killer—or at the least, is working with the killer."

"Why does he think the tournament officials will pony up?" Conner asked, reading as he talked.

"The negative publicity has already hit them hard. Imagine if a third person is killed, and word gets out that the tournament officials could've stopped it, but didn't, because they didn't want to part with any of their profits."

"That would be devastating."

"That would be the end of the Masters. Tenniel and the rest of the board don't have any choice, and they know it. They've already started assembling the cash."

"And you're going to let them pay?"

"It's the safest course of action," Liponsky explained. "We don't want to see anyone else get killed, either. Of course, when the drop goes down, we'll be watching."

"That goes for the FBI *and* the Augusta PD," O'Brien added.

Conner's eyes returned to the faxed message. "There's still one thing I don't understand. Why are you telling me about this?"

Liponsky and O'Brien exchanged another look.

"Read the fine print," O'Brien advised.

Conner's eyes darted down the page. Details about the murder . . . threats and intimidation . . . demands for unmarked bills . . .

"Down here," O'Brien said. She pointed to the key line at the bottom of the page.

Conner read the sentence in question, then gasped.

The killer demanded that the million in cash be delivered to a yet-to-be-designated location late that night—

By Conner Cross.

Alone.

21

"Wow," Conner said, staring at the paper clutched in his hands. "Double wow."

"That was pretty much our reaction," O'Brien replied.

"But why me?"

"Actually," Liponsky said, "we were hoping you might be able to answer that question for us."

"I'm clueless," Conner said.

"Our first thought was that you're the killer, and you're planning to take the money and run. But Lieutenant O'Brien assures that that is . . . well, only one possible explanation."

Conner looked at O'Brien. "You did that for me? I'm touched."

Artemus Tenniel emerged from somewhere in the rear of the office. To Conner's surprise (and partial horror), the man smiled faintly and placed his hand on Conner's shoulder.

"I know we've had our differences in the past," Tenniel said quietly. "But I'm hoping you'll be able to put that aside for the time being and do what's right."

Conner shrugged his shoulder free. "What's right, meaning—helping your sorry butt out of a tight spot. Being the bag man for the Augusta National."

Tenniel was unfazed. "Needless to say, if word of this situation gets out—it could destroy the tournament. Permanently."

"That would be a tough end for the bastion of tradition and excellence."

"Yes, it would. So we'll pay the money. But it must be kept confidential. The club has been having some serious financial problems of late."

"Say it ain't so."

"I'm afraid it is. Our funds are unaccountably lower than average this year, and thus far we have been unable to determine why. Believe me when I say we can't afford the losses we'd suffer if the tournament were canceled."

As astonishing as it seemed, Conner knew it was possible. Whatever other faults and foibles the Masters might have, it was well known to be one of the few major professional sporting events in the universe that hadn't succumbed to greed. The tournament resolutely refused to compromise itself to obtain a corporate sponsor or celebrity huckster. And it forewent millions in potential television dollars in order to restrict commercials and dictate standards to broadcasters. The Masters had a long and unbreachable litany of commandments announcers were required to observe. Thou shalt not refer to the gallery as a mob—or even a crowd. Thou shalt not refer to golfers' earnings. Thou shalt never liken the holes at Augusta to those at any other course.

"Don't you have insurance?" Conner asked.

Tenniel seemed taken aback. "Yes. I mean . . . I suppose we do." For the first time in Conner's experience with the man, he seemed unsure of himself. "Of course, that's not the preferable way to proceed but . . . now that I think of it, we do have some insurance. Quite a generous policy, as I recall."

"As you *recall*?"

"Haven't looked at the thing in years." Tenniel turned abruptly and returned to his desk.

"So," O'Brien said to Conner, "are you on board?"

Conner looked at her, then at the fax, then back at her. "You're asking if I'll risk my neck and go out all by myself to make this drop, possibly facing the killer on my own against impossible odds and getting myself killed in the process?"

"That probably isn't how I would've phrased it, but . . . yeah."

"Sure," he said, handing the fax back to her. "Sounds like fun."

BY ONE IN the afternoon, Conner was ready to tee off for the third—and penultimate—day of the tournament. He spotted Fitz several yards before they actually met. He was running a fast interception course, obviously intending to cut Conner off before he made it to the first tee.

Conner checked his watch. "Almost one, Fitz. We'd better get to the tee-off."

The caddie's lips were pursed tight. "I'd like a word with you in private first."

"I'd love to, Fitz, but see, I'm in this golf tournament—"

"That's why I want to talk to you."

"—and if I don't show up on time, they'll disqualify me."

"If you don't play any better than you have so far, you'd be better off disqualified."

"That would be humiliating."

"It would be a mercy killing. Now, listen up, buster, and listen up good."

Conner scrutinized the stern expression on Fitz's face. "Is this another trip to the woodshed?"

"You're damn right. And long overdue, too."

"Look, Fitz—I'm in no mood for a lecture."

"Just shut up and listen."

Conner did precisely that.

"How long have you been on the tour now?"

As if Fitz didn't already know. "This is my third year."

"And in that magnificent stretch of time, what exactly have you accomplished?"

Conner tilted his head to one side. "I like to think I've developed a sense of personal style."

Fitz grimaced. "And what exactly has that gotten you?"

"I have a following."

"Charles Manson had a following. So what? What else has it gotten you?"

Conner frowned. "Hearty chuckles?"

"I'll tell you what it's gotten you. Absolutely nothing."

"I have my own personality, Fitz, and I plan to keep it. I'm not going to turn into one of those PGA zombies."

"I'm not talking about your attitude, sorry though it is. I'm talking about your game."

"You said I have one of the best drives in the business. As good or better than Tiger Woods."

"Yeah, but your putting game stinks. Because putting requires concentration, focus, resolve—all the qualities you've held back. And for that matter your driving game is erratic, because it can't overcome your unfailing tendency to make stupid decisions!"

"Aren't you being a bit harsh?"

Fitz ignored him. "This tournament is a perfect example. Your performance has been abominable."

"Now wait a minute. There have been some pretty damn extenuating circumstances, Fitz. My best friend died!"

"I know that. Why do you think we're having this talk?" His eyes were narrow and electric. "John McCree made a lot of personal sacrifices to get you on the tour. And you're throwing it all away!"

Conner's lips parted wordlessly.

"Sorry to be blunt, but that's the reality of it, kid. John gave you a lot, and you haven't given him anything in return." Fitz whipped off his shoeshine boy cap. "Look—I don't know what it is with you, Conner. I don't know what made you the way you are. I don't know if it's because you lost your mama so early or because your dad was too hard on you. Maybe you're just some kind of genetic mutant, which is the theory I personally favor. But whatever it is—you need to get over it."

Conner wanted to defend himself, but there was a distinct catch in his throat. "I've had a lot on my mind lately," he finally whispered.

"Stop making excuses. It's make or break time, pal, you're a lightning rod, like it or not. If you don't show these people what you can do today, you might as well hang up your golf shoes for good."

"What exactly is it you want me to do?"

"Stop wasting your talent. Stop screwing around. Listen to your caddie. Push yourself. Before it's too late."

"And you expect me to do all this for you?"

Fitz drew in his breath. "I was hoping you might do it for John."

Conner felt a distinct itching in the back of his eyeballs.

"His fondest wish was that an Oklahoma boy would make good at the Masters. Why don't you see if you can make his dream a reality?"

Conner didn't know what to say.

"Well? Say something! Will you do it?"

Conner pivoted around, his face expressionless. "I think it's time to start."

Fitz trailed behind him as they made their way to the first tee. Conner pulled a golf ball out of the zippered pocket in his bag; Fitz selected a club.

Conner gripped the club, his hand just above Fitz's, then froze. "I— I don't know what to do," he said, barely audibly.

"Course you do. What do you mean?"

"I mean—I don't know how to be any . . . better."

"That's fine. I do." Fitz pushed the club into Conner's hand. "Now go hit the damn ball."

"I was thinking I might use the other—"

"Conner!"

Conner took the proffered club and prepared to shoot. He popped the ball onto the tee and fell into position.

"Loosen your grip," Fitz said.

Conner frowned—but he did it. He focused, concentrated, then started his backswing . . .

"Adjust your stance."

Conner's teeth ground together—but he did it.

"Now swing."

Conner let 'er rip. The ball sailed up beautifully, forming a graceful rainbow arc, then landing not five feet from the green.

It was a perfect shot. The spectators applauded with enthusiasm.

Conner gave Fitz a long look, then, at last, smiled. He threw his arm around the older man's shoulder. "Fitz, I think this could be the start of a beautiful friendship."

22

CONNER FINISHED EACH of the first six holes either one or two under par. He established a new personal best, and did a great deal to rehabilitate his previously pitiful standing.

By the seventh hole, a buzz began to circulate throughout the tournament. By the time he was ready to start the back nine, Conner had acquired his own gallery, following him from hole to hole. The word was out—Conner Cross was where the action was.

At first, it was a tough adjustment. Conner was not accustomed to having spectators follow him so attentively. But he had to admit—it was kinda fun.

"Just ignore them," Fitz said, clamping a firm hand down on Conner's shoulder. "Block them out of your mind."

"Why would I want to do that?" Conner said, grinning and waving as he approached the seventeenth. "They love me."

"They won't if your game starts sucking again."

That brought Conner down to earth in a hurry.

"You're here to play a game, so play it. Focus all your energy, all your attention, on the game. That's what matters."

"Right. Got it." It was tempting to put on a show for the spectators. In fact, his class clown instincts almost demanded it. But Fitz was right. The game was what mattered. He was playing well and he was relishing the moment. He was in the zone, as the sportscasters say. Something had clicked.

And he knew what it was, too. For the last many years, he'd been playing for himself—someone who wasn't all that demanding. But now, for the first time, he was playing for someone else. Now he was playing for John.

And Jodie.

And he wasn't going to let them down, either.

Conner scanned the fairway. "Do they still have that stupid tree in exactly the wrong place on the left of the fairway? Obstructing the green?"

"They do," Fitz confirmed.

"Do you think they'd have that thing removed, if I put in a formal request to the Augusta National committee?"

"Let me put it this way, Conner. Back in the Fifties, President Eisenhower put in a formal request that the tree be removed—and it's still there."

"Well, sure. But he didn't have my winning personality."

"Go around the tree, Conner. Lay up."

"I hate laying—"

Fitz raised a finger. Conner never finished the sentence. He laid up. And finished the hole two strokes under par.

CONNER FINISHED THE day's play with exuberance. He'd never played so well—and he knew it. He spent half an hour gassing on with the reporters under the spreading maple tree, talking about his game—and how the day's performance had been for John. He also credited Fitz, which was certainly a new page in his playbook.

By the time he reached the clubhouse, he was sky-high. "Hail the conquering hero!" someone shouted, as he entered, and there was a spontaneous round of applause. Some of the players cheered.

Actually *cheered*, Conner thought silently. For *me*.

Vic the bartender slid him a glass of his favorite—on the house. This treatment was so unusual Conner felt he should slug himself just to make sure he wasn't dreaming. Everyone swarmed around him; everyone wanted to be his friend. And he had a pretty good idea why, too.

He didn't need to see the day's postings to know where he stood. He would still be behind Ace, the leader—but the gap was much narrower. If he played tomorrow—the last day of the tournament—like he had today, he could catch up. He could even conceivably win.

Conner steadied himself against the bar. Just the thought of it made his head reel—literally reel. Conner Cross, champion of the Masters, sipping mint juleps in his green champions jacket.

It was too wonderful to imagine. But it was possible.

"Hey, Conner, way to play, man." It was Harley Tuttle.

"Thanks, Harley. How'd the day go for you?"

"Oh, 'bout like always. I think I'm still running fourth or fifth." He shrugged modestly. "Like my daddy used to say—always the brides-maid, never the bride." He took a sip from his drink.

Conner grinned. "I'm sure your luck will turn around soon."

"Maybe. But the way you played, man—that was spectacular. I saw what you did on the seventeenth on the closed circuit."

"You mean the cameras were following me?"

"Didn't you know? Hell, yeah—I think CBS covered your entire back nine."

Conner didn't know what to say. He was flabbergasted.

Some of the other pros offered congratulations. Conner chatted with everyone in sight, anyone who came near. Whether they were in the tournament or not. He was feeling generous and egalitarian. He did notice, however, that his chief competition, Ace, didn't seem to be in the clubhouse.

Probably out on the driving range, Conner mused. When he heard how well Conner was playing, Ace probably panicked and realized he needed some more practice.

Well, it was a nice daydream, anyway.

Fanboy Ed wasn't anywhere in sight. Did he just leave, since John wasn't in the tournament anymore? Or was he doing something else? Conner wasn't sure why he cared, but for some reason, Ed's absence bothered him.

Barry, on the other hand, was present, even though he had ab-solutely no reason to be. He was out of the tournament, and it showed. He looked as if he hadn't budged from his barstool all day. He was barely able to sit upright. Conner actually felt sorry for him. He didn't know why—possibly because for once, Barry had his mouth shut. But it was becoming increasingly apparent that Barry had a serious drinking problem, and needed help.

Conner knew it well; he had a stockpile of paternal memories on the subject.

And where was Freddy, come to think of it? Sure, he'd been plan-ning to leave town, but now that the cops had made that impossible,

Conner thought he might show up at the clubhouse. But there was no sign of him. He wondered if O'Brien had exchanged any heated words with the man yet, or if she was still laying back. Hard to know. She was a very cool lady—very cool, and very several other things as well.

And speak of the devil . . .

He saw O'Brien entering the clubhouse, carrying a large black valise.

"Well," she said, "I don't know whether to snap the cuffs on you or buy you a bottle of champagne."

"I know which I'd prefer," Conner replied.

O'Brien grinned. "Didn't take you for a champagne drinker."

"I'm not. But that thing with the cuffs could be kinda kinky."

"As I recall, you didn't enjoy it that much last time." She edged closer to him and lowered her voice. "Are you ready to go?"

"Go where?"

"I see your triumph has addled your wee brain. The sun has set, Conner. And you have a date tonight, remember?"

"Cool. Your place or mine?"

"Neither." Leaning close, she opened the valise a crack, so only he could see inside. It was filled with cash. More cash than Conner had ever seen in one place in his entire life.

"Get some coffee for the road," she said, snapping the bag closed. "It's show time."

23

NIGHT HAD FALLEN, and it seemed appropriate somehow that there was no moon. In stark contrast to the glistening hustle-bustle of the day, the Augusta National course was now dark and gloomy, somnolent. Much too quiet. Almost spooky.

Conner strode into the darkness, O'Brien on one side, Agent Liponsky on the other.

As they marched toward the fifteenth green, Liponsky gave him a last minute briefing. "The faxed instructions just say that you're to be on the fifteenth green with Tenniel's cell phone," Liponsky explained. "Evidently the killer already knows the number. Once you're in place, we have no idea what he might have in mind."

Somehow Conner didn't much like the sound of that. "Care to speculate?"

"Either he plans to meet you there, which I doubt, or he plans to send you somewhere else. We'll be using scanners to try to pick up the conversation on your cell phone, of course. And we'll try to trace the call, although that can be tricky with mobile phones. And we won't be far away."

"Didn't the fax say I had to come alone?"

"Yes. And you will, too. We just won't be far off, that's all."

Conner frowned. "Sounds dangerous."

"It'd be a lot more dangerous to send you out there with no backup, believe me."

"What if this guy gets pissed off?"

O'Brien cut in. "We won't give him any reason to get pissed off. We'll keep our distance, and we'll stay hidden."

"Then what's the point of being here at all?"

"Because eventually, this blackmailing murderer is going to instruct you to put the money somewhere. And then he's going to try to get away with it. Once he does—and you're safely out of the way—we'll make our move."

Conner nodded, just as they arrived at the fifteenth green. "Just remember that part about 'safely out of the way,' okay? That's the most important point."

Liponsky didn't smile. "Look, we're talking about a killer who's already taken two lives and is threatening to take more. We have to do everything possible to apprehend this person."

"Meaning what exactly?"

"I think I've made myself clear. I want to bag this creep. So follow my instructions and don't screw it up. Got it?"

As soon as he could tear himself away from Liponsky's fiery glare, Conner took O'Brien aside. "I'm not sure I like this Special Agent Liponsky."

She nodded. "That's because you have a problem with women in positions of authority."

"No, that's because I think she'd tear my heart out and eat it if it allowed her to catch this killer."

O'Brien smiled wryly. "I'll try to keep her talons in check."

"Don't forget to wear your Kevlar."

The group reassembled. Liponsky pushed a small black palm-sized device into Conner's hands. "Keep this in your pocket. No matter what happens. Don't let the killer see it."

"What is it?"

"It's a PDA."

Conner blinked. "A Public Display of Affection?"

"A Personal Digital Assistant." Liponsky paused. There was no light of recognition in Conner's eyes. "Think of it as a souped-up pager. A signal device. It works via satellite, so even if the killer manages to disrupt phone transmissions or ties up the line, you can still get through."

Conner stared at the tiny plastic box with its myriad buttons. "Looks complicated."

"It isn't. Here's all you need to know. As soon as you've made the drop, push the red button."

"Red button. I can do that." He looked up. "As soon as I see the killer."

"Wrong. Pay attention. You may never see the killer. As soon as you've deposited the bag wherever it is he wants it, you push the button. That'll be our signal to close the cordon—to make sure no one gets out."

"All right. Red button. Got it."

"Keep it in your pocket the whole time. If the killer is watching, he doesn't need to know you've signaled."

"If—" Conner looked up abruptly. "You mean you think the killer could be watching?"

"It's possible."

"You mean—" He turned his head skyward. "Even now?"

"It's possible."

"How?"

Liponsky shrugged. "How should I know? Maybe he's up one of those trees. Maybe he's planted video cameras. Maybe he's in a hotel hot tub laughing his head off at our expense. I can't know." Her voice dropped. "But I have to be ready for all contingencies."

Liponsky pushed the black bag filled with loot into Conner's hands. "Here's the McGuffin. Take good care of it." She raised an eyebrow. "And by the way, I feel compelled to say that if you're having some cockamamie thoughts about taking off and keeping the cash yourself—forget it."

"Me?" He stared at O'Brien. "What have you told her about me?"

"Everything."

"Well, that explains it." He opened the bag, just to establish in his mind that the money was still there.

It was. A million dollars in cash. Amazing.

O'Brien checked her watch. "Almost time. We'd better scram."

Liponsky nodded. "Right. We have to stay out of sight."

O'Brien laid her hand on Conner's shoulder. "Good luck, slick."

Liponsky laid her hand on his other shoulder. "Don't screw it up."

TWENTY MINUTES LATER, Conner remained all by himself at the fifteenth hole, leaning against the flag. It was painfully dark out here, and painfully quiet as well. He would've given a great deal for some company—as long as it didn't involve getting whacked on the head with a golf club.

Inevitably, his mind reeled backward through the sights and sounds of the last few days. He remembered that stupid food fight at the champions' dinner. A harmless bit of revelry. Who would ever have thought that would be the last time he'd see John alive? He couldn't imagine a world that didn't have John McCree in it.

And he didn't particularly want to, either.

That train of thought led him in no time at all to Jodie. Sweet Jodie. His first love. An aching in his heart that never quite subsided.

He closed his eyes tight, wincing at the memory of that last sight of her, floating in the fountain, a thin tissue of blood issuing from her throat. God—who could have done such a thing? And why? Who could possibly be so cruel? It was like tearing the wings off a butterfly. Taking such a beautiful creature and—

His reverie was abruptly interrupted by a harsh beeping noise. He had drifted so far away, it took him a few moments just to register what the sound was.

The cell phone. The one Liponsky had given him. In his pocket.

The killer.

Conner pulled the phone out of his pocket and pushed the Talk button. "Hello."

The voice that came back at him was harsh and metallic. It echoed, like someone was putting their lips too close to an electronic bullhorn. Obviously, the killer was using a voice disguiser. "Hello, Conner. Having a good think?"

Conner looked all around him—the course, the trees, the green. He didn't see anything. No signs of movement; no signs of life. Was he out there? "Who is this?"

"Your worst nightmare. Ready for a quick jog?"

"I gave up exercise years ago. Just before I took it up."

"Well, you're in luck. I want you to run, Conner. I want you to run like the devil himself is chasing you. I want you to be on the third green in five minutes."

"The third green? Do you know how far away that is?"

"Of course. That's why I chose it."

"Forget it. I'm not doing it."

"If you're not on the third green in five minutes, someone else will die. Someone you know personally. Maybe closely."

"You son-of-a—"

"Watch the language, Conner. On your mark—"

"Just explain to me why—"

"Get set—"

"But first, tell me—"

"*Go!* Try not to leave a divot on the green. Five minutes and counting."

Conner snapped the phone shut, shoved it in his pocket, and ran. Thank goodness he was wearing his sneakers. If he could make it to the third green in five minutes, it would be nothing less than a miracle.

He bolted across the fairway, criss-crossing in a southwesterly direction. Fortunately, he'd been playing this course since Monday, so he had a pretty good idea how to shortcut to the third. But five minutes? Was the lunatic serious about killing someone else, or was that just a threat he hauled out so Conner would play his sick little game? Conner couldn't be sure—but he couldn't take the chance, either. If running would save someone's life, then run he would.

Conner raced up a steep slope near the tee-off for the seventh, bounded over a short fence lining the cart trail, and kept on running. He didn't know what he was running for or running to, but he was determined to make it. Huffing and puffing, he careened across another fairway, then raced up toward the flag for the third hole. He collapsed on the ground, then checked his watch.

Seconds to spare.

The cell phone buzzed again.

"Congratulations, Conner," the scrambled voice said. "You've outdone yourself. Really. I'm genuinely impressed."

"You have no idea how happy that makes me," Conner gasped.

"I can see I'm going to have to make this more challenging for you."

"That's really not necessary—"

"I want you at the eleventh tee-off in five minutes. No, make it four."

"Look, you sorry sack of—"

"If you don't make it, Monica Cartwright dies."

"Monica—" Conner paused, his mind racing. "Who's she?"

"She's the woman you picked up in the bar and slept with Monday night, you heel. Didn't you even ask her name?"

"Must've slipped my mind."

"Would you prefer I choose someone you know better?"

Conner gritted his teeth together. "No."

"Fine. On your mark, get set, *go!*"

Conner flew. He raced back the way he had come, this time jogging left on the seventh fairway, making a beeline for the start of the eleventh.

He crossed a water trap with a flying leap . . . and almost made it. His sneakers came down in the water, wet up to his knees. Didn't matter. He didn't have time to stop, much less complain.

He had to keep running. His throat felt dry; sweat was flying off his brow. He felt a painful stitch in his side, but he forced himself to keep going. He could see the end in sight. The tee-off was just around the corner.

Conner pulled up to the tee-off, gasping for all he was worth. He was drinking in air in huge gulps, feeling as if he might faint at any moment. But he had made it, damn it, with time to spare. He'd made it—

His eyes wandered to the sign posted at the top of the tee-off spot. The big sign with a red twelve painted on it.

Twelve? His heart sank.

He'd taken a wrong turn.

Without stopping to think, Conner flew backwards through the twelfth fairway. How much time did he have left? He couldn't be sure; he'd forgotten to check his watch before he left. But it couldn't be much.

His chest pounding, his feet aching, the stitch in his side ready to split, Conner finally loped to the eleventh tee-off. He collapsed on the ground, face first. He had no energy left. Not even enough to stand.

The cell phone beeped. "Yes?" he gasped.

"Not bad, Conner. Not bad at all."

Conner swore silently. Could the creep really see him? Or was this just a charade to make him think so?

"Look," Conner said forcefully, "I'm tired of playing games. Tell me where you are and I'll bring you your damn money."

"Sorry, old boy. That's not the way we're going to play it."

"I'm tired of running around!"

"A pity. Because you see—we've only just begun."

"Forget it. I'm not doing it."

"I'm sorry to hear that, Conner. Though not as sorry as Monica Cartwright will be."

"Listen to me. You can't—"

"I can and I will. I haven't killed anyone for almost twenty-four hours. I'm overdue."

Clenching his jaw, Conner forced himself to his feet. "Fine, you sorry son-of-a-bitch. Where do we go now?"

24

LIEUTENANT O'BRIEN HUNCHED over Agent Liponsky's shoulder, watching her work. Liponsky had headphones on, plugged into the cellular scanner.

"Are you getting anything?"

Liponsky shook her head. "Not much. Scattered words. It was coming in clear at first, then it dissipated."

"How can that be?"

"Can't be certain. Conner is moving a lot. Maybe they both are. That makes it harder to catch the signal. It's also possible the killer is using a frequency scrambler."

"Where would he get one?"

"Are you kidding? Pawn shops, Internet, wherever. This is the United States. You can buy anything you want. Pick up a couple of Uzis while you're at it. Hell, next week you'll probably be able to get them at Wal-Mart."

"Surely this creep isn't smart enough to use a frequency scrambler."

"Don't be so sure. He hasn't made any mistakes so far. And he's the one who decided to communicate by cell phone, remember. It's not as if this happened by accident. And it's not as if he wouldn't know the FBI would be involved at this point."

O'Brien frowned. "You know where Conner is?"

"Yeah. He doesn't know it, but that PDA is emitting a constant signal. We know his position at all times."

"Is that wise? What if the killer picks up the signal?"

"He won't. And this way, my team can follow Cross from a distance.

As soon as he signals that he's made the drop, they can surround the area instantly. The killer will have no chance to escape."

O'Brien shook her head. "Still seems risky to me."

"Relax, Lieutenant. We're professionals. We know what we're doing."

"Easy to say."

Liponsky observed the note of concern in O'Brien's voice. "Look, Cross knew there was an element of risk."

"An element of risk? Is that what you call it? He's putting his life on the line out there! And you're screwing around, assuming the killer won't know you're breaking his rules. Sure, Conner knew there was risk. But he didn't know you were going to be giving the guy an excuse to blow him away."

"Lieutenant, it might be best if you waited somewhere else. I promise I'll keep you posted."

"I'm not going anywhere."

"Please, Lieutenant. Don't make me pull rank."

"You'll have to pull a lot more than that to budge me."

"Don't fight me on this, Lieutenant. If you won't go of your own volition, I'll have to remove you."

O'Brien arched an eyebrow, her feet planted firmly in place. "You and what army?"

AFTER THE TEE-OFF for the eleventh, Conner was ordered to the pin of the fourth green in six minutes, the cart trail between the first and the second in five, and the north rough of the eighteenth in three. Each time, he was certain he had nothing left; he couldn't possibly move any faster. And each time he managed to get back on his feet and force his sneakers into action.

He collapsed under a spreading magnolia in the designated rough, his throat dry, wheezing, gasping for air like he couldn't recall ever doing in his life. Why was that sick bastard on the other end of the line doing this? What was the point? Just to get his jollies? Or was there something more, something Conner hadn't begun to imagine yet?

He wondered where his backup was now. They couldn't possibly be keeping track of all this hustle-bustle across the course. Maybe that was the point. All Liponsky and O'Brien could do was wait for his signal and try to surround the area quickly. There was no telling whether they'd make it in time to catch the creep. Much less in time to prevent him from drilling Conner, just for the fun of it.

Conner wasn't surprised when he heard the phone in his pocket beep. He flipped it open and shouted: "Look, you sick son-of-a-bitch! I'm tired of your stupid games!"

"Temper, temper," the electronic voice said. "There's a two hundred and fifty dollar penalty for harsh language."

"The PGA can go screw itself. And so can you."

"Do I detect a note of irritation? Aren't you enjoying our little game?"

"No, I'm not. And I'm not going to do it anymore."

"Really. Then I'm afraid I'll have to deal with your sweetheart Monica."

"Yeah, and I'll have to pour your money into the fucking water trap, you asshole! How would you like that?"

The metallic ringing subsided. The line was silent for several seconds.

"That would be a mistake, Conner. I need that money."

"For what? Another trip to Fiji?"

There was a pronounced pause on the other end of the line. It had been a long shot, but it seemed to have hit home. "I need the money," the voice repeated.

"Then come and get it, you bastard!"

"Calm down, Conner. Calm down. Perhaps it is time to get on with it. Do you know which direction is north?"

"At the moment, I don't even know which direction is up."

"Sorry. After the way you've been playing this week, I thought you'd know the roughs like the back of your hand."

"Why don't you go—"

"Toward the tee-off, Conner. Get up and walk toward the tee-off."

"Then what?"

"Just do it. And don't disconnect the line. Let's chat awhile."

"Oh, goody." Conner pushed himself to his feet, brushing the dirt and debris off his pants. He didn't get the half of it, and when it came right down to it, he supposed it didn't matter much, either.

"All right, Conner. Keep walking till you're about halfway down the fairway."

"I already am." Why didn't Mr. Murder know that? Did that mean he couldn't see Conner? That he'd been bluffing all along? Or that he could see Conner before, but now he'd gone somewhere he couldn't? Conner couldn't make any sense of it; it made his head hurt, just trying.

"Fine. Veer west at the post. That would be to your left. Do you remember which is your left hand, Conner? That's the one you keep too stiff when you swing."

Conner gritted his teeth and prayed to heaven he got ten seconds alone with this creep before the cops showed up. "I'm turning."

"Good. Keep walking. You'll go about a hundred feet."

"Fine. Should I pace this off?"

"I don't think that'll be necessary." The metallic voice faded for about twenty seconds. "See anything unusual?"

"As a matter of fact, yes." Staring straight ahead, Conner saw a white golf cart—parked in the middle of the rough. "What's that thing doing out here? The cart track isn't even nearby."

"I made special arrangements for you, Conner."

"What now—you want me to drive the cart backwards down the freeway?"

"Nothing nearly so elaborate. Just put the money on the seat and disappear."

Conner stopped a few paces from the cart. "You mean—leave the money? Here?"

"What do you know—you're brighter than you look."

"But I thought I was going to give it to you."

"And you will, Conner. You will. Drop it on the cart."

Damn. What was this fiend planning? He hated to let go of the loot until he knew where the man was. "I don't feel good about this. What if someone else gets it?"

"Like who?"

"I don't know. A vagrant, maybe."

"At the Augusta National? Put the money on the damn seat!"

Conner did as he was told.

"Now scram."

"What—that's it?"

"You heard me. Clear out. Fast."

"But I thought—"

"If you're anywhere near here in one minute, the deal's off. And Monica's dead." The line disconnected.

Damn! He didn't have any choice. Conner slipped his hand in

his pocket and pushed the red button on the PDA. Then he started running.

"We got his signal!" Liponsky shouted.

O'Brien pressed close to the viewscreen. "Where is he?"

"On the eighteenth hole. Just south of here." She stared at her screen for a moment. "The signal's moving. He probably dropped the cash and ran." She flipped a switch and spoke into her microphone. "All right, boys and girls—move. Double time."

Somewhere in the darkness of the Augusta National golf course, a team of twelve FBI agents began closing in.

"I want a cordon around the eighteenth in place in thirty seconds," Liponsky shouted. "Start big, then close. Whatever you do, don't let anyone escape. Got it? I don't want any screw-ups. I want this killer *caught!*"

She removed the headphones, then turned to O'Brien. "Well, Lieutenant? Shall we go see what we've bagged?"

Conner was still running fast when he saw Liponsky and O'Brien approaching from the opposite direction. O'Brien stepped forward, taking Conner by the arms. "Are you all right?"

"I'm fine. Exhausted, but unharmed. My leg muscles are aching."

"Is there anything I can do to help?"

"Well, a shiatsu massage followed by a full-body oil rubdown might do the trick. Or if you'd like, we can skip the massage."

O'Brien shoved him away. "Pervert."

"Well, you did ask."

Liponsky stepped between them. "Did you see the killer?"

"Sorry, no. Just heard him. And he was using some kind of voice disguiser."

Liponsky grimaced. "That's what I thought. Doesn't matter. We'll grab him when he comes for the mil."

"Good," Conner said. "Mind if I hang around?"

"I suppose not."

Conner's eyes turned back toward the eighteenth. "I have a message to deliver."

O'Brien arched an eyebrow. "With your lips? Or your fist?"

Conner looked away. "No comment."

THE FBI CORDON remained out of sight but kept a tight lock around the golf cart sitting in the west rough off the eighteenth fairway. The team had settled into place mere seconds after Conner sent the signal. They were certain no one could have gotten in or out. Moreover, they could see that the black money bag was still resting on the seat of the cart.

"He has to come sometime," Liponsky said, peering through high-powered infrared binoculars. "Otherwise, what's the point?"

"Maybe the killer spotted your team and made himself scarce," O'Brien suggested.

"No way. These are some of the best-trained agents in the business. They know how to be invisible. Particularly on a nearly pitch-dark golf course in the dead of night."

Fifteen minutes had passed since Conner had made the drop, and the bag was still on top of the seat, just where Conner had left it. Despite all his elaborate preparations, the killer didn't seem to be in any hurry to collect his prize.

"It doesn't make any sense," Conner said. "The time to grab the bag was immediately—before I had a chance to call in the reinforcements. Why would he do this if he doesn't want the cash? Besides, he told me he did. He said he needed the money."

"He's just being cautious," Liponsky whispered. "Making sure the coast is clear before he makes his move. As soon as he's sure no one's watching, he'll go for it. That's why we have to stay quiet—and stay out of sight."

"Fine," Conner said, folding his arms. She was the professional; they'd play it her way. But for some reason, he wasn't convinced. A glance at O'Brien told him she wasn't particularly convinced either.

FIFTEEN MORE SLOW, tedious minutes passed. Conner wondered if all stakeouts were this exciting. Sitting in the dark, doing nothing. Not exactly a thrill-packed adventure. He wasn't even angry at the creep anymore. He just wanted this night to be over.

On cop shows, stakeouts never lasted more than a minute or two before the culprit appeared. It seemed reality was something else again. Conner supposed it hadn't actually been *that* long. In truth, he'd only been waiting a little over half an hour, but he was ready to call it a day and run to the clubhouse for a sandwich. Maybe a margarita to wash it down. From their position near the eighteenth, Conner could see the clubhouse. He could even smell the food—or so he imagined. It was just too tempting to resist.

"Look," he said quietly, "not that this isn't the most exciting time I've ever had with my clothes on, but I think I'm going to call it a night."

"Shh," Liponsky whispered. She was peering through infrared binoculars.

"No, seriously, I can't take it any longer." Conner started to push up to his feet.

Liponsky grabbed him by the shoulder and yanked him back down. "I think I see someone."

Conner froze. Could it be? Finally—?

Liponsky whispered into her mouthpiece, which transmitted to the earpieces each of the agents was wearing. "See 'im? Yeah, me too. On my signal."

A few moments passed. Conner began to perceive a tall silhouette weaving its way across the fairway. It was hard to be certain, but—

Yes! The silhouette took a sudden veer to the left. It was definitely moving toward the golf cart.

"That's it," Liponsky whispered breathlessly. "One . . . two . . . three . . . *move!*"

All at once, a dozen figures appeared out of nowhere, surging forward, forming an increasingly tight circle around the mysterious figure.

The man stopped suddenly. He'd spotted them. But he didn't turn away, didn't run. He just stood still, as if staring in disbelief.

"Get him!" Liponsky shouted.

The agents rushed forward, tackling the man. Without resistance, he fell to the ground like a wet sack of potatoes.

Conner couldn't stand the suspense. He ran forward, desperate to see who it was. He pulled away a few of the agents on top, straining to get a better view of . . .

Barry Bennett. And he was potted. Totally.

"Whass goin' on?" Barry slurred. His eyes were wild and he seemed dazed, which was not all that surprising, given the circumstances.

"Cuff him!" Liponsky shouted, just over their shoulders. One of the agents rolled Barry onto his stomach, pulled back his wrists and slid on the cuffs.

"Look, Liponsky," Conner said, "I think possibly you've—"

"Did someone read him his rights?" Liponsky shouted. "I don't want any procedural errors screwing up my collar. We've got to read him his rights."

The same agent who'd done the cuffs whipped a card out of his shirt pocket and began to read. "You have the right to remain silent . . ."

"Look," Conner said, trying again, "I think maybe you've made a mistake."

"I don't make mistakes," Liponsky fired back. "Criminals make mistakes."

"Yeah, I'm sure. But I don't think Barry is your man."

"What makes you so sure?"

"I know him. He's on the tour."

"That doesn't mean he can't be the killer."

"Look at him, will you? He's smashed!"

"What?" Liponsky's head jerked down toward the ground.

"He's drunk! If you don't want to take my word for it, smell his breath."

"I can smell it from here," O'Brien said, somewhere behind them.

"Iss thiss my cabin?" Barry said with a hiccup. "I been trying to find my cabin . . ."

Conner rolled his eyes. "You're a little off-track, Barry."

The tiniest trace of concern flickered across Liponsky's brow. "This could be a front. An acting job to put us off."

"No one's that good an actor, Liponsky. He's wasted. Probably been drinking all day. And there's no way the man I was talking to on the phone was drunk."

Liponsky bit down on her lower lip. "There must be some explanation."

"Yeah, there is. You screwed up."

A look of horror suddenly spread across her face. "Oh, my God. If he's not—"

"What?" Conner said. "What is it?"

Without another word, Liponsky raced toward the parked golf cart.

She ran like there was no tomorrow, probably doing twice the time Conner had out on the course. She didn't stop running until she practically collided into the cart.

"Oh, no!" she cried. "No, no, *no!*"

Conner and O'Brien followed close behind her. "What is it?" Conner asked.

She didn't need to answer. One look was all it took.

She was holding the black bag in her hands. And it was empty.

25

AN HOUR LATER, Conner was back in the clubhouse listening to O'Brien try to explain what had happened.

"But how did he get the money? You had the place surrounded."

"Above ground, yes," O'Brien said. "Below ground, no."

"Below ground? I don't get it."

"Turns out there's a fairly extensive sewer system under part of the golf course. Including the part the eighteenth hole is on."

Conner nodded. "That's true. I remember Fanboy Ed telling me about it. That's how he got in."

"Who?"

"Never mind. Seems the Augusta National has heavy water demands—for watering the course and whatnot. So they built this underground sewer system. Tunnels are small—but passable."

"So I hear from our dear friend Agent Liponsky. She's got agents crawling through every branch of the system. But they haven't found the culprit. And I don't think they're going to, either. He probably grabbed the money seconds after you put it down, then hightailed it."

"But how did he grab the money without being seen?"

O'Brien reached out across the small round table, then popped a handful of beer nuts into her mouth. "Turns out the golf cart was just a decoy. It was parked over a manhole cover—an access tunnel to the sewer system. The insides of the cart had been hollowed out so a person could crawl up through it, pull the seat cover off, cut the bottom of the bag, take the money, and disappear—without ever being seen above ground. The bag never moved—but our extortionist got the cash just the same."

"That's pretty damn smart."

"I would have to agree with you on that point. He outfoxed us but good."

"A genius golfer. Who the hell would that be?"

O'Brien gave him a sharp look. "Do you know something I don't? What makes you so sure the killer is a golfer?"

"It was my conversation with him," Conner explained. "While he was running me all over creation. He talked like a golfer—talked about divots and bogies. And stuff not just any golfer would know—like about PGA penalties. And he was familiar with my golfing performance this week—even though the TV people never got close to me before today." He shook his head thoughtfully. "No, I'm sure of it. Our killer is a golfer. Or at the very least, someone intimately connected to this tournament."

"Any suspects?"

"I already told you what I thought—you need to talk to Freddy."

"Funny you should say that. I was thinking pretty much the same way you are, that the time had come, even if I didn't have anything on him and it might tip him off that he was under suspicion. So after we got back from our moonlight fiasco, I gave Freddy a call. He's disappeared."

"What? As in—?"

"As in, no one knows where the hell he is, even though he was specifically instructed to stay put."

"This is very curious."

"It's more than that. Get this, Conner—no one knows where he was tonight."

"O'Brien, I think you need to pick him up."

"Way ahead of you. I've got an APB out. We'll get him."

"Good. So . . . how is Liponsky taking the news?"

"Not well. Her home office is all over her for botching the nab." A smile spread across her face. "As a fellow law enforcement officer, of course, my hearts bleeds for her."

"I can see that. Mine, too."

O'Brien pushed herself out of her chair. "I've got to check in with my office. I'll be in touch."

"Sure I can't buy you a drink?"

O'Brien hesitated. For half a second, Conner almost thought she might go for it. "Rain check," she said. She left the clubhouse.

Well, Conner asked himself, what next? What exactly does one do as a follow-up to acting as the bag man for a million-dollar extortion scheme?

Fortunately, he didn't have to think about it for long. The question was answered for him when the PGA's main man Richard Peregino entered the bar and made a beeline for Conner's table.

Conner braced himself for another lecture about PGA standards. What had he done this time, he wondered? Mussed a sand trap while discovering a corpse? Worn the wrong color socks to deliver the payoff?

Without waiting to be invited, Peregino pulled out a chair and sat at his table. "Can I talk to you, Conner?"

Conner, Conner noted. Not Cross. "It's a free country. Unless you're in the PGA, of course."

Peregino didn't smile. "I need your help."

Conner tried not to appear astonished. "You need *my* help?"

Peregino nodded. "We think there's a leak."

"What, in the plumbing?"

"No, you—" He cut himself short. "To the press."

"A leak about what?"

"About the extortion scheme. The threat from the killer."

Conner shrugged. "Shouldn't they know? It seems like a matter that might be of some public interest. Isn't that what the press is for?"

"No, it isn't. There's already been way too much turmoil surrounding this tournament, what with one murder on the course and another not far away. If they find out about this, it could be the end of the Masters."

Conner nodded. That was a distinct possibility.

"At the least, there'll be a call for us to terminate the tournament. They'll accuse us of risking lives to keep the income flowing."

"Aren't we?"

"No. We're demonstrating that we won't be pushed around by some bully with a big knife."

The distinction seemed pretty thin to Conner. "Tenniel told me he couldn't afford to cancel the tournament, regardless of how big the knife was."

Peregino ignored him. "This issue has ramifications that go well beyond the Masters tournament. This could affect the whole PGA."

"How so?"

"The PGA has an image to maintain. We have a tradition of excellence, of athleticism pushed to—"

"Stop, stop," Conner said, holding up his hands. "I've heard this rhapsody before. What you're saying is, you want the PGA to be associated with middle-aged guys in knit leisurewear, not psychopaths whacking players in the head with their Pings."

"That would be one way of putting it, yes."

"So what do you expect me to do about it?"

Peregino tapped his finger against the aromatic candle centerpiece. Conner could tell he was dreading asking him for a favor, a fact which gave him a great deal of pleasure. "Given your performance on the course today, you're likely to have some press swarming around you tomorrow. In fact, a great deal of press. You're now considered a contender. A strong contender."

Conner's head reeled. A strong contender? Him? Talk about music to your ears . . .

"I'm sure they'll be firing questions at you—including questions relating to the murders. I would . . . um . . ." His fingers absently twiddled a sugar packet. "I would take it as a personal favor if you would not mention what happened tonight. You know. About the . . . the . . ."

"The payoff?"

"Well, yeah . . ."

"The extortion scheme?"

"Yeah . . ."

"The bungled FBI operation."

"Yes, Conner. All of those. Is there any chance you could keep your lips sealed? At least until we have a chance to get the killer behind bars?"

"What's in it for me?"

"Why did I know it would come to this? All right, here's the deal. You keep mum about the blackmail, and I'll wipe your slate clean."

"What does that mean?"

"I'm talking about your lengthy record of PGA infractions and violations. I'll erase the whole ugly mess. Like it never happened."

Conner gave him an indignant look. "Peregino, I'm surprised at you. You're the PGA Ethics and Morality cop. And now you're trying to buy me off."

"I wouldn't put it that way . . ."

"Tell me, Peregino—is this ethical?"

A familiar look returned to Peregino's eyes—the look of contempt. "It's necessary. So—are you in?"

"I don't know. What do I care about my PGA record? It hasn't done me any harm so far."

"Get with the program, Cross. I've got enough material to kick your butt off the tour two times over. And don't think I won't do it, either." He paused, letting the words sink in. "It would be a shame if that happened now, wouldn't it? Just when it looked as if you might actually win a major tournament."

"You're going to kick me out on the last day of the tournament, for alleged violations that happened well before? No way."

"Don't be so sure."

"I'll go to the press. I'll tell them everything. Including that you tried to blackmail me into silence."

"Maybe you will. Maybe you won't. But even if you do—you won't finish the tournament."

Conner felt a hollow spot in the pit of the stomach. "I'll give it some thought."

"I need an answer now, Cross. So I know whether to approve you for play tomorrow."

Conner pondered before answering. "Well, here's the straight scoop, Peregino. I made a promise to Jodie McCree, and if I'm going to keep that promise, this tournament needs to continue—with me in it. So I don't see any reason to volunteer any information to the press."

"Good thinking."

Conner held up a finger. "I won't lie. But I won't volunteer anything."

"Good enough." Peregino pushed himself up from the table. "Uh . . . thank you. For doing the right thing. You'll feel good about this."

I feel, Conner thought, like I've been dickering with the devil. But that's life on the PGA.

"If you'd like, we could hold a mock press conference. Let you practice dodging questions."

"Gosh, that does sound—" Conner's eyes were diverted by a figure moving rapidly down the corridor outside the bar. "Excuse me, Peregino. Gotta run."

Conner jumped out of his chair and bolted down the hallway. "Wait!"

The figure at the end of the corridor stopped. Conner increased his speed, catching him near the outside door.

It was Ed Frohike, the President of the John McCree Fan Club. "How ya been, Ed?"

Ed's face was a mix of surprise, confusion, apprehension. "I'm fine."

"I haven't seen you around the last day or two. Where ya been?"

Ed answered awkwardly, diverting his eyes toward the floor. "Well, you know. Without John in the tournament . . . it hasn't been so . . . interesting for me."

"I'm sorry to hear that. What are you doing here today?"

"Oh . . ." He craned his neck. "I . . . just had to get my things."

"Your things?"

"Yeah. My backpack. Clothes and stuff. I've got 'em stored in a cabinet in the men's room."

"Really?" As far as Conner could tell, he was wearing the same clothes he'd been wearing all week. "Is there something wrong? You seem nervous."

"It's just—I don't want to be caught. I'm not really supposed to be here, remember. Hidden in a crowded bar is one thing, but out in the hallway, exposed . . ."

The more they talked, the more uncomfortable Ed seemed to become. "You mentioned to me that you used the underground tunnels to get onto the grounds."

"Did I?"

"As a matter of fact, you kind of bragged about it. So let me ask you a question. How did you find out about the tunnels?"

"How did I find out?"

"That was the question, Ed. Got an answer?"

There was a brief pause. "I found a diagram on the Internet."

Conner did a double-take. "What?"

"On a Web page run by an underground golf groupie. Calls himself the Ping."

"The Ping?"

"Yeah. After the once-tournament-illegal clubs. He loves golf, but he's got kind of a counter-culture approach to it."

"I guess so."

"Anyway, he published the schematics on his Web page and encouraged people to use them to break into the oh-so-exclusive Masters." His face fell. "Guess I'm the only one who did."

Conner declined to enlighten him. "Did you tell anyone about the tunnels?"

"No. Well, other than you."

And Conner hadn't told a soul.

Ed took a step toward the door. "Well . . . if you don't mind . . . I really should make myself scarce . . ."

Conner stepped aside obligingly. He didn't really want to, but he supposed he had no grounds—much less authority—for holding Ed any longer.

After Ed disappeared, Conner decided to walk outside. There was no point in hanging around the bar any longer, and after all he'd been through, he was ready to call it a night.

The sky was still as dark as it had been earlier. But for a few halogen lamps dotting the landscape, it would be just as dark as it had been out on the golf course. He still had to focus hard to see anything.

How had it come to this? he silently pondered. How had buddying up with John led to investigating his murder a million years later? How had falling in love with golf led to delivering a bag full of money at the Masters? How had falling in love with Jodie led—?

He stopped himself short. There was no point in going there. No cheese down that tunnel. It was all over. All over and done—

His thoughts were interrupted by a high-pitched noise buzzing just beside his ear, followed by a crackle of thunder.

He whirled around. *What*—?

He reached up and touched his left ear. His hand came back with blood on it.

Someone had taken a shot at him.

26

A LL AT ONCE, Conner's brain sputtered into action. He dove forward, seconds before another shot fired somewhere north of him. He took cover behind a hedge, then scrambled close to the front of the building.

A moment later, he heard footsteps moving rapidly away from him.

Conner bit down on his lip. There was almost nothing stupider than chasing someone who was trying to shoot him. But if he didn't—

He might never find out who it was.

He didn't have time for protracted analysis. He pushed himself around the corner of the clubhouse and ran in the general direction where he'd heard the shots and the footsteps.

There was something moving over there, toward the cabins. He could just barely see the outline of a figure moving fast. Conner steered himself toward it, bracing himself for the next crash of thunder.

Conner took a hard left around the first cabin and continued barreling forward, panting and wheezing. He had almost forgotten how much exercise he'd already had tonight, until his aching thighs reminded him. He felt winded before he'd crossed the first hundred feet; he broke out in a cold sweat long before that. But he forced himself to keep moving.

The shadowy figure was well ahead, but Conner was gaining on him. Come on, Cross, he told himself. Pedal to the metal. Don't let this creep get away. He was still telling himself that when something big and solid slammed into his face.

Conner hit the ground hard. His head hit the grass; fireworks went off before his eyes.

What the hell—? His hands groped for the glistening steel object that had knocked him over.

A golf club. The SOB had thrown a golf club at him!

Conner pulled himself together and started running, ignoring the intense throbbing he now felt in his head. If there were any chance he could catch this creep, he wasn't going to let it slip away.

He'd passed three more cabins when he spotted the silhouette. Hah!—the fool had made the mistake of stopping, checking to see if the coast was clear. He was history now.

Conner poured on the speed. Hell, a few more nights like this, and he'd be ready for the triathlon.

The figure ahead saw him coming and started sprinting, but it was too late. Conner tackled him like a pro quarterback, wrapping himself around the man's legs and bringing him down with a thud.

Conner sat on top of the squirming man, then rolled him over onto his back to see who it was.

"Ace? Ace Silverstone? Why did you do it?"

"Conner Cross!" the other man fired back. "Why the hell are you sitting on me?"

Conner kept a firm arm on Ace's throat. "You were trying to kill me!"

"You're even crazier than I thought."

"You were firing a gun."

"I've always suspected you had some mental problems, Cross, but you've outdone yourself this time."

"Don't feed me that. I saw you. I heard the shots."

"I heard those shots, too. That's why I came outside. What was going on?"

Conner stared at the man's wide, seemingly innocent eyes. Was it possible he'd made a mistake? If it had been Ace, where was the gun? He began frisking him.

"This your idea of a good time, Cross?"

Conner patted him down all over, but he didn't find a weapon. "What did you do with the gun?"

"What gun? I've never had a gun. What are you babbling about?"

"Someone took a couple of shots at me. I've been chasing him all the way from the clubhouse."

"Well, it wasn't me. Assuming this isn't all some bizarre psychosis created by your paranoid brain. May I get up now?"

Conner hesitated. Was it true? Had the killer slipped away after he'd been decked by the golf club? "How long have you been outside?"

"Barely a minute. If that long. Since I heard the first shot."

"If you just came outside, why are you sweating?"

"I've been exercising. You should try it sometime, Cross. You are an athlete, in theory, anyway." He pushed up with his hands. "Now get off me, you oaf."

Reluctantly, Conner rose, releasing Ace. It was just possible, he supposed. The killer could've escaped. Ace could've gotten caught in the crossfire.

"You'll be lucky if I don't file a complaint with the PGA," Ace said, brushing himself off.

"Don't bother. The PGA loves me. Today, anyway."

"You ought to consider getting some counseling, Conner," Ace said, as he hastily made his way back to the cabin. "You really do have a screw loose. Maybe several."

Ace went inside, closing and locking the door behind him.

Conner wanted to kick himself. Once again, he'd had a chance to catch the killer. And once again, he'd somehow managed to screw it up. How much longer could this go on?

He pointed himself north, toward his own cabin. It'd been a hell of a night, and he needed rest. He was playing in a tournament tomorrow, after all. The last day of the Masters. The Big Enchilada. If he could keep his head together, could keep on playing like he had today, it was just possible he could be heading back to Watonga in a spiffy green jacket.

But somehow, he couldn't get his brain to focus on the tournament. No matter how hard he tried, his mind kept wandering back to the same thought.

The killer was still at large.

And it seemed his current target was Conner Cross.

27

Sunday

THE NEXT MORNING, Conner lathered himself up as he sang at the top of his lungs: "Some enchanted evening . . . you will meet a stranger . . ." Funny, he thought, how much better your singing voice sounds in the shower than in real life.

A good night's sleep had washed away the fatigue and frustration of the night before. This morning, he was determined to focus his energies on the tournament. It was the last day of the Masters—and he was in fourth place. It was possible . . . just barely possible . . .

He stepped out of the shower, still high as a kite. He took the towel handed to him and began to dry off, humming a happy tune. He could envision the entire victory scene—the ball drops into the hole on the eighteenth, a stunning hole-in-one, the crowd grows wild, screaming and throwing confetti on the course, the other pros scoop him up and hoist him aloft, pouring champagne over his head. "For he's a jolly good fellow, for he's a jolly good—"

Wait a minute. He took the towel handed to him—by whom?

Lieutenant O'Brien stood by the bathroom door, her arms folded, visibly unimpressed. "Are you about done, or should I call for a backup band?"

In a panicked flurry, Conner whipped the towel around his waist. "What the hell are you doing in here?"

"I knocked. No one answered."

"I was in the shower!"

"I gathered that."

Conner grappled with the towel, trying to secure it. "You don't have any business being in my cabin! Much less my bathroom!"

"Excuse me. Didn't you tell me I could"—she tried to simulate his seductive voice—"drop by anytime?"

"Yes, but I meant—"

"Get your clothes on, cowboy. We've got work to do."

"*I've* got work to do," Conner said, pushing past her. Where did he leave his clothes, anyway? "I've got a golf tournament. And I don't want to be distracted."

"Relax, your tee time isn't until afternoon. And in the meantime, we need you."

"You need me?" Conner picked up his boxers and a pair of pants. He started to drop his towel, then realized she was still watching. "Could you possibly turn your back for just one tiny moment?"

O'Brien obliged.

"Haven't I done enough already?" Conner asked, yanking his clothes on. "I ran all over the golf course. I delivered your money. I helped tackle the drunk."

"Ha ha."

"Plus, someone was taking pot shots at me last night."

"Oh?"

"Yeah, oh."

"Did you call the police?"

"I didn't see the point. He got away. And besides, I was exhausted."

"That was stupid. Who knows—we might've found something." She frowned. "This is disturbing. Particularly in light of the latest development."

"Well, just don't tell me about it, okay?" Conner said, pulling on his shirt. "Fitz says focus is the most important part of playing pro golf. He says focus could be the secret to improving my putting game—which definitely needs improvement. So I intend to stay focused. Don't be distracting me or luring me out to play cops and robbers, okay?"

"You're not interested?"

"I'm not."

"You don't want to know what's happened?"

"I don't."

"We've received another fax."

Conner slowed. "Am I mentioned?"

O'Brien's head bobbed up and down. "Oh, yeah. Big time."

*　*　*

FIVE MINUTES LATER, Conner was in the downstairs level of the clubhouse. It was Tenniel's office, but the passage of another day had created further changes; now it resembled a set from a TV cop show. Conner noted that there were twice as many agents, as before, twice the equipment—and twice the tension.

On the other hand, one component from the previous day was missing: Agent Liponsky.

"I understand she's been removed from the case," O'Brien explained.

"I'm all torn up," Conner replied.

"I figured you would be. They've put some guy named Stimson on the case. I like him better."

Conner arched an eyebrow. "Cute?"

"Think Ben Affleck."

"Wonderful. So where's the fax?"

O'Brien handed him a copy of the faxed message that arrived a few hours before, while most people, including Conner, were snoring in their beds. It had been sent from a convenience store, just as before. The clerk in attendance vaguely remembered sending it but never got a proper look at the man who brought it in. The customer's face had been obscured by sunglasses, a hat, and a high-collar coat, an extremely unhelpful description confirmed by the security camera.

Conner scanned the fax. It appeared to have been typed, or perhaps word-processed, on the same machine as before—and without distinguishing characteristics. "Want to give me the highlights?" he asked.

"Why? Can't read anything longer than a beer label?" She jabbed a finger toward the bottom of the page. "He wants another million."

"You're joking!"

"You hear anybody laughing?"

Conner turned and spotted his nemesis Andrew Spenser hovering in the background. "He says if we don't supply him with more money, people will start dropping like flies. Players, spouses—even spectators."

"But we paid the man!"

"Apparently he wants more."

"Then why didn't he just ask for two million in the first place?" Conner frowned. "Something here doesn't make sense. Are you sure it's the same extortionist?"

"Positive," O'Brien answered. "The message has been scrupulously analyzed. It matches the first one in every possible way."

"Doesn't matter anyway," Spenser said firmly. "We're not paying it."

"But what if he—" Conner began.

"We can't keep doling out a million dollars a day, just to keep an extortionist at bay."

"But if you don't—"

"It would be different if we felt the money would ensure everyone's safety. But clearly, this man cannot be trusted. He intends to keep milking us endlessly."

Conner handed the fax back to O'Brien. "I think maybe you'd better discuss this with Tenniel before you make any rash decisions."

"This *is* Tenniel's decision," Spenser corrected him. "He's laid down the law. Not a cent more."

"Playing the tough guy, huh?"

"Confidentially, I don't know that we have much choice. I think Mr. Tenniel mentioned our financial difficulties to you."

"Did anyone confirm if you have insurance coverage?"

Spenser seemed surprised. "Of course we do."

"Maybe the safest thing would be to cancel the tournament, then collect damages for your loss."

"It's not that simple. The policy doesn't pay off in the event of disruption or cancellation by us. Only if the tournament is rendered impossible or canceled as a result of forces outside our control. Like an act of God. Or a court order."

"Or maybe being shut down by the police." Conner turned toward O'Brien. "Why don't you do it? Give them the excuse they need."

"I'm ahead of you," she said. "I floated that idea by my boss this morning. He didn't go for it."

"Why not?"

"Not sure exactly. I think maybe he has friends who are members of the Augusta National."

"Give me a break."

"Still—we're working on it. But for the moment—no cancellation."

"Let me tell you something, people," Conner said. "I don't like what I'm hearing. This is a very dangerous game you're playing."

"Don't look at me," Spenser said, holding up his hands. "It's outside my control. We can't pay off this blackmailer if we don't have the money."

"Perhaps we should make a withdrawal from your private stash, Andrew."

All heads in the room turned. Artemus Tenniel had quietly entered the room. And his expression was not a happy one.

"My . . . stash?" Spenser said, pressing his hand against his chest. "Good heavens—whatever are you talking about?"

"Game's up, Andrew." Tenniel slapped a thick blue folder on the table beside them. "The police found this among the late John McCree's belongings. They forwarded it to me this morning."

"Really? And—what could that be?" Slowly but surely, Spenser's stoic resolve was eroding.

"It's a report of a subcommittee of the board of directors. The financial oversight subcommittee, to be precise. John McCree was the chairman. They were trying to figure out why profits have been down of late. To that end, they had a comprehensive audit performed."

"Do tell?" Spenser stammered. "I didn't know of this."

"I'll bet you didn't," Tenniel shot back.

"Okay," Conner interjected, "I'll bite. What did they find out?"

Tenniel's face was the picture of controlled rage. "They discovered that Mr. Spenser here has been skimming off almost ten percent of the club's fluid income."

"Fluid income?"

"Cash. Green fees, pro shop grosses, membership dues—which are not at all insignificant. He took everything he could get his hands on."

"It wasn't me," Spenser pleaded. "There must be some mistake!"

"Please don't insult my intelligence, Andrew. There's no one else it could have been. All the club's income flows through you."

"Perhaps there was an error in the accounting—"

"The fact is, Mr. Spenser has pocketed an amount in the high six figures—in less than two years."

Conner whistled. "That's some major-league embezzlement."

"I tell you, I didn't do it!" Spenser protested.

Conner checked the date on the cover of the report. "That would explain why John went to talk to you the night he was killed, Spenser. He'd just received the audit report, and he wanted to confront you. Boy, I'll bet that was a heated conversation."

"I'm telling you, there was no conversation."

"Don't bother lying, Spenser. I've got an eyewitness." Conner took a step closer to the man. "What happened when you found out John had the goods on you? I bet you went into a major meltdown. I bet you were ready to do anything, even—"

Spenser's eyes widened with horror. "You're crazy, I tell you! I haven't done anything improper."

Conner turned quickly toward O'Brien. "Are you thinking what I'm thinking?"

O'Brien nodded. "Covering up an extensive embezzling scheme. Pretty damn good motive for murder."

"Murder?" Spenser said. "*Murder?*"

"Makes sense," Conner said. "Spenser, where were you Tuesday night? Say around nine-thirty."

"I—I—Well, I don't remember exactly."

"No alibi?"

"Alibi? I don't need—" He stopped suddenly. "That's it. I refuse to say another word. I want an attorney."

"The last refuge of a scoundrel."

"Don't think you're going to hide behind some shyster's coattails, Andrew," Tenniel said forcefully. "I won't let you get away with this. I will hound you until every cent is repaid and you are behind bars."

Spenser's eyes narrowed. "Don't stir up any trouble you can't handle, Artemus."

"Is that it, then? You think I won't prosecute because I don't want a scandal at the club." He leaned forward ominously. "Don't be so sure."

Spenser backed away. "If you'll excuse me, I'm leaving." He headed rapidly toward the doors. "But let me warn you. I will not tolerate this unwarranted encroachment on my good name. I have a reputation in this community, and I will not stand idly by and see it sullied. If I learn that you have made any libelous accusations, I will instruct my attorneys to seek redress to the full extent of the law." He skittered out the door and disappeared in the corridor.

"Well," Conner observed, "he's terrified."

"True," O'Brien agreed. "But unfortunately, that doesn't prove anything."

"Maybe not, but he had a hell of a motive."

"I'm beginning to think a lot of people had motives. What I need is proof. And I need it fast. Before this maniac strikes again."

28

O'BRIEN GLANCED AT her watch, then gave Conner's shirt sleeve a gentle tug. "Well, Slick, what say you and I do a little spelunking?"

Conner's eyebrows rose. "Madam, there are gentlemen present!"

"I'm talking about the sewer tunnels. You know, our killer's escape hatch."

"Didn't Liponsky's dudes scour the tunnels?"

"Looking for a murderer, yes. Looking for clues, no."

"And why would you want me along?"

"Because you're my golf expert. What other reason could there be?"

THEY MADE THEIR way to the rough on the north side of the eighteenth hole. After diligent searching, they found the manhole cover that blocked the access into the tunnel system.

"Looks dark," Conner commented, peering into the stygian hole. "I'd better go first."

O'Brien pulled a pencil-thin flashlight out of her back pocket and tossed it to him. "Take this, Slick."

Conner flipped the flashlight on. "Here goes nothing."

Advancing feet first, he lowered himself into the narrow passage. "Luckily I had a light breakfast." Once he was in waist-deep, he kicked around, searching for something to hold onto. He found a rusted iron ladder descending the side of the tunnel. "This should help."

Cautiously, he placed one foot on the first rung of the ladder. It squeaked and wobbled, but held. The next foot followed. He could feel the strain on the metalwork, but the ladder didn't break free.

"I'm going down," he announced.

"I'll alert the media," O'Brien replied.

Conner worked his way down the rickety ladder. About ten feet under ground level, he reached the bottom. He scanned the area with his flashlight, etching a 360 degree circle with the thin beam of light.

"There's some kind of recess down here," Conner shouted up. "Big enough to stretch your legs. Even move around a little bit. And I can see two tunnels going in different directions. Man, they're small."

"Big enough to pass through?" O'Brien shouted back.

"Oh, yeah. But it won't be fun. They're maybe three feet in circumference, tops."

"All right. Look out, I'm coming down."

Conner moved to the side of the ladder. "Be careful. That ladder has seen better days, and the wall is slick and slimy. Don't hurt—"

Conner was interrupted by a swift whooshing noise down the length of the access tunnel. O'Brien had foregone the ladder altogether— and jumped. She landed in a crouched position, executed a perfect barrel roll on her left shoulder, and ended up on her feet. "You were saying?"

Conner blinked. "That was impressive. Where'd you learn that move?"

"I have a brown belt in tae kwon do."

"Who doesn't?" He grinned. "Was that just to impress me?"

"No, that was because I hate to get my fingers slimy." O'Brien snagged her flashlight and scanned the two tunnels. "Let's take the north tunnel. They tell me that one leads off the Augusta National grounds. It seems the most likely route for a felon on the run."

O'Brien crouched down, then duck-walked into the tunnel, using her hands for balance. "I'll take the lead."

"You're the boss." Conner knelt down and followed, waddling behind her.

Once they were five feet from the entrance, the tunnel was pitch black. The only illumination came from O'Brien's flashlight. Conner's fingers came down on something wet and slimy, but he couldn't see what it was. "Am I the only one getting creeped out here?"

"No," O'Brien admitted. "This is like something out of Edgar Allan Poe."

"And then some. If I hear any bats, I'm leaving."

O'Brien laughed softly. "Bats are okay. But if you hear rats, I'll join you."

"Rats? You think there might be rats?"

"Rats? In a sewer? What a crazy idea. Of course not."

They continued trudging down the tunnel. Conner assumed there had to be an end somewhere, but he couldn't see it. "Now if this were a Stephen King novel," he suggested, "we would be in hell now, except we don't know it, see. We'd just keep trudging along this dark, slimy tunnel for eternity, never reaching an exit."

"Wonderful imagery," O'Brien commented. "Very Sisyphean. You read about Sisyphus in college, didn't you?"

"Oh, yeah. Sure." Conner paused. "Is that something to do with your sorority house?"

O'Brien laughed again. "You're smarter than you look, Conner."

"Gee, thanks."

They continued moving along the tunnel. Conner wasn't sure how much time had passed. It seemed like hours, but the voice inside his head told him it was probably more like ten minutes. His ankles were already beginning to ache. Miss Tae Kwon Do up there might be able to duck-walk for hours, but he felt certain he'd be getting shin splints after fifteen minutes.

He was thinking about suggesting they sing "One Hundred Bottles of Beer on the Wall," when he heard O'Brien let out an abrupt cry.

"What is it?" he asked urgently.

She didn't answer, but he did hear what sounded like a scraping or crashing sound, followed by a heavy thud. "*Oww!*"

"O'Brien! What's wrong?"

She didn't answer.

"O'Brien?" His voice was tinged with concern. "Talk to me!"

"I'm all right," she answered. "More or less, anyway. There seems to be a small crater here in our otherwise reliable tunnel. Some of the brick gave way and my foot crashed down into it."

"Are you okay?"

"Ankle feels twisted." He heard more scraping noises, followed by a strong grunt. "Can't seem to get my foot free."

"Let me help." Conner scooted forward until he bumped into her prostrate figure. He slid his hands under her arms and gently tugged. She didn't budge.

"Damn. I'm stuck. I think I feel blood trickling down my foot."

"We'll figure something out. Don't panic."

"Thanks. I wasn't planning to."

Conner took the flashlight from her. There was, in fact, a small crater beneath them—small, but bigger than he might've guessed. O'Brien's foot had wedged itself neatly into it.

He tested some of the surrounding brick and mortar. It felt loose and crumbly. "I think I can get you out of here." He hesitated. "Um . . . I have to . . . um . . ." He cleared his throat. "Have to, you know. Reach between your, um, legs."

"What are we, in kindergarten? Just do it already."

"Right, right." Conner inched forward till he was directly behind her. With O'Brien blocking his path, the only way he could get to the crater was by folding himself on top of her and reaching down in front. His hips hung on her left shoulder as he pried her foot loose. He was forced to prop his body on top of hers, his chin resting against her knee. The whole thing struck him as some bizarre variant on good ol' 69, but he opted to keep the thought to himself.

"Having any luck?" O'Brien grunted. Conner suspected she was probably in more pain than she cared to let on.

"Yes," he answered. "But it's slow work."

"What do you weigh, anyhow?"

Conner bristled. "Two hundred. Two-oh-five, tops."

"Are you sure? Maybe you should lay off the frozen margaritas."

Conner grimaced. "Remind me again why I'm busting my butt to help you?"

After about two more minutes of making like a gopher, Conner managed to create an opening large enough to withdraw her foot. Gently, he helped her out of the rocky crevasse. Her foot was bleeding.

"Think you can walk on it?"

"Assuming I can get out of these tunnels into someplace where you can walk, yes."

"Stiff?"

"A little."

"Here. Let me massage it." To his surprise, she didn't protest. He wrapped himself over her again and began rubbing the sore calf and foot.

Her foot was soft and warm, and despite the bizarre circumstances, Conner felt himself responding to her touch. "You have . . . um . . . very nice feet."

"My momma always said it was my best feature."

"Well . . . I wouldn't go as far as that." He continued massaging the sore muscles, working his way slowly up her calf.

"You can quit if you're tired."

"No. I don't mind." Taking her shoulders, he adjusted her slightly, pulling her up into his lap. Again she didn't resist.

She turned slightly and so did he, till they were almost face-to-face. Even if he couldn't see her very clearly, he could definitely feel her presence.

"O'Brien," he said.

"Yes?" she whispered.

Whatever it was he was planning to say, he forgot it. He leaned forward slightly, and once again, to his amazement, she did not draw back. Their lips met.

"How's your foot?" Conner asked, when at last their lips parted.

"Foot?" she replied, and a second later, they were kissing again. The brush of her lips sent warm shivers cascading down his spine.

Abruptly, she broke it off. "I'm sorry," she said, placing a hand against his chest.

"Sorry? Why? I'm not."

"It's just—I just—" She paused. "I shouldn't be doing this."

"But—why?"

"I'm still on duty."

"We'll call this a coffee break."

"But—I can't—for all I know—"

"What are you saying?"

O'Brien grabbed the flashlight and began brushing herself off. "It wouldn't be appropriate, Conner. You're still a suspect."

Conner felt as if he'd been thrown overboard and dashed against the rocks. So that was it. Despite all they'd been through, she still held out the possibility that he was the killer.

"Anyway," she said, changing the subject, "let's move on."

"Right. Fine. Whatever you—" Conner stopped in midsentence. As O'Brien turned, the beam of the flashlight washed across the crater. "Give me that thing."

Conner took the flashlight and aimed it into the now even larger crevasse. There was something down there. Something shiny and metallic.

Conner reached into the opening. He knocked some dust and rubble out of the way and managed to come up with a palm-sized metallic silver box.

"This doesn't look like part of the sewer system," Conner said. "But I don't know what it is."

"I do," O'Brien said anxiously. "It's an electronic voice disguiser. Our killer must've left that behind." She took the box from him and carefully wrapped it in a handkerchief.

"But why did he leave it down here?"

"I don't know. Probably an accident. Maybe he fell into the crater, too. Maybe he dropped the thing without realizing it. Whatever the reason, it's a big break for us."

"What—another serial number to trace?"

O'Brien shook her head. "I'm hoping for something even better. Fingerprints."

29

A N HOUR LATER, CONNER abandoned the search through the tunnels. When he made his goodbyes, O'Brien grabbed his arm and said, "Go get 'em, boy. Win this one for the Gipper."

"I never knew the Gipper."

She squirmed. "Then win it for some other dead sports guy."

Conner smiled. "I'll do my best." She gave his hand a squeeze, and then he was off.

Just before he arrived at the first tee-off, Conner spotted Fitz, who stepped forward to intercept him.

Fitz motioned him to the side. "I want a word."

Conner checked his watch. "Could we do this after I sign in?"

Fitz shook his head. "Do you have any idea what's waiting for you up there?"

"This is just a wild guess, but . . . my golf clubs?"

"Yeah, that—and three camera crews and about a thousand golf fanatics."

Conner went bug-eyed. "No!"

"Yes! And they're all here to see you."

"But—why?"

"You're the man of the hour. The latest phenom. The underdog who bounced back from personal tragedy to batter down the favorites. You've got a story no reporter—or fan—can resist. You're practically a folk hero."

Conner probed the side of his mouth with his tongue. "Do I detect a certain note of cynicism?"

"I'm not cynical about your performance yesterday. I thought that was incredible. I always knew you had it in you. I just didn't know if I'd live to see it."

"Then what's your problem?"

"The problem is I don't want you to blow it after you've come so close."

"And of course, it goes without saying that I would *normally* blow it."

"Don't put words in my mouth. You pay me to look after you, and that's what I'm doing. Every athlete has a tendency to choke when he thinks he's being watched, and today you're going to be watched big time."

"I won't choke."

"I also know that you, more than most, crave attention and love to play to a crowd. Especially a crowd that adores you. Especially a female crowd that adores you."

"I won't get distracted."

"There's going to be a ton of pressure. Those reporters will be badgering you, telling you that Ace just bogeyed the thirteenth or Harley just got a hole-in-one on the ninth. Trying to get your reaction. You have to put all that out of your head."

"I know this already, Fitz."

"You have to keep your brain on the game. Ignore the leader board. Concentrate on the game, and nothing but—"

"Fitz, please." Conner held up his hands. "You can skip the pep talk. I'm ready."

"You say that, but you—"

"Fitz, I'm telling you—I'm ready."

"Yeah, but—"

"Fitz." He laid his hand on the older man's shoulder. "Listen to me. Did you trust Gary Player?"

"Well, of course, but—"

"Did you trust Jack Nicklaus?"

"Well, sure—"

"Did you trust Arnold Palmer?"

"Who wouldn't?"

"Good." Conner looked him firmly in the eye. "Now trust me."

* * *

CONNER SAILED THROUGH the first nine holes of the course, beating his previous day's score by two strokes. Even his putting, usually the worst part of his game, was perfection itself. The crowd behind the gallery ropes stayed with him the whole distance, but if Conner was aware of their presence, he never indicated it.

Conner showed no signs of letting up on the back nine. He blitzed through the water holes of Amen Corner, all the while staying dry as a stiff martini. He listened patiently as Fitz made recommendations about clubs and tactics. As they finished the fifteenth, no one in the area—including Conner—could miss hearing one of the commentators announce that Conner Cross now had the best score in the tournament.

As they approached the sixteenth hole, one journalist sidled up to Conner and engaged him in a brief whispered conversation. Fitz, who was out of earshot, was clearly not amused.

At the seventeenth hole, Conner set up his tee shot, but hesitated before hitting the ball. He gazed out at the horizon, surveying the fairway, testing the wind. After a few more moments, he waved Fitz over for a consultation.

"C'mon," Fitz whispered. "We don't want to pick up a stroke for delay of the game."

"I won't be long." He cast his eyes dreamily toward the fairway. "Fitz, what would you say . . . if I went for it?"

Fitz didn't need an explanation of what that meant. "I'd say you'd lost your mind."

"Well, now, let's give it some thought."

"Conner, please don't blow it when you're doing so well. I thought you were past all this macho, going-for-it stuff."

"This isn't machismo, Fitz. It's plain strategy."

"The smartest strategy is to lay up. Take the dogleg left, then get to the green on your second shot."

"Normally, I would agree, but today . . ." His eyes turned back toward Fitz. "Today I think that would constitute an extra stroke I can't afford."

Fitz's eyes narrowed. "What did that reporter tell you?"

Conner leaned closer. "It's Ace. He's four holes behind us. He dropped two strokes on the first two holes, but after that, he's been mirroring my performance the whole way. And I'm sure I need not remind you . . ."

Fitz completed the sentence. "That he started the day two strokes ahead."

"Which means we're tied. Or will be, if he continues to play as he has, which seems likely. I need to pick up a stroke."

"But there's no straight shot. You think your ball can go through those trees?"

"Over them."

"Over them! Are you kidding?"

"It's possible. Theoretically."

"But it's so risky, Conner."

"It has to be. Otherwise, Ace will simply duplicate it. It has to be something so risky he won't dare try it himself."

Fitz nodded grimly. "This would certainly qualify. I don't think anyone's gotten to the green in one on this hole in the history of the Masters."

"On the other hand, no one has more experience than me at trying."

"Trying and failing."

Conner raised his club. "So what do you say?"

Fitz ruminated for several seconds. "I . . . I think you should do what you think is right," he said finally. He paused a moment before adding: "I trust you."

"Thank you, Fitz." Conner took the proferred club and strolled calmly to his tee-off spot.

He drew in his breath and tried to remember everything he had ever been told about this game. Loosen your grip. Keep your weight on both legs. Swing smoothly, with a strong follow-through. And he remembered one other piece of advice as well, something his old buddy John McCree had said a million years ago and a million miles from here.

If it isn't fun, what's the point?

A tiny smile crept across his face, and he knew what he was going to do.

Conner went for it.

30

THE BALL CLIMBED into the sky, becoming a tiny dot against the fluffy white clouds overhead, reaching ever higher, passing the water hole, soaring over President Eisenhower's tree, and not coming down until it was only a few precious feet from the green. Pandemonium erupted. The crowd screamed, and the applause didn't die for minutes. The commentators went apoplectic, then launched into a spew of hyperbole. Everyone in sight seemed to be pouring out their love and affection, all in Conner's direction.

Except Fitz. Fitz was remaining notably stone-faced.

As they strolled to the eighteenth and final hole of the course—and the tournament—Conner whispered into Fitz's ear. "Hear that? They love me."

Fitz nodded stolidly. "It's true."

"They think I'm magnificent."

"Who wouldn't?"

"Everyone!" Conner stopped. "Except you." He peered at his caddie. "You're afraid this will go to my head and I'll blow it on the last hole."

Fitz averted his eyes. "It's a sin to tell a lie . . ."

Conner laughed, then slapped the man on the back. "It's not going to happen, Fitz."

"You won't let the crowd get to you?"

"Crowd? What crowd?" He winked. "I'm here to play golf."

And after Conner Cross eagled the eighteenth, no one in the world could doubt it.

*　*　*

CONNER SPENT A good half-hour with the reporters under the giant maple tree, then retired to the locker room to change. He'd played fabulously well—the best game of his career. It showed in his score, too. He'd finished at 274—only four strokes above Tiger Woods's all-time best Masters four-round score of 270. He was definitely a contender. But there were still fourteen players on the course, including Harley Tuttle, who had placed in almost every tournament that year, and Ace Silverstone, who had been leading the pack since the first day. All he could do was cross his fingers—and wait.

He changed into his street clothes and ambled upstairs to the bar. He'd never felt less like drinking in his entire life, but he knew the bar was where the action would be—and the players. When the final scores were posted, the barflies would be the first to know.

A few minutes after Conner sat down, Harley Tuttle entered the bar. He made his way toward Conner.

"Well," Conner said. "Do I dare ask how you did?"

"I can tell you this," Harley replied. "I didn't beat you."

Conner felt a quickening in his heart, a tightening in his gut. "How much difference?"

"Two strokes. That eagle on the seventeenth nailed it for you. Man, that took some balls."

"Thanks."

"I'll probably end up in fourth or fifth place," he said downheartedly. "I blew it on the fifteenth. Totally underestimated the distance. Should've known better." He shook his head. "Like my daddy always said, Measure twice, saw once."

"Hey, you've got nothing to feel low about. This is your first year on the tour, and you've placed time after time. You must be racking in the bucks big time."

"It has been a good year financially," Harley conceded.

"So stop with the making morose. Get yourself a beer."

"Thanks," Harley said, grinning. "I think I will."

Conner scanned the room, wondering where Fitz was. If the news came in, and if it was what he dreamed it might be—he wanted Fitz to be a part of it. He could never have won the tournament without Fitz's help, and he knew it.

Barry Bennett was standing by the front window, staring out at the course. He seemed wistful but, for once, sober. "The last player is coming off the course," he announced. He turned toward the throng. "Ladies and germs, the Masters tournament is finished. It's all over but the crying."

Yes, Conner thought, but will it be crying salty tears or crying for joy? That was the question.

Several of the players were kind enough to say a few words to Conner on their way to or from the bar. "Good luck," one said. "We're rootin' for you," said another.

Conner thought about that. He wondered if anyone really was rooting for him. Would people like to see him triumph, just for the novelty of it? Or had he made himself so thoroughly obnoxious that the thought of a Conner Cross championship sent shivers down their spines? It was hard to know.

He was almost embarrassed. There were so many things going on right now. His best friend and his first love had been murdered. The killer was blackmailing the tournament officials. Last night, someone had taken a few potshots at him. And here he was, sitting in the bar, possessed by one thought: his golf score. It shouldn't matter. He shouldn't even care.

But he did care. And it did matter. Maybe it wouldn't seem important if he hadn't come so close. But he had—and now all he could think about was how wonderful it would be to slide his arms into the sleeves of one of those lovely green jackets.

LESS THAN FIVE minutes later, Conner saw one of the scoring officials entering the hallway outside. There was a large white posterboard under his arm that couldn't possibly be anything other than the final scores. The official walked to one of the walls outside and began adhering the poster with sticky white tape.

Conner polished off the last of his ginger ale. It seemed the time had come.

31

C ONNER SLOWLY PUSHED himself away from the table. You
will not run, he told himself. You will remain calm, cool, and
collected, no matter how desperately you want to mow down
everyone standing between you and that poster. You will make Fitz
proud.

You will make John proud.

He wasn't even out of the bar when he saw Fitz making his way in.

One look at Fitz's face was all he needed. It told the whole story.

He hadn't won.

As Conner approached the final rankings, the crowd parted wordlessly, creating a path for him. It seemed Ace had rallied on the last five
holes, matching Conner's score on every hole but the seventeenth, and
bettering it twice.

He'd beaten Conner—by a single stroke.

JUST AS THE sun was setting on the Augusta National, two men were
huddled on the porch outside one of the cabins. The hour was late and
the night was still. There were no sounds, no whispers of life; no one
seemed to be about—except on that porch. And even there, the men
were doing everything in their power to prevent anyone from noticing.

"But why here?" one of them asked. He was just as nervous now as
he had been several days ago, when they first met back at the bar on the
outskirts of town.

"Just do it," the taller one fired back. "Quick! Before someone
notices."

The first man pressed his weight against the door and tried the knob. It didn't turn. "Door's locked," he murmured. "See? This is pointless."

The other man pushed him out of the way. "What are you, a man or a moron?" With one mighty leap, he flung himself against the door, shoulder first. The aged and weathered wood cracked, then began to splinter. Another hard thrust against the warped wood, and the door was open.

"Easy as pie," he said, massaging his shoulder. "Now get in, before someone spots us."

Both men quickly skittered inside. One of them—the one who didn't want to come in the first place—reached for the light switch.

"Stop!" his companion insisted. "Do you want everyone to know we're in here?"

"No. I just want to be able to see where the hell I'm going."

"Then use this." A small rectangular object flew through the air. The other man held up his arms, not knowing what it was he was about to intercept. When it arrived, it almost clubbed him in the face.

"A flashlight," he murmured. "Thank God." He pushed forward on the plastic switch, casting a thin beam of light through the cabin. "So now that we're here," he said, addressing his cohort, "*why* are we here?"

The other man smiled thinly. "We're here to finish what we've started. To close all the loopholes. To end it once and for all."

"You love that crap, don't you?"

"Love what crap?"

"Talking in riddles. Even when you know there's not the slightest chance anyone will know what the hell you're talking about."

"Don't be ridiculous."

"You're really into it. You think it makes you seem deep, don't you? Well let me tell you something—it doesn't. It just makes you seem like a jerk-off."

"You wound me."

"Cut the bullshit."

"Why the sudden hostility?"

The other man moved forward, the flashlight illuminating his path. "I'll tell you why. I've gone along with you all the way on this. You know I have. And what's it gotten me?"

"For starters, a hell of a lot of money."

"But at what cost? The cops are everywhere. They're closing in."

"On you, maybe."

"That's my point. What the hell good is the money if I never get a chance to spend it?"

"I think you're overreacting."

"I don't care what you think. I didn't sign on to take these risks. And if you expect me to do it any longer, you're going to have to pay me a lot more than you have so far."

"I did try."

"Trying's not good enough, you manipulative son-of-a-bitch! I'm two seconds away from telling the cops everything I know. Maybe offering a deal. Turning state's evidence in exchange for immunity. What do you think about that, asshole?"

"You're so predictable."

The other man's head twitched. "Predictable? What's that supposed to mean?"

"Just that. You're so easy."

"You're saying you predicted this?"

"Of course I did. How could I not? You're about as subtle as a plane crash. I saw it coming . . . and prepared accordingly."

He tried not to let it show how much the man's words, his eerie tone of voice, bothered him. "Do you think you're scaring me? Is that it? 'Cause if it is, you're barking up the wrong tree. I'm done with being scared of you."

"I know," the other said, and all at once the merriment faded from his voice. "That was your big mistake."

The golf club whipped around so quickly he could barely register what it was, much less take action to avoid it. If it hadn't been for the flashlight, he would've had no chance at all. As it was, he didn't have nearly time enough. He stumbled backwards, barely missing the lethal club as it whisked around just inches before his face. He bumped into the bed, then lost his balance and fell backwards, tumbling onto the king-size comforter.

He heard the familiar sound of rushing wind and knew the club was in action again. He rolled around, but this time he wasn't quick enough. The golf club narrowly missed his head, but still managed to slam into the side of his neck.

He tried to scream, but found that the injury to his neck had somehow throttled his windpipe, cut off his air. All he could manage was a pathetic gurgling noise, hardly enough to summon help. He heard the whistling of air again and threw himself back, slamming his head against the bed's backboard. It wasn't enough. This time the club caught him square on the chin, shattering a few teeth and leaving him so dazed he could barely think, much less move.

"Damn it, you spoiled everything!" his assailant cursed. "I wanted one quick clean shot—like the first time. The mark of a professional."

The man sprawled on the bed was aware of the other man's movement. He felt the sharp dip, the signal that the other man had climbed onto the mattress and was slowly making his way to him. His head was swimming and red flashes fired before his eyes. He was barely conscious, and knew he wouldn't be that for much longer.

"All right then," the taller man said, snarling, as he hovered just overhead. "You wanted to make it messy? Fine—we'll make it messy."

He heard a scraping noise, and in the dim light of the flashlight—where was that thing now anyway?—he saw the other man extract a thin knife from its sheath.

"Time's up," the killer said, as he drew inexorably closer. "Now watch this last stroke. It's one of my best."

CHAPTER

32

B ACK AT THE clubhouse, Conner licked the salt from the rim of his fourth margarita. Things couldn't be any worse than this, he told himself. It just wasn't possible.

It would be different if this had happened to the Conner of a few days before. He had never taken these tournaments seriously, never allowed himself to get too attached to the idea of winning. When he lost, it was no great shakes; hell, he hadn't even been trying hard, right?

But somehow, somewhere in the midst of the excitement and horror, in the loss of his closest friends and the woodshedding of his caddie, he had lost that detachment. Whether he wanted to admit it or not, he had allowed himself to dream of winning—and found that he liked it.

He had been so *close*, damn it! So close. For all he knew, he might never play this well again. And it hadn't been enough. He'd given the game everything he had—and come up short.

He couldn't fault the other players. They had been tremendously supportive. Even Ace had offered a few kind words. Conner had secretly harbored the hope that this tournament might increase his fellow players' respect for him and his skills, and that at least appeared to have happened.

But who was he kidding? It wasn't the same as winning. Not by a mile.

He lifted the margarita to his lips. Could he down this in a single shot, he wondered?

"Conner, may I speak to you?"

Conner peered upward. His vision was already somewhat blurry, but not so much that he couldn't make out the figure of Lieutenant O'Brien standing just in front of him.

What was she here for? he wondered. To offer her condolences?

"What's up?" he said, trying not to sound as blotto as he was. "Come here to lick my wounds? 'Cause if you have, I could make a few alternative suggestions . . ."

O'Brien looked distinctly uncomfortable. "I'm not here alone."

Conner squinted, trying to bring his long-range vision into sharper focus. He spotted at least four uniformed police officers standing behind her. "What's up, O'Brien? Is the Augusta National hosting the policemen's ball?"

"Not exactly," O'Brien said. She whipped her cuffs out from behind her jacket. "You're under arrest."

This had a more profound sobering effect than a dozen cups of coffee. *What?*

"You heard me," she said, tugging at his shoulder. "Get up."

"But—but—" He allowed himself to be hoisted. "I told you I didn't do it."

"And for some stupid reason, I believed you. I guess I let my professional judgment get clouded. It won't happen again."

"But I'm telling you, I didn't do it. I wouldn't kill my own best friend."

"I didn't think so before, but—" She stared at him for a tense moment, and Conner realized that there was something more behind this arrest. "There's been another murder," she said directly.

"*Another* one?" Conner was stunned. "But—I didn't have anything to do with it. I couldn't've. I haven't left the clubhouse for hours."

"Right. C'mon, Conner."

"I'm telling you, it wasn't me. What about Freddy? Have you found him yet? He's the one you need to talk to."

"That would be extremely difficult," O'Brien said, as she snapped the cuffs over Conner's wrists. "He's dead. As if you didn't already know."

FOUR

The Killing Stroke

◆ ◆ ◆

Dwight D. Eisenhower loved the Augusta National. Because of his friendship with cofounder Cliff Roberts, he was not only a member but a frequent visitor. After he became president, Eisenhower's visits were so common that Roberts had a residence built for Ike on the club grounds. Because Eisenhower liked to fish, Roberts had already built him a pond nearby and stocked it with black bass and bluegill. Eisenhower spent the happiest days of his life at the Augusta National, where he could fish in the morning, then find ready partners to play golf all afternoon and contract bridge all night.

Eisenhower's visits to Augusta were not, of course, without controversy. In 1957, when Eisenhower ordered the federal troops into Little Rock to protect the black students integrating Central High School, he reportedly made the call from Augusta. In reaction to this move, obviously controversial in the deep South, the Augusta Chronicle *blasted him for "running the country from a country club."*

In 1955, when Eisenhower ran for reelection, opponents circulated a poster that read: Ben Hogan for President. If we're going to have a golfer, let's have a good one.

33

CONNER PROTESTED, BUT to no avail. With the help of two
uniformed officers, O'Brien hauled Conner out of the bar and
led him down the corridor. All the pros in the vicinity stood
agape, watching but not speaking, as the cops dragged him out of the
building.

"There goes my short-lived reputation," Conner muttered, as he
was escorted down the stone path that divided the clubhouse from
the cabins.

"Move!" O'Brien said curtly.

"You can't just haul me away like this! I don't even have a tooth-
brush. Let me stop by my—" His head jerked around. "Hey, the lights
are on in there! Someone's in my cabin!"

O'Brien looked at him levelly. "And this surprises you?"

"Damn straight! I even locked my door tonight! What's going on?"

O'Brien pondered for a moment, then shrugged. She gave one of
the uniforms the signal. They led Conner back to his cabin.

Before he was even close, Conner could see that something serious
had occurred while he'd been waiting for the postings and swilling margaritas. All the lights were on in the cabin, and uniformed men and
women were swarming all over it. A dozen people, maybe more. Some
of them Conner recognized—because he'd seen them before, out on the
eighteenth hole in the sand trap where he'd found John's body.

The previous crime scene.

O'Brien took him by the cuffs and led him inside. The crime scene
techs parted as she approached, making a path for her without even being
told. "We received an anonymous call about an hour ago," she explained.

"Said there'd been some kind of disturbance in your cabin. Violent, from the sound of it. When we arrived, we found the front door wide open. And this is what we found."

She made a tiny gesture which was altogether unnecessary. Conner couldn't possibly have missed the grisly main attraction.

It was Freddy E. Granger, golf pro and proud father of a recently married Southern belle. Only this time, he was sprawled across Conner's bed. His throat had been cut—like Jodie's, only not half so neatly. He must've struggled, Conner surmised, because the cut was jagged and irregular, like a dull knife working its way through a particularly tough piece of meat. Blood was everywhere, on the headboard, on the bedspread, on the carpet, and the walls. It had been a week of horrors, but this was the most grotesque, most hideous spectacle Conner had ever seen in his life, bar none.

"My God," Conner said. He turned away, holding his stomach, feeling his gorge rising. "You can't think—You can't think that I—"

"We don't think. We know." O'Brien pushed him away from the bed, then jerked him toward the door. "You have the right to remain silent. If you decide to waive that right, anything you say can and will be used against you . . ."

34

Back at Augusta police headquarters, Conner sat in an interrogation room surrounded by half a dozen law enforcement officers. O'Brien had apparently won the coveted right to take the lead; she sat opposite the small table from him, a look of disbelief permanently etched on her face. Two men in uniforms stood behind her, their mouths closed but molded into something like a sneer. There was an older matronly woman administering the cautions and operating the tape and video equipment. And finally there were two huge burly men guarding the door.

"I'm tired of playing cat and mouse," O'Brien said impatiently. "Just come clean. Tell us the truth. Then everybody can go home."

"Everyone except me, you mean."

O'Brien did not smile. "Well, Conner, I don't see you going home for a good long time, no matter what you say."

"You really know how to inspire a guy."

She leaned across the table. "You must be racked with guilt by now. Killing your oldest and best friend—and his wife?" She shook her head sadly. "I can't imagine what you must be going through."

"I've been telling you—I didn't kill anyone."

"And I have to admit—I bought it for a while. I went along with you. Played your game. But the game's over now. You've been caught red-handed."

"There's no red on my hands. Not a trace of blood. If I committed this murder, where's the blood?"

O'Brien was unimpressed. "I learned how to wash my hands back in kindergarten, Conner. It's not a big trick."

"How did I manage to not get any blood on my clothes?"

"Practice makes perfect." She drummed her fingers on the tabletop. "Give it up. No one's buying it anymore."

"Look, talk to the people at the clubhouse. Talk to the bartender. Talk to Harley or some of the other pros. I've been in that clubhouse for the last three hours. I never left once."

"We're checking your story. We know you were in the clubhouse. But no one was really keeping tabs on you—a fact you no doubt counted on. So far no one can be certain you didn't slip away for a short while. After all, five minutes is all it would've taken."

"But it doesn't make any sense. Why would I want to kill Freddy?"

"I don't know. Why did you kill John and Jodie?"

Conner's face screwed up with anger. "I didn't!" He leaned forward, voice angry. "I didn't kill anyone!"

His shout rang through the tiny interrogation room, bouncing off the coarse plaster walls. Get a grip on yourself, Conner warned himself. This is exactly what they want. They want you to lose control, to babble.

Conner tried to calm himself. He leaned back in his chair. "I'm not saying anything more."

"Do you want an attorney?"

Conner blew air through his teeth. That really would be the last resort, wouldn't it? He might as well stamp I'M GUILTY on his forehead in big black letters. "No, I want you to let me go and leave me alone."

"Yeah, that'll happen." O'Brien turned her head and gave a quick nod to one of the men standing behind her. Seemed it was time to change lobsters and dance.

The other man, a dark-haired middle-aged guy with eyes as deep as a water well, introduced himself. "I'm Sergeant Hopkins," he said. "For the record, I'm taking the lead in the interrogation as of twenty-two-oh-six P.M." He looked at Conner and smiled pleasantly. "What was it, Mr. Cross? Professional jealousy?"

Conner peered at him uncomprehendingly. "What are you talking about?"

"Motive, that's what I'm talking about. I've got no problem with guilt; it's obvious you did it. Finding John McCree's body yourself was a nice touch; that threw us off for a while. But you had clear means and opportunity. The only thing I can't figure is motive."

"So I killed John because he was a better golfer? That's really pathetic."

"To me, maybe. But to someone who spends his whole life knocking those balls around—who knows?" He tilted his head to one side. "Or maybe it was the woman."

"The woman? Which woman?"

"Jodie McCree. She was your girl, once upon a time, wasn't she? Don't bother denying it. We've investigated this thoroughly."

"That was years ago!"

"And I'll bet it was digging into your craw every single day, wasn't it?" His face darkened, and his eyes actually seemed to recede. "I'll bet your hate festered like an open wound, getting worse and worse every day, until finally you just couldn't stand it any longer. You saw them both at the tournament, maybe sitting across the table at the champions' dinner, and you couldn't stand it any longer. You had to do something. You had to strike back against the people who had wronged you. Isn't that how it happened?"

"No!"

"You'll feel better if you confess. Really. Just let it all go. You can't imagine how much better you'll feel."

Giving Hopkins a few shots in the face would also make him feel better, but he wasn't going to do that, either. "You're barking up the wrong tree, Fido."

"So it was all a coincidence. Just a strange twist of fate that you found the body. That your golf club was the murder weapon. That you were on the scene when Mrs. McCree was killed, too. That you don't have an alibi for either murder."

"I didn't know I'd need one—since I didn't know there were going to be any murders!"

"Weren't you a bit jealous of your old buddy John? When he went off to that big West Coast college? When he married your old girlfriend? When he won all those golf tournaments, and you couldn't seem to win anything?"

"I've done all right this week."

"Sure—'cause John McCree is out of the way."

"That's the stupidest—"

"When he was around, you were psychologically incapable of playing a good game. But once he was gone . . ."

"What is this, Psych 101? You're on a gigantic fishing expedition. You don't know anything. And you don't have anything on me."

"Other than a bloody mutilated corpse on your bed," O'Brien replied. "How do you explain that?"

Conner frowned. "I can't. But it wasn't me."

"Why would anyone else want to kill Freddy Granger?"

"I don't know."

"And even if they did—why would they do it in your cabin?"

"I don't know. Maybe the same reason they took my golf club. To frame me."

"And why would anyone want to do that?"

"I don't know!"

"Is this going to be your story at trial? Because I have to tell you— it's pathetic. No one's going to believe you."

"How could I know the answers to these questions? I wasn't there! I didn't do it!"

"Gee, maybe no one did it. Maybe it was suicide. Maybe Freddy slashed his own throat."

Conner didn't feel this remark merited a response.

"Or maybe it was just an accident. Maybe he slipped in the shower."

Conner looked over at O'Brien. "Do I have to listen to this?"

"Or maybe his death was staged," Hopkins continued. "Maybe he isn't dead at all. Maybe this was some wacky fraternity stunt."

"Would you just shut up!" Conner shouted. Once again, his voice echoed through the tiny room. "I've had it with you, understand? I did not kill my friends! I did not kill Freddy Granger! And—And—" All at once, Conner's shouts faded.

"Yes?" Hopkins said expectantly.

"And—*damn*." Conner fell back into his chair. "I think I know who did."

O'Brien pushed her way back to the interrogation table. "What are you saying?"

"I know who the killer is."

"Yeah," Hopkins snorted. "So do we."

Conner's eyes became soft and unfocused. "How stupid could I possibly be? It's been right in front of my face the whole time."

Hopkins pressed his hand against his forehead. "This is ridiculous. I refuse to be distracted by this ploy. I want to—"

O'Brien cut him off with a wave of his hand. "No. Let's hear him out."

"It's so simple," Conner said, still lost in his own thoughts. "Why didn't I see it before?"

"Conner . . ." O'Brien took a step toward him.

"This is a load of crap," Hopkins groused.

Conner was lost in thought. "Maybe there's a way . . ."

"Can't you see what he's doing?" Hopkins bellowed. "He's just buying time."

O'Brien bit her lip. "I'm not so sure . . ."

"It's obvious. He's a con man, through and through. He has no sense of right or wrong. He's a golfer, for God's sake!"

"Oh, well then!" she exclaimed. "Snap on the shackles."

"I'm telling you, O'Brien, he's playing you for a fool. *Again!*"

O'Brien gave him a stony stare that shut him down in a heartbeat. "I said we're going to hear him out. And you—*Sergeant*—will follow my lead. Got it?"

Hopkins buttoned his lip, a sullen expression on his face.

"Good." She turned back to Conner. "Look, if you're serious about this, we're going to need proof. Otherwise—"

"Maybe we could create some proof," Conner said. His brain was racing, tying to put all the disparate pieces together. "Maybe—if I could call Fitz."

"Fitz? Why?"

"I'm allowed one phone call, aren't I?"

"And you want to use it to call your caddie?"

"Man's best friend." Conner sat up and leaned across the tiny table. "Look, everybody—I know this seems crazy. But—just go along with me, one more time. Let me play out one last round—under O'Brien's close supervision, of course."

O'Brien raised an eyebrow.

"I can't be certain," Conner continued. "But it's just possible we may be able to bag a killer."

CHAPTER

35

ABOUT HALF AN hour later, Fitz wandered into the clubhouse bar—but it wasn't the Fitz to whom everyone on the tour had grown accustomed over the years. His normally dapper, immaculate appearance had disappeared; he was dirty, disheveled, smudged. His cap was on crooked and his face was stubbled. He looked exhausted. For once, all his years showed in the deep lines etched in his face.

He leaned against the bar, looking as if he could barely hold himself upright. "Club soda," he ordered. "Quick."

The bartender, Vic, popped open a bottle and poured the drink posthaste.

Most of the pros were still hanging around the bar, swapping stories or commiserating over the tournament results. Tomorrow morning their planes would take them home, but for the moment, they were free to amuse themselves. Ace sat at one table, surrounded by well-wishers and hangers-on. Harley sat at another, his fifth place trophy resting on the table just before him. Barry was back at the bar, swilling to his heart's content. And on the other side of the room, one table was occupied by the three top men in the tournament officialdom: Tenniel, Spenser, and Peregino. A heated conversation was taking place at that table, with lots of angry, exasperated sputtering and arguing. Trying to determine what was going on at that table was the second-most popular topic of conversation in the room.

The first, of course, was Conner Cross being hauled off by the cops for triple homicide.

Ace saw Fitz at the bar, saw his condition, and made his way toward him. "Everything okay?" he asked.

"No," Fitz said breathlessly. "Everything is definitely not okay."

"Conner?"

Fitz nodded. "The police have him in custody. They're about ready to lock him up and throw away the key."

Ace shook his head sympathetically. "I can't believe it. Sure, Conner was kind of a wild man—but killing three people? Incredible."

"He didn't do it," Fitz said.

Ace smiled. "You're a good-hearted, loyal man, Fitz."

"I'm not speaking out of loyalty. I'm speaking out of fact. He didn't do it."

"Is there anyway I can help?" Harley Tuttle had come to the bar. "I'm sorry—I couldn't help but overhear. But, if there's anything I can do, I'm ready."

"That's very kind of you," Fitz said.

"Conner has been very kind to me. More than once. Taking me under his wing. Introducing me to the boys on the tour. Like my daddy used to say, A friend in need is a friend indeed. I owe Conner."

"I owe him, too," Barry said with a hiccup, on the other side of the bar. "I owe him a bloody lip."

Fitz scowled. "Shut up, you miserable drunk."

Barry was nonplussed. "I don't know why you've stayed with that creep. I'm sure you could get other offers, even at your—your—" He hiccupped again, then declined to finish his sentence.

"I'm sorry to interrupt," said a gentle voice from somewhere behind him. It was Artemus Tenniel. Spenser and Peregino were trailing in his wake. "We've heard the most awful rumors about Conner. If you could possibly enlighten us—"

"The police have charged him with murder," Fitz said, giving him the quick and dirty version. "But they're wrong. And Conner says he can prove it."

"Prove it?" Tenniel seemed dubious. "How?"

"By finding the murder weapon. The knife that was used on Jodie and Freddy."

"Indeed. And how exactly would Conner know where that weapon is—if he's not the murderer?"

"He knows where the weapon is because he knows who the murderer is." Fitz's voice dropped to a hush. "He's figured it out."

"How?" Ace asked.

"I don't know, but he did. He's certain. And he says he knows where the killer would've hidden the knife. Says the scum would use it to try to divert suspicion to Conner, like he's been doing all along. So Conner figures there's only about a half a dozen or so places it could be. And he's had me running all over the grounds, checking them before it's too late."

Peregino cleared his throat. "And *have* you found it?"

"No. Why do you ask?"

Peregino pulled back quickly. "Oh, I don't—I—" He paused. "Just curious. You know. Could affect the image of the PGA."

"I haven't checked all the places yet," Fitz said. "After I wet my whistle, I'll get back at it. I'm not letting this killer railroad Conner."

"You're a good man, Fitz," Spenser said, patting him on the shoulder.

"Don't work too hard," Ace added. "You have to take care of yourself, too."

Fitz nodded, then took another swallow of his drink. "I made a promise to Conner, and I intend to keep it."

Everyone nodded sympathetically. Gradually, the group dissipated. A few of them left the clubhouse. A few minutes later, Fitz was alone with the bartender.

He polished off the last of his drink.

"How about another?" Vic asked.

"Nah," Fitz said, casting his eyes about the now much emptier room. "I think that'll do it." He paused. "Yes, I think that did just fine."

36

THE DOOR OPENED, and a thin stream of light spilled into the locker room. One shadowy figure quickly entered, then closed the door behind him, returning the room to darkness. He moved quietly, careful not to make a sound, and deliberately, advancing toward his goal. He had a job to perform, and the sooner he got it done and got out of there, the better off he would be. He placed a key in a small lock. Then he opened the locker door, careful not to let it squeak. He reached inside and a moment later . . .

He removed a long, blood-stained serrated knife.

"That's a nasty looking thing. Couldn't you at least have cleaned it before you stuck it in my locker?"

The man with the knife spun around, his eyes squinting in the darkness. He didn't have to squint for long. He heard a click, and barely a moment later, the locker room was illuminated by three overhead fluorescent bulbs.

Conner Cross stood at one end of the locker room staring at the man at the other end—who was holding a knife.

Harley Tuttle.

"Son-of-a-bitch," Harley whispered, just under his breath. "What the hell are you doing out of prison?"

"Is that something your daddy used to say? Or did you think it up on your own?"

"I heard you were arrested. In custody."

"I got a temporary reprieve, Harley. Just long enough to catch the real killer."

"Really? Then you'll be interested in this." He stepped forward, holding out the knife. "I found this lying on the floor. I don't know how it got—"

"Harley, please. Don't bother."

"Don't bother?" He twisted up his face. "I don't get you, Conner."

"Don't bother lying, Harley."

"But what—" He did a double-take. "Oh, my God. You don't think—you're not imagining—that *I* committed those crimes?"

"Yes, Harley. As a matter of fact, I am."

"Conner, that's crazy. Look, I can explain."

"I'm sure you can. But first, let me take this." He surged forward and, before Harley had a chance to protest, snatched the blood-stained knife. He wrapped it in a towel, then set it on a counter out of Harley's reach. "Don't want you to get any crazy ideas. Like maybe going for four."

"Conner—are you telling me you honestly believe—"

"I believe this. You killed John. You killed Jodie. You killed your accomplice Freddy, poor schmuck. And you masterminded the extortion plot."

"Conner—you're insane."

"I've been certain for some time that the killer was a golf pro. It made sense. It had to be someone who could lure him out to the eighteenth hole in the dead of night. And when the killer had me running all over the course by remote control cellular phone, his knowledge of the course, his terminology, his knowledge of the game all convinced me he had to be somebody on the tour."

"But even if that's true," Harley protested, "why would you accuse me?"

"I didn't at first. I thought it was Freddy. After all, it was his club that found its way into my bag, right? He's the only other player here using Excaliburs, and his height would explain why the shaft was shorter than mine. But then you went and killed Freddy, screwing up my theory."

"Conner—you're talking like a crazy man."

Conner ignored him. "I was certain the key to the mystery lay in understanding the meaning of *Fiji*. It was the last thing Jodie heard John say before he died. She thought it was important—and so did I. I tried to bait the killer into commenting on it over the cellular phone, but he didn't go for it. So I was left wondering—what could it mean? Was it an acronym? A code word? A geographical reference?"

"I'm sure I don't know," Harley said impatiently.

"Oh, I think you do. But I couldn't figure it out—until this evening, when I heard a cop make a remark about a fraternity stunt. It was all I needed to jog my memory. A bit of trivia left over from my college days. John was a member of the Beta Theta Pi frat house. They're called Betas. But there's another fraternity house in the Greek system called Phi Delta Gamma—right, Harley? And its members are called—Fijis."

"You're mad. Stark raving mad."

"John was a Beta at Stanford, but I felt certain he knew some Fijis—maybe even one who didn't want to be known. So I had a lieutenant friend of mine call the university and get faxed some pages from the Fiji frat house annual for the years John went to school there. And guess what we found?"

Harley wasn't smiling any more. "I'm waiting."

"It wasn't easy. You were a good deal heavier then, and you've changed your name. But once I saw the photos enlarged, there was no doubt in my mind. That kid who used to be called Myron Caldwell is now Harley Tuttle."

"You're certifiable," Harley said. He made for the door. "I'm leaving."

Conner shoved him back. "Granted, you've done everything imaginable to change your appearance. Dyed your hair black, shaved your beard. Ditched the glasses and the earring. Just the same, I made you."

"This is ludicrous!" Harley protested. "Even if I could do such a thing, why would I want to?"

"You know, I was curious about that myself. So as soon as I ID'd your picture, I got faxes of your—or Myron's—college records. Seems you were quite a promising golfer back in college, which of course increased the likelihood that John would've bumped into you somewhere. But it also turns out you ran into a spot of trouble during your junior year. You got arrested and charged with several offenses—sexual offenses. Including statutory rape."

"You're full of it," Harley said. Once more, he pressed forward, trying to escape.

And once more, Conner shoved him back. "I've got proof."

"You've got nothing!" Harley's voice was rising.

"Wanna see the police report?" Conner whipped a green sheet of paper out of his pocket. "There it is, big as life and twice as ugly. Statutory rape. My God—how can you live with yourself?"

"You're out of line, Conner."

"If it had just been petty theft or hot-wiring cars, that would be one thing. Most kids get into a little trouble before they grow up. But sex with minors?"

Harley's face flushed red. "You don't know what you're babbling about."

"I think I do. And it makes me sick." He shoved Harley backward. "Come on, you disgusting son-of-a-bitch, *talk*."

Harley's neck tensed. "I'm not—"

Conner shoved him again. Harley slammed into the lockers. "You're a pervert, Harley. A pervert who takes advantage of children. A child molester." He kept pounding away at him, shoving him back again with each word. "You're sick, Harley. You make me want to puke."

"It was just a frat party, for God's sake!" The words came tumbling out, like lava spewing from a volcano. "That's all it was!"

Conner stopped hammering him. Finally, he had the man talking.

"We had some fun, they had some fun. All us horny frat boys, all those equally horny sorority girls running around in their skimpy nighties. We were all drunk and turned on and—and—I don't know. I guess things got out of control. But no one forced anyone to do anything."

"But someone turned you in."

Harley bit down on his lip. Conner could imagine his inner turmoil. A part of his brain knew he should remain silent, but another part was desperate to speak in his defense. "Someone called the cops. They showed up, and—" Harley cast his eyes toward the floor. "I assumed everyone there was a sorority girl, meaning they were eighteen or older. But it turned out one of them—the one I was with—was somebody's little sister. Fifteen. And the cops found out."

"So you were arrested."

"My attorney said I could get off easy if I pled guilty. So I did. Two years probation. I never served a day in jail. It was no big deal."

"No big deal—unless you were planning on a career in the PGA. Because, as I've been reminded all week long, the PGA has very strict morals and ethics regulations. And there's no way in hell they'd let a convicted sex offender on the tour."

"It just wasn't fair! One stupid mistake, and it was all over. All my plans, all my prospects, all those years of practice—all down the dumper. Myron Caldwell had come to a dead end."

"So you became . . . someone else."

Harley flopped down on the nearest bench, tired and resigned. "Myron disappeared. I changed my looks, changed my name. Eventually created a body of false IDs and fake background records. Then, when I thought enough time had passed, I entered the PGA qualifier. And made it."

"And so this year you joined the tour."

"That's right. But I've been careful. Damned careful. I never went anywhere near anyone I thought might be able to make me. That's why I was so uncomfortable the other day when that crowd followed us all over the course. That's why I didn't socialize much. And I've thrown tournaments. I figured a guy who consistently places fourth or fifth can remain relatively anonymous—but a champion receives entirely too much publicity. I didn't want a crowd watching me; I didn't want to be on television. So I contented myself with placing. Just high enough to rake in the bucks—never high enough to attract attention."

"It's also why you skipped Pebble Beach, isn't it? Too close to Stanford."

Harley nodded. "I had everything planned so carefully. And then—" He stopped short.

"And then, Monday afternoon, I introduced you to John."

"That's right." His face twisted. "Didn't recognize him at all. But he recognized me. I could tell it the second he laid eyes on me."

"John was like that," Conner said quietly. "Never forgot a face."

"No, he didn't, damn him. And I knew he'd feel honor-bound to report me, too. That's what the PGA requires, isn't it?"

Conner nodded solemnly. "So you killed him. Before he had a chance."

"What choice did I have?" Harley spread his arms wide. "My career was on the line. I'd put too much work into this to let it slip away—again!"

"But why the golf club switch? Why frame me?"

"Why not? It was your damn fault I was in this mess. And it was convenient, since you were using the same brand clubs as Freddy. I thought the best way to keep the cops from looking around too much was to give them an obvious suspect. So you were elected. I did the dirty deed with your club, knowing full well it would be traced back to you."

"But how did you get it?"

"Ah, that's why I needed Freddy. I didn't want to do anything that would attract attention to me. I needed help."

"Why Freddy?"

"I knew he needed cash, bad. He hadn't placed in a tournament in two years, and he was throwing it away hand over fist on his daughter's wedding. He was such a weasel—it didn't take much to get him in my back pocket. I slipped him some bucks and he agreed to separate you from your clubs."

"The peephole."

"Yup. That was the dodge he used. And you fell for it. Left your clubs on the driving range. I removed your nine-iron and replaced it with Freddy's—after scraping off the serial number. And then I lured John out to the eighteenth green—"

"And killed him in cold blood. Buried him in the sand trap."

Harley didn't deny it.

"And Jodie?"

Harley took a deep breath. "I didn't plan to kill Jodie," he said quietly. "But I passed her at the wedding reception Friday night and she was muttering Fiji over and over under her breath. It was only a matter of time until she figured it out, or told someone else who figured it out. I couldn't take the risk. I tried to get Freddy to help, but of course he was too much of a weakling. So I took care of her myself."

"One sin begets another. And Freddy?"

"That greedy bastard couldn't be satiated. Once he realized what I had done with your club, he thought he had me under his control. He demanded money, more than I could provide. That's why I concocted that extortion scheme—I needed the cash to pay him off. And even after I made away with the million—he wanted more! Can you believe it? I tried, but even as I sent the second fax, I knew Tenniel would never go for it. So there was only one course left to me. Freddy had to die."

"Which you happily arranged. Framing me in the process."

Harley shrugged. "Best to be consistent, don't you think? It was the logical thing to do."

"I suppose it was you who took the potshots at me last night."

"You mentioned *Fiji* on the cellular phone. I realized Jodie must've talked to you before I killed her. I didn't intend to kill you just to shut you up. If I'd wanted you dead, you'd be dead. I needed you alive to be my scapegoat."

Conner stared at him, his cold demeanor, his guiltless expression. "You've killed three human beings—*three*—and for what? So you could be a pro golfer? For the bragging rights of being on the PGA tour?"

"Yes, damn it! Not to mention the money. I've made almost a quarter of a million bucks in three months. Think of that! Three months! Imagine what I stand to make in the years to come. I've worked all my life for this. I've spent my spare time practicing, day in, day out. While other kids were out screwing around, I was knocking a ball into a tin cup, mastering my stroke, perfecting my swing. I had a right to be on this tour. I deserved it. I earned it! And I wasn't going to let them take it away from me. Not again!"

Crackers, Conner thought to himself. Absolutely altogether crackers. And golf drove him there. "Come on, Harley. We're going to the police."

"I'm not going anywhere."

"Don't make this harder than it has to be."

"I'm not going to the police."

"Then I will."

"And tell them what? That you have some screwy theory designed to get you off the hook? You don't have any proof."

"I have the knife."

"Of course you do. You're the killer." Harley laughed. "But no one saw me with it. And no one ever will."

"I'll tell them what I know."

"And who's going to believe you? You're just a screw-loose, shaved-head gonzo golfer. You can't prove anything."

"I think I can. See, we found your voice disguiser in the tunnels, where you dropped it. It has fingerprints all over it. And I'm betting they'll match the ones we take from you at the police station a few minutes from now."

"I can explain that away."

"Don't be so sure." Conner reached into his pants pocket and removed a small tape recorder. "This has been recording ever word you've said since I turned on the lights."

Harley's face hardened like steel. "Give me that."

"I don't think so."

"I said, give me that."

"Or what? You'll brain me with one of my golf clubs?"

Harley reached inside his jacket and slowly removed a small revolver. He pointed it at Conner's head. "You won't leave here alive."

37

CONNER STARED AT him. "You're a veritable arsenal, aren't you?"

"Like my daddy used to say, A smart man comes prepared."

"Yeah? Well, here's something my daddy used to say: You're about to be in a hell of a lot of trouble, son."

"Give me the tape recorder, Conner."

"What else have you got? A flame thrower in your socks? Maybe a bazooka in your boxers?"

"Give me the tape recorder, Conner. Now!"

"I really don't want to do that, Harley."

"And I really don't want to blow your brains out, Conner!" His voice was thin and strained. Sweat dripped down the sides of his face. "But I've already killed three people. One more won't make much difference!"

"Harley, let's talk about—"

"Give it to me! Now!"

"Be reasonable—"

"*Now!*" Harley's arm wavered up and down. His trigger finger twitched. "I said, *now!*"

Conner crouched down and laid the tape recorder on the tile floor. He gave it a gentle kick. The tiny recorder slid between them, stopping about two feet in front of Harley, who picked it up and dropped it into his coat pocket.

"Thank you," Harley said, wiping his brow. "I don't like to leave loose ends."

Conner pursed his lips. "And what about me, Harley?"

"I don't suppose you'd just give me your word not to tell anyone what you know?"

Conner didn't answer.

"No. I didn't think so." He raised the gun eye level. "I suppose I should make this look like a suicide. 'The golf club killer, racked with guilt, ends his killing spree by taking his own life.' "

He held the gun out at arms' length and squinted, aiming carefully, zeroing in on Conner's right temple . . .

"Freeze, asshole."

Harley's head whipped around. "Wha—?"

Lieutenant O'Brien was perched in one of the windows, behind and above him. "Drop the gun. Pronto."

Harley pivoted slightly.

"Don't do anything stupid, Harley. I've got you dead to rights. Now drop it!"

Harley opened his fist. The revolver dropped to the floor with a clatter.

"Now give it a kick. A good one."

Harley complied. The gun went flying across the locker room, well out of sight.

"Now put the tape recorder on the bench."

Harley did it.

O'Brien jumped down from the window ledge, careful to keep her gun trained on Harley. "Mr. Tuttle, you are officially under arrest."

Harley recovered his mask of innocence. "You're making a big mistake."

"I don't think so."

"Conner Cross is the killer! He's been trying to frame me. He's desperate to divert suspicion to someone else."

"Save the performance for the trial, Harley. I've been in that window listening for the past ten minutes." She pressed her gun into the small of his back. "Now march. I've got a jail cell with your name on it."

"All right. I'll go. No need to get rough." His body slumped. "Shouldn't you get the knife? It's your best evidence."

Her eyes diverted for barely a fraction of a second, but it was all Harley needed. In the blink of an eye, he whirled around, ducking in case she fired the gun, and bashed his elbow back into her face.

O'Brien went reeling backward, blood spurting from her nose, her head smashing into a row of lockers. Before she had a chance to react, Harley lunged forward, twisted her wrist, and wrested the gun away from her.

Conner sprang forward, but before he could reach Harley, the murderer had locked his arm around O'Brien's throat and pointed the gun at her head. "Back off!" he shouted.

Conner froze in his tracks.

Harley pressed the gun hard against O'Brien's right temple. "I mean it! I'll blow her head to kingdom come!"

"Don't do anything stupid, Harley. Killing her won't help you."

"Killing both of you will," he muttered.

Conner turned his attention to O'Brien. "Are you all right?"

O'Brien's eyelids fluttered. Blood still oozed from her nose, which looked as if it might be broken. Dark circles were forming around her eyes. "I'm all right," she said, not very convincingly.

"Enough chatter!" Harley barked. "Move!" He tried to edge toward the door, holding O'Brien's body in front of him like a shield. But O'Brien seemed barely conscious, dead weight. Each step was harder than the one before.

Conner watched carefully, waiting for an opportunity to do something without putting O'Brien at risk.

Harley made it to the exit. He released his grip on O'Brien's throat and she fell in a crumpled heap at his feet. He cocked the gun again, then pointed it toward her head. "This is where you get off, sweetheart."

Conner sprang across the room. Even as he did it, he knew there was a good chance Harley would readjust his aim and drill him before he arrived. Didn't matter. He wasn't going to stand still while this madman killed another one of his friends.

Harley twisted the gun around, but Conner slapped it aside just in time. The bullet flew up and to his right, impacting on one of the lockers. Conner hit Harley again, and the gun dropped to the floor.

"You—stupid—*idiot!*" Harley reared back his fist and took a shot at Conner's chin. Conner ducked, and the blow missed him. Harley lost his balance and fell forward, giving Conner a perfect shot at his gut, which he took. Harley clutched his stomach, gasping for air.

Desperate, Harley reared his foot back and kicked O'Brien in the ribs, hard. A sharp cry spilled forth from her lips.

"Stop!" Conner knelt beside her.

Harley saw his opportunity and took it. He turned tail and bolted out the door.

Conner cradled O'Brien in his arms, slightly elevating her head. "Nikki! Talk to me. Are you all right?"

Her eyelids fluttered, then opened. "I'll be fine," she said. She wiped some of the blood from her face. "I just didn't want that creep to drag me clear across the golf course."

Conner brushed her hair from her face; some of it had gotten caught in the coagulated blood. "I was so worried—"

"Later," she said. To his surprise, she pushed herself upright. "Let's get that bastard before he disappears and becomes someone else."

With Conner's help, O'Brien rose to her feet. She collected her gun and made her way out the door. She seemed a bit unsteady, but she was holding together.

"There!" Conner said, pointing. Harley was making tracks across the first fairway. He already had a substantial lead on them. He probably planned to cut through the rough, then find his way to another one of those sewer access tunnels, Conner mused. He could slip off the grounds and disappear before they had a chance to call in backup.

O'Brien raised her gun and fired, without success. "Damn. He's out of range. And if he gets off the grounds, our chances of finding him are about nil."

Together, they started running. Conner led the way, but O'Brien held her own. Still, he knew it was hopeless. Harley had too great a lead on them. They'd never catch him like this.

O'Brien fired another shot, but it had no more effect than the first time. He was too far away.

Still racing, they crossed the driving range. Conner saw some clubs resting beside a bucket of balls. A crazy idea flitted through his brain.

"You keep running," he told O'Brien. He stopped, grabbed the longest range club in the bag, tipped over the bucket of balls, and concentrated. Well, he thought, Fitz says I could hit a dime at two hundred yards. Let's see if he's right.

He swung, sending the first ball over O'Brien's head and landing about ten feet in front of Harley, who saw it, paused momentarily—then kept on running.

You'll have to do better than that, Conner. He took another swing, this time coming in a bit short. Damn. He didn't have much time. At the speed Harley was running, he'd soon be out of Conner's range, too.

Conner took another shot, then another, then another, all in close succession. Golf balls were raining down around Harley. He started zigzagging, tracing a serpentine path down the course, trying to avoid the hail of golf balls. But he kept running.

The next shot struck pay dirt. It came barreling across the course like a line drive and crashed into the back of Harley's head. He screamed out, then stumbled and dropped to the ground.

Harley shook his head fiercely, regathering his wits. Gritting his teeth, ignoring the pain, he pulled himself back to his feet.

But the golf balls kept coming. Conner fired them off nonstop, one after the other. Harley kept running, but he wasn't making nearly as good time as before. Conner hit him in the back, then in the leg, just behind his left knee. He was moving even slower, but he was still moving.

Conner took a deep breath. He knew he only had a few more chances left. What was it Fitz had tried to tell him the other day? Imagine the target. See it in your mind's eye. Then swing.

He concentrated and tried to do everything he'd been told. He knew where Harley was. He knew where Harley was going. He knew where he wanted the ball to be. He pulled back the club . . . and fired.

The ball crashed into the back of Harley's head, bringing him down hard. And this time, he did not get back up. A few moments later, O'Brien caught up to him. She whipped his hands behind his back and snapped on the cuffs. "It's over, scumbag."

A few moments later, Conner arrived at the scene. O'Brien was sitting on top of the prostrate and bound Harley Tuttle. "Looks like you have the situation well under control," Conner commented.

"I let this jerk get the drop on me once," she said, wiping more blood from her face. "I wasn't going to let it happen again." As if to demonstrate, she pressed down on the back of Harley's head and shoved his face into the dirt.

"Bit rough for a Southern belle, aren't you?" Conner asked.

"My momma didn't raise any wussies." O'Brien drank in air, trying to catch her breath. "Besides, see for yourself—this creep is wearing white shoes, and it's still a week before Easter. There's just no damn excuse for that."

"Of course not."

"Thanks for your help, Conner. I hate to admit this, but—you may not be the total toad I thought you were."

Conner beamed. "Sweeter words were never spoken."

"That was pretty slick work with the golf balls."

Conner shrugged. "Well, after all—I am a professional."

She nodded. "Good thing he wasn't close to us. Then you'd've had to putt."

All Over but the Shouting

◆ ◆ ◆

Eisenhower was not the only president to take in the Masters. Lyndon Johnson came one year, even though he didn't golf. Johnson was indifferent to the game and the Masters, but his advisors thought there might be some political advantage in being seen there.

Unaware of his utter lack of interest, a reporter stopped him between holes to ask what his handicap was.

"Congress," Johnson replied.

38

Monday

MONDAY MORNING AT the Augusta National clubhouse presented a scene worlds apart from what it had been the night before—really, what it had been since John McCree's body turned up in a sand trap. The pervasive gloom was gone. Spirits were buoyant and boisterous; smiles were the order of the day. A surprising number of the pros were still around, even though the tournament was over.

All the hustle-bustle, all the questions and rapt attention gravitated around one central nexus—Conner Cross. For once, no one could get enough of him. Everyone wanted to hear what he had to say.

"So he pulls this gun on me," Conner explained to the rapt throng. "Then he looks at me, real cold-like, and he says, 'You'll never leave here alive.' But that doesn't scare me. I stare right back at him, right down his throat, and I say, 'The game's over, you two-bit psychopath. I'm taking you in.' " Okay, so maybe this wasn't exactly how it happened, but it made a hell of a good story.

"What did you do then?" someone asked.

"I distracted him with some song-and-dance about the cops swarming around outside, then I got the drop on him."

"Wow." Even Barry Bennett had stayed sober for this story. "All by yourself?"

"Well, I did have a tiny bit of help. From that female cop you've seen running around the grounds. She showed up at just the right moment. Of course, later, I saved her life."

"She must be eternally grateful to you," Barry said. His elbow jabbed its way into Conner's ribs.

"Yeah," Conner said, grinning. "No doubt." But where was O'Brien anyway? He hadn't seen her since they finally finished all the paperwork and the arraignment. Surely, he would see her again—wouldn't he? After all they'd been through . . .

"So tell us the part about the golf balls," someone urged. "Did you really pound one into the back of his head?"

"Like a ballistic missile." Conner loved this part; it was a modern myth in the making. "I took a bead on the creep, aimed, and fired. Right on target. I never missed." Well, not more than eight or ten times, anyway. "Took him down in one."

"Amazing," Barry murmured. Several of the others concurred.

"Conner Cross! I want a few words with you!"

Conner turned and, to his horror, found himself flanked by none other than Derwood Scott.

"Derwood," Conner said coolly. "Imagine. Somehow I thought for sure I'd seen the last of you."

Derwood's face was flushed and puffy. "Not by a long shot, Cross. I've got a bone to pick with you. Several, in fact."

"Derwood—the tournament is over."

"And you've made a real hash of it, haven't you? You blew through this place like Hurricane Hilda."

Conner could see his admiring throng suppressing their laughter. "I don't know to what you are referring, Derwood."

"How about your cabin, for starters? It looks like a disaster area. The place is wrecked. Stains all over the floor and the bed."

"That would be blood, Derwood." Apparently Derwood hadn't been apprised of the latest developments.

"And the locker room is equally wrecked. One of the windows is shattered. One of the lockers has a bullet hole."

"Cool," Ace said. "Can I have that one next year?"

"It's not funny!" Derwood insisted. "You trampled all over the driving range. You used equipment that didn't belong to you!"

Conner coughed in his hand. "There were some mitigating circumstances, Derwood."

"I'm tired of your excuses, Cross. You think the world revolves around you, that the rules don't apply. Well, you're wrong. I said if you crossed the line I'd see to it you were bumped from the tour, and I meant it. From now on—"

Derwood felt a firm hand fall on his shoulder. "Derwood, be quiet."

Standing behind him with his usual impassive expression, Artemus Tenniel gave Derwood a look that spoke volumes.

"But sir," Derwood sputtered. "He's broken the rules!"

"Yes, Derwood. I know."

"We can't allow these unrestrained encroachments on our standards. It's a slippery slope, sir. If we allow one slacker to get away with it, before long, the whole tournament—"

"Derwood, for once, close your mouth and use your brain."

The crowd gasped, watching with amazement—and amusement.

"Have you forgotten," Tenniel said, "that Mr. Cross helped catch the man who was blackmailing us?"

"Well . . . he hardly had much choice."

"Mr. Cross quite literally put his life on the line to keep this tournament afloat. I think perhaps that merits some special consideration."

"But sir—"

"Furthermore, in case you haven't heard, he helped catch the criminal who killed two of our members and one of their wives, again at considerable risk to himself."

"But sir—his dress, his behavior—"

"Given the magnitude of Mr. Cross's contribution, I think we can afford to give him a bit of leeway, don't you?"

"But, sir—!" Derwood pulled himself erect. "No, sir. I can't do that. Rules are rules. It's my job to enforce them. And I will. I'm prosecuting Conner Cross to the full extent—"

"Put your manhood back in the bottle, Derwood. I'm afraid I'm going to have to let you go."

"What?" More futile sputtering followed. "But—you can't do this! I'll go to Spenser—"

"Who I already fired, ten minutes ago. Next time, Derwood, think twice before you align yourself with an embezzler."

"But sir—!"

"It's over, Derwood. Go pack your bags."

Derwood looked as if the top of his head might pop off at any moment. His whole body clenched, top to bottom. Finally, he stomped out of the bar.

Once he was gone, Tenniel looked down with the most beatific smile Conner had seen in his entire life. "I'm sorry you had to witness that, Mr. Cross."

"Aw, that's all right," Conner said magnanimously. "I think maybe you were a bit hard on Derwood, though. Sure, he's a blowhard, but I hate to see him lose his job."

"I'm afraid I can't agree with you there, Mr. Cross. You see, I've spent most of the night studying the audit report that was submitted to your late friend, Mr. McCree, and I've become convinced that Derwood Scott was a partner in the systematic embezzlement being perpetrated by Andrew Spenser. At the very least, he knew what Spenser was up to but didn't report it. Either way, I'm afraid he can no longer be employed by the Augusta National." Tenniel turned his eyes toward the crowd. "But this isn't what I came here to talk about. If I could have everyone's attention, please?"

The room fell silent. Tenniel never even had to raise his voice.

"I think it goes without saying that the Masters tournament is greatly indebted to Conner Cross."

Conner felt his heart fluttering wildly. Could this really be happening? To him? At the Masters?

"There is no way we can possibly thank you for all you've done. You, sir, are a hero, in the truest sense of the word. You embody all that the Masters tournament has come to represent—a standard of excellence in all respects: body, mind, and soul. If you would do me the honor, I would like to shake your hand."

Conner stumbled to his feet and extended his hand. Was this possible? Did this mean Conner was forgiven for the crack about the Easter bunny suit?

"Thank you, Mr. Cross. But of course, a mere handshake doesn't go nearly far enough. I'm pleased to have the honor to announce that the board of directors has just held a special meeting and has unanimously voted to award Conner Cross the Bob Jones Sportsmanship Award for exemplary performance both on the course and off."

Conner didn't know what to say. He was utterly floored. He couldn't think of anything that didn't sound stupid, so he mumbled a "thank you" and left it at that. He felt as if he were walking on air. His eyes were even getting misty. Could the other guys see? This could be totally embarrassing . . . but somehow, he didn't care.

The other pros surrounded Conner. One by one, his peers, many of the golfers he respected most in the entire world, offered their congratulations. Conner was so unaccustomed to this kind of treatment he didn't know what to do. So he just stood there gaping, as the parade passed by.

And at the end of the line, he found Fitz.

Fitz pressed his hand into Conner's. "I've caddied for a lot of fine players," he said, and there seemed to be a bit of a catch in his voice. "I've caddied for men who won the U.S. Open, the British Open, the Masters—the whole tour. But I never before had the honor of caddying for someone who won the Bob Jones Award. Congratulations, son." Fitz gave him a quick wink. "I knew I could trust you."

Conner walked with Fitz outside, where a throng of reporters were waiting. En masse, the journalistic assemblage pressed forward, rolling cameras and pressing microphones into his face. "What will you do now?" and "What does this mean to you?" and "Where will you put the trophy?" Conner was too stunned to put on a show; he figured he'd be lucky if he managed to sound coherent.

A female reporter sidled in from the left and positioned herself in front of him. "Dozens of men have won the Masters," she said. The rest of the crowd stopped to listen. "But only three have won the Bob Jones Award. Many golfers have sought it, without success. How do you explain this?"

Without hesitation, Conner put his arm around the shoulder of the older man standing at his side. "Those other guys didn't have Fitz."

39

THAT NIGHT, CONNER dined in the Augusta National's private ballroom, which he had never even seen before. He was being treated to a seven-course meal—a special extravaganza arranged by Artemus Tenniel. Caviar, pâté fois gras, steak tartare, and several other dishes Conner didn't actually like but felt classy as hell eating. There were no patrons, no members. Conner had the place to himself—himself, and his special guest for the evening.

Lieutenant O'Brien was out of uniform and wearing pearls and a black decolleté gown—and looking very uncop-like in it, too, as Conner couldn't help noticing.

Somewhere between the soup and the sorbet, O'Brien asked, "So . . . what are you going to do with the trophy?"

"I'm sending it to Stanford," Conner answered, as he poured her another glass of champagne. "They're going to put it in a display case with all of John's trophies. They're going to call me John's prodigy. Part of his living legacy." He smiled. "I think John might like that. He always wanted an Oklahoma boy to make good at the Masters. He just didn't know exactly how it would happen."

O'Brien nodded. "By the way—thanks."

"For what?"

"You know perfectly well for what. For saving my ass. And the rest of me, too."

"My pleasure," Conner replied. "And may I say—it's a very fine looking—"

"About time you noticed."

"I noticed a long time ago. It's just that the badge and the gun kept blocking my access."

"Why, Conner," she said, fluttering her eyelashes. "Are you making a pass at me?"

"I don't know," he answered. "Are you going to arrest me again and haul me back to the police station?"

Nikki peered back at him. Their eyes met across the table. She placed a hand delicately on his arm. "Actually . . . I'd rather haul you back to your cabin."

Conner's eyes glowed like light bulbs. Maybe he could learn to like the Masters tournament after all.

EPILOGUE

*A*fter his term of office ended, Eisenhower visited Augusta eleven times, returning again and again to the home away from home that gave him so much pleasure during his presidency. In May, 1961, at a gala party, Eisenhower thanked each of the forty members who had contributed funds to pay for Ike's Cabin on the club grounds. In October of 1965, he and Mamie celebrated their fiftieth wedding anniversary, and were given by the Augusta National members an elaborately carved, eighty-four-ounce gold bowl. Bobby Jones himself drove in from Atlanta to serve as toastmaster, but by that time he was suffering from a rare and severe neurological disorder, and the journey tired him so much that he had to stay in bed during the party.

On his last visit, Eisenhower is reported to have gazed out at the gorgeous greens and rolling hills and said, "This place is so beautiful. Never in my life have I been so happy as I was right here."

He died in 1969. At his funeral, in addition to notables such as President Nixon and president of France Charles de Gaulle, were Cliff Roberts and many others from the Augusta National, Ike's old gang, all together for the last time.